Weird...

VOL. 2, NO. 5   **ISSUE 35**

Features

Stories

Poetry

From the Editor's Tower

Welcome to *Weirdbook* #35!

Though April showers may come your way
They bring you Weirdbook that looms in May

(Al Jolson is probably rolling in his grave right now.)

It's time again! Weirdbook #35 is here, and we're bringing you another cavalcade of the bizarre, the frightening, the adventurous, and the fantastical! In others words what you are holding is the fix for your weird jones.

This issue contains 17 stories and 5 poems. These were selected from the over 350 submissions that I received last October. I ended up choosing what I felt to be the 58 best stories and poems. In doing this I went overboard in spending my publisher's hard earned cash by stuffing each issue to bursting with over 80,000 words of content in each issue. That is because I received so much wonderful material that I couldn't bring myself to let any of it slip by. So hopefully we'll manage to sell a few extra issues in order to cover the cost overrun.

It's my deepest and sincerest wish that each and every issue of Weirdbook delivers an enjoyable and satisfying reading experience. Thought is continuously given to balancing the content of each issue, and I hope that each tale is a pleasant surprise.

I don't know if I've mentioned this before, but we will soon be publishing our very first themed Annual. This year's theme is "Witches," and the Annual will be out in time for Halloween.

And, as always, I want to think everyone who has submitted to the magazine, everyone who has supported the magazine, and (of course) everyone who reads the magazine. Bless you all!

In closing I want to dedicate this issue to the memory of my step brother Stephen Leibrand, who left us a few weeks ago, so much sooner than he should have. You were a fine man and your passing has left a void that won't be filled.

Till next issue.

—Doug Draa

Staff

PUBLISHER & EXECUTIVE EDITOR

John Gregory Betancourt

EDITOR

Doug Draa

CONSULTING EDITOR

W. Paul Ganley

WILDSIDE PRESS SUBSCRIPTION SERVICES

Carla Coupe

PRODUCTION TEAM

Steve Coupe
Ben Geyer
Helen McGee
Karl Würf

The Pullulations of the Tribe
Adrian Cole

I was engrossed in the paperback, a battered crime pulp labeled *A Fist-ful of Femme Fatales*, so it took me three grabs to get a hold of the ringing phone. I paused in my chewing to mumble a response, but when I heard the voice on the other end, my mouth opened, the gum dropped into my lap and the paperback flopped onto the floor.

"How you doing, Razorface?" Only certain people called me that. The voice was breathy, laced with sex. FiFi Cherie, nightclub singer *extraordinaire*, never usually rang me in my den.

I made some kinda noise so she knew I was still on the end of the phone.

"Hope I didn't startle you." I could just picture her face, half screened by that long drop of shining black hair, silky and shimmering. She laughed huskily and then slipped back into the voice I was more used to, that of Ariadne Carnadine, my sometime partner in crime fighting. She knew well enough I was a sucker for her alter ego, the singer who melted hearts in her club, *Diamonds Are Forever*.

"I was thinking of dropping by at the club," I said.

"That's sweet of you, honey, but one of the reasons for the call is that I have to fly over to Europe for a few days. Gay Paree. The business won't run itself and this deal needs the personal touch."

"You've just ruined my week."

"I'd take you with me, but I know what flying does to your digestive system."

Not to mention the rest of my system. Any kind of plane was my idea of hell on earth, or above it. "There were others reasons you rang?"

"Yes. I have a little problem for you to solve. Specifically for FiFi."

"How could I refuse? So what gives?"

"You know I like to choose my singers very carefully. I like to find the best of the new talent." It was true—she had a good ear and had pulled some real charmers from the many wannabes who auditioned in her club. "The thing is, at least two potential new kids on the block have gone missing. I got word to them after their auditions that I wanted them back, with the likely prospect of a contract for them. Usually, that kind of offer is something they'd bite your hand off to get."

"I know it."

"So it's weird that I've heard nothing. I'm organizing a Big Jamboree at *Diamonds Are Forever* soon and anyone who's anyone in this town will be there. It's a real prestige event. Big opportunity for these girls, so it's very strange that they've disappeared. I put the word out and had some of my people check things. No sign. Nothing. Both girls have left town quick. I don't like it, Nick."

"Rival concern?"

"I'd know if it were. No, this is weird. Will you poke around for me, see what you can dig up?"

"It'll cost you. A whole weekend."

"Don't sell yourself short," she purred, using her FiFi Cherie voice again.

"Okay, let's say a month."

"Now you're being greedy."

* * * *

Ariadne had furnished me with details about the two young singers, both of them from the city, kids who ought to know their way around and who should have been streetwise enough to look after themselves. Neither had an agent, which was maybe a good thing, as the music agents I knew were the land equivalent of great white sharks.

I did a bit of legwork for a couple of nights, drawing blanks until I got my first sniff of something in a rundown club down on the waterfront. Called *The Gunrunner Club*, it was run by an ex-pro boxer, Mo Karstein, whose main claim to fame was that he'd gone ten rounds with the world champ of some ten years back. He'd had his lights punched out, but that wasn't the point—he was still a local hero.

Mo poured me a double, on the house, and pointed me in the direction of one of the bar floozies, a sleepy-eyed vixen by the name of Selene. She must have used more paint than the entire cast of a Broadway show and wore a pink wig that looked like the insides of a mattress had exploded over her. When I walked up to her and gave her a cheery wave, she grinned at me like she had hit pay dirt.

When I told her who I was and that I wasn't looking for a good time, just information, she shrugged and swigged resignedly at her gin cocktail. I slapped a good few greenbacks on the bar and they disappeared like they'd never existed.

"Mo tells me you do a bit of singing," I said.

"He's being kind. We used to have a thing, and he humoured me. These days he sees that I'm all right. Let's me take a turn at the mike when there's not too big a crowd. Don't tell me you're interested in my voice, mister."

"My guess is, you know a good voice when you hear one, right?"

"Sure. I got a good ear."

"I'm looking for two kids who can sing. Word is—they're good. Maria Mozzari and Suki Yosimoto. Names mean anything to you?"

I always watch the eyes. They usually give the game away. I could see this lady recognised the names—her eyes narrowed slightly, she looked away for a moment, then back at me, composed again.

"Listen, I'm no bank, lady. But I'll give you a fair price. What do you know?" I shoved a few more greenbacks at her. She counted the money, folded it and shoved it somewhere private.

"A few nights back, the place was jumping. Rock and roll night and more than a few fresh customers from outside. We all had a good time. Two of the new faces were hoods. It wasn't just the suits that gave it away. I can smell hoods a mile away. Not sure whose mob they were from. Maybe outta town. Carrying enough hardware to start a war."

"You talk to them?"

"Nah, but I listened in over the shoulder of the bozo who was trying to carry me off into the night. Fat chance. I was holding him up."

"So what did these guys talk about?"

"Something was going down. Big action. They were posing as talent scouts. Like I'm an opera diva. Talent scouts! White slavers more like. Anyways, they was watching the girls' acts. I watched them. Weird thing was, they didn't take a load of notice of all the naked flesh on display, you know, the tasteful dancing and stuff. Most guys had their eyes and tongues hanging out. These two were listening."

"For the singers?"

"Sure. You mentioned two names." She looked around as if it would be a bad idea to repeat the names like they were a curse or something. "When they did their acts, these guys perked up."

"The girls were good?"

"Yeah. Like I said, I got a good ear. These two had class. I'd give a lot to have a voice like that. And they had the chassis to go with the voices. Sleek. I hated them."

"What happened?"

"I heard one of the hoods say these two would be right for some woman. I guess she was their boss. She had a fancy name." She swigged her gin as if it would fuel her memory. Her eyes blinked in concentration. I motioned for the barman to top up her glass.

"Cadenza?" she said. "Was that it?"

I felt as though a sudden cold wind had blown across the room. "Carmella Cadenza."

"Yeah, that wuz it. Mouthful. Sounds like some piece from Hollywood. Anyway, the hoods muscled their way over to the stage and spoke to the girls and I reckon they bought them drinks. That wuz it. Cleared off soon after."

"You said these guys were talking about something before that."

"My head was full of booze—when isn't it?—so I didn't get much more than the drift of it. Something about power. The girls wuz gonna help this Cadenza woman get some kind of power."

The cold wind blew colder. I'd crossed paths with Carmella Cadenza before and it had taken a certain amount of strange power to foil her unsavoury ambitions. She'd lost out, but my guess was she was the kind of woman who'd go looking for an alternative means to get what she wanted, none of it any good for the rest of us. If she was kidnapping young women, there were several potential reasons that sprang to mind, all of them unpleasant.

"You look like you could do with a stiff drink, mister," said Selene, like she was mounting a half-hearted attempt to seduce more cash out of me.

"You have any idea where these hoods and the girls went? Does anyone?"

She shook her head. "I'll ask around. Come back tomorrow. I'll have something for you, even if it's only a warm bunk."

* * * *

I spent the next day mooching around town and I was beginning to get the feeling that I'd have to go back to *The Gunrunner Club* and see if the delectable Selene had dug up anything for me, other than a warm bunk. With more than a little reluctance, I was heading in that direction, when a voice behind me pulled me up short.

I turned to face the cracked smile of a grizzled old sailor, Sten-Gun Stan, mechanic to the eccentric Henry Maclean, a youngster who spent a lot of his time cruising about in an unlikely tin can he called *The Deep Green*—a submarine of sorts, in which I had once experienced the very dubious delights of underwater travel.

"Been looking for you," he said. Stan's crumpled jacket reeked of oil like he'd just finished greasing the engines on that infernal machine of his.

I let him direct me to one of the buildings along the sidewalk, a place where auctions were held from time to time. Today was one of those times, and a crowd had assembled within, shoulder to shoulder, so I wondered what they were pedaling.

"Keep a low profile," said Stan.

"You expecting trouble?" I asked, but it was a dumb question. Whatever he and Henry were up to would likely have questionable ramifications.

"Henry's after something. There's a whole load of musical instruments up for bids, most of it junk, some of it the real deal, and one item in particular of special interest. Henry has set his heart on it, but we think there are others who want it, too."

"Others?" The word dripped with painful possibilities.

"Toughs working for someone higher up the food chain. You got your hardware?"

"Does a dog have fleas?"

He grinned and we muscled our way further in, ignoring the scowls and grunts of annoyance from the press of bodies. I saw Henry a few rows ahead. As usual, he was dressed in a tee-shirt, a patterned thing that would have looked more in place on a West Coast beach, his mop of blonde hair standing out like a sunflower in a bed of nettles.

I also saw the big guy in a trench coat tucked in directly behind him. My guess was, he was up to no good. I could smell it on him. Henry and I eased our way towards him and got as close as we could. So far he hadn't noticed us.

"Cover my back if things liven up," said Henry. I wasn't sure what he was expecting—this was the last place you'd want to start a gunfight or any kind of fight for that matter. We were hemmed in by the crowd.

There was a stage at the front, and the auctioneers, a team of three guys, were getting through their wares, slick and fast, gabbling in their own weird language, and as far as I could see, bids were flying in from all directions, snapping up the various gewgaws on offer.

"This next one's ours," said Stan, referring to a grubby programme he'd picked up. He pointed to a photo of what looked like a guitar, although it was pretty damn weird—vary narrow, elongated base and a stretched neck. My guess was it was one of those hybrid things from the Orient, and it would make twisted sounds, gimmicky and off the wall. Yeah, that would attract Henry's interest.

The bidding started low like no one was that interested. Henry waited for a while, then slipped in a bid of his own. It was countered by a thickset guy across the hall from us. He looked like the double of the big trench coat who was now pressed up behind Henry, like a leech about to attach itself. Two big uglies in trench coats. I wasn't liking this.

Henry and the guy across the room exchanged bids, lifting the price up to a sum that surprised me and got the crowd buzzing. Then I saw the guy behind Henry say something to him, into his ear. It must have been a threat. *Drop out of the bidding*, something like that. I saw Henry stiffen, but Stan had squeezed ahead of me.

The guy across the room had upped the bidding and held the initiative. Stan had almost got himself into a brawl, but he pressed up behind the trench coat. The guy stiffened and slumped. Stan started to indicate to those around him that some guy had fainted. Pretty soon a space had cleared and the guy was stretched out on the deck, dead to the world. Henry must have slipped a needle into him, a needle loaded with enough dope to knock out a horse.

Henry immediately upped his bid for the guitar and I looked across at trench coat two. His face was a picture. Not a pretty one, at that. He snarled a higher bid, but there had to be a ceiling on what he was allowed to offer. Henry bettered it. He sure wanted that guitar.

Now, I knew Henry was an eccentric, to put it mildly, but there was something going on here that was somehow important in the grand scheme of things. I could taste the atmosphere, and I'm not talking about the cigarette fug. The trench coats were the type of guys I'd had more than a few brushes with—my gut feeling was that they worked for someone, or something, very out of step with the run of the mill Mob in this town. If they got hold of that guitar, it was going to be bad news for the rest of us. Serious bad news.

Trench coat two upped his bid by a big heap of dollars. I knew Henry was beaten. I waited to see if he would raise the bid. Stan turned and looked at me, his face grim. I was getting the feeling that he and Henry would end up doing something stupid to get that guitar. I didn't think it would be a good idea to start trading bullets with the trench coats, wherever that might take place. Likely they'd have a bunch of reinforcements outside.

I put in a bid that was way over what the trench coat had offered. I could see him looking across at me, his eyes narrowed like he was focusing some kind of insane energy through them that would excoriate me and melt my bones down into glue. My bid had done the trick, though. It was one big pile of dough, but it had won me the guitar. Henry and Stan fought their way to me, both their faces beaming.

"That's a lot of money, Nick," said Henry.

I don't make a big thing of it, but I have a lot of money tucked away in a very private bank. How I got it is a long story, and this isn't the place to go into all that (maybe some other time) but let's just say it was no problem for me to scoop the guitar without denting my private hoard.

By the time I'd got the guitar and had it wrapped up, the two trench coats were gone, though I didn't expect it to be the last we saw of them.

* * * *

Sten-Gun Stan, Henry and I found a quiet little dive not far from the waterfront where we could chew over the events of the day. As far as we knew, we hadn't been followed.

"So what gives with this weird guitar I've just spent an arm and a leg buying?" I asked them over a round of iced beers. "My guess is, it's one of those artifacts of power I keep stumbling over."

"Exactly!" said Henry, glancing around into the gloom of the bar. Nothing much stirred. It would be like that until round about midnight when a scuffle or two might break out.

"Well, I don't want the damned thing," I growled. "I know you were keen to get hold of it, so you're welcome to it, Henry. Where did it come from?"

"It's been lost for a while. I'm not sure, but it was used by a rock band who bought it off some old freak who was supposed to be guarding it for— well, even freakier guys. The thing has power and must have spooked him so he took the money. It was a bad omen for the band. They ended up on skid row and the guitar disappeared until now."

"What is it?"

"It's a dual purpose mechanism," he said, leaning forward and injecting as much mystery and unease into his voice as he could. "If you play it one way, gently, it can open certain—doors. It's also a weapon. If you play the Entropic Chord, it can be very dangerous. Destructive. You can imagine what it would be like in the wrong hands. Like the forces of darkness. Those thugs we bumped into at the auction were their hired hands."

"So what are you aiming to do with it?"

He looked embarrassed. "Well, it's a kind of a rescue mission. Tricky and it could be a bit of a mess, but I have to take it on."

"Rescue?" I said, sipping my beer. "Who's in a jam? Anyone I know?"

Stan was grinning. "No need to go all shy on us, Henry. Tell the man!"

"It's a friend of mine—"

"A girl," said Stan, enjoying Henry's discomfort.

"How's she different from all your other surfing girlfriends?" I asked.

"Apart from being exquisitely beautiful," Stan said on Henry's behalf, "she has the sweetest voice you've ever heard. Supernatural if you ask me."

"She's missing," said Henry. "I've heard nothing from her for almost a week. It's not like her."

"She's not run out on you?"

Henry shook his head. "No, no. She wouldn't. I think she's been abducted."

Those remote alarm bells that ring at the back of your mind sometimes were starting to ring louder in mine. A singer, abducted? This sounded familiar.

"I think I know where she is," Henry went on. "She's not here, in our world. Nor the Pulpworld. She's in a place that's kind of in between. A secret place held together by dark magic. The guitar can open a door to it. I'm going in after her."

"In your submarine?"

Both Henry and Stan were shaking their heads. "Not possible," said Henry. "This realm is protected. Can't get anything in, other than flesh and blood, or something strongly tainted with magic. The guitar is neutral—whoever uses it suffuses it with power. It's the one thing I can take with me. So I owe you, big time, Nick. Now at least I have a chance of finding Suki."

I didn't quite drop my drink, but I did set it down unsteadily on the table. "Suki? Would that be Suki Yosimoto?"

Henry's face lit up. "You know her?"

"She has a friend, another singer, name of Maria Mozzari?"

"Yes! They're inseparable."

"Both missing, yeah, I know." I told him about the connection with FiFi Cherie's night club and the little job I'd been given. Henry's grin widened, but I wasn't feeling so good about all this.

"So we're in this together," he said as if some of the clouds around him had thinned.

"I'm not sure I care for this escapade. You say nothing can be taken into this other realm? What about my guns, my knives? I'm naked without them." It was true. I could handle myself in a fist fight, but from my experience of other realms, you needed a whole lot more than brawn to take on the kind of critters you'd find in there. And if Carmella Cadenza was behind this, she'd have a bodyguard to match the Pope.

"We've got the guitar," said Henry. "And the element of surprise. They won't be expecting us."

"Well, that warms the cockles of my heart," I said.

* * * *

In my apartment, I prepared myself as meticulously as I could for this little jaunt into Whereverland. No guns? Hell, I must be getting senile. I stripped to the waist and applied a certain type of paint in a certain type of way across certain parts of my torso. Once it was dry I put on a shirt I only wore for certain occasions, one that was supposed to be charmed against the agents of darkness (although I had some doubts as to its veracity) and finally I slipped on a necklace and snapped wristbands on each arm. Looking at myself in the mirror, I grimaced. If my pal Rizzie Carter, the local Police Chief, saw me in this get up he'd think I was heading on stage for a pantomime, but it was worth it if it could deflect the kind of nastiness I was about to bump into.

I met up with Henry again in an insalubrious part of town. He wore the tightest pair of black leather pants I'd ever clapped eyes on like he'd been poured into them and a black shirt to match—it even had black buttons.

"Less chance of being seen," he explained. Across his shoulder he'd slung a black leather case, long and narrow, the prized guitar secreted within. Overall he looked like a runaway from an Iron Maiden concert. I thought maybe I looked a bit like Robert Mitchum's kid brother, but I doubt if Henry had ever heard of the guy.

Darkness had already dropped over the city as Henry led us through the streets to a remote place where, mercifully, not many of the lights overhead worked. There were a few people about, night owls, but they paid us no heed. Henry was heading for the place where Suki Yosimoto had last been seen, as far as he knew. I had some pretty good contacts in these rat-runs, but Henry had his own eyes and ears.

"You'd be surprised what they'll do for a peek at *The Deep Green*," he grinned. "She's a legend."

We entered an old building that looked like one good sneeze would bring the whole place down on our heads. It must have housed every pest known to man—woodworm, dry rot, wood beetle, concrete cancer, you name it, this was their heaven. We threaded our way through the piled dust and debris, our way barely lit by one flickering street light outside.

Henry unzipped his case and slid out the guitar. It had a weird blue glow to it, faint as moonlight in fog, so we were able to see our way into the heart of the collapsing masonry. This would not be a good place to get buried. My bangles and baubles were proof against sorcery, not a ton of falling bricks.

Unfazed, Henry slipped the guitar strap over his shoulders, paused to take in a deep breath, and then gently stroked the strings. The sounds he made were like whispers, susurrating around us, echoing back like ripples on a pond as they touched the walls. We waited in sudden silence after the sounds faded.

Ahead of us was a solid wall. It groaned and we both ducked instinctively. Dust belched from abrupt cracks in the surface and before we knew it, the whole goddam shebang was toppling forward, with us under it, like mice about to be pinned in a trap. However, as the bricks reached us, they parted like a miniature Red Sea, and thundered down on both sides of us. What we were left with was a thick cloud of dust and a tall, black gash, empty as space.

Coughing fit to bust our lungs, Henry and I went into that darkness. It was a vacuum, soundless, but at last, we could breathe. Behind us, the dust and rumble of settling masonry died away and it was like someone had slammed shut a mighty door.

Henry, his face smeared in muck, grinned. "We're through," he said.

I didn't know whether to be relieved or unnerved. I settled for glad to be alive and we moved on, the light slowly changing from inky black to dark grey. Henry put the guitar away and it fused with his back, making him look like some kind of malformed troll. One disguise was as good as another.

Henry had earlier told me as much about this realm as he knew. It was, he said, like a bubble between worlds, limited in dimensions, held together by ancient spells and sorcery created eons in the past by creatures—demigods, he said—who generally shunned the light and occasionally needed someplace to hole up while the powers of light went on the rampage, looking to exterminate them.

By the septic glow of the light somewhere ahead I could see we were in some kind of tall, rocky maze, the sheer walls rising up into total darkness. This was either one big, monolithic building, or a subterranean catacomb of dubious dimensions. I just hoped that Henry had some inkling of where we were headed. I'd have been lost within a dozen paces. All we had was the dim light and there was no clue to its source. What I did figure out was that we were not alone.

Something or more likely some*things* were plodding about, probably down more than one of those narrow runs in the stone. High up in the darkness, something else flapped and scraped along, a big bunch of bats maybe, or creatures with similar wings. And claws. They always had claws.

As we wove our way deeper into the maze, I got the distinct impression that the shifting, scraping things beyond us were moving in a certain pattern. My guess was, we were being herded.

"I think you're going to need your guitar," I whispered to Henry.

He grinned back at me. Jeeze, he was enjoying this. It must be his youth. Barely gone twenty and he was up for anything. I ached for my twin Berettas, although I had a feeling that in this place they would be less effective than water pistols.

Something emerged from the murk ahead of us. It looked like a pile of rags on small stilts, with one arm as twisted as the branch of a warped tree, flapping at us. The other arm gripped a crutch, another distorted branch which just about supported the thing. Light gleamed briefly under a long confusion of hair and beard in what I took to be a couple of eyes. They were the only features in an unrecognisable face.

Henry did unstrap the guitar, slipping it out of the case slowly. I was relieved to see the faint blue glow, which suggested to me that the thing was primed. "We're in luck," he said. "It's the Raggedy Man."

Luck? This mobile heap of garbage was a sign of *luck*?

"The legends say if you find him, he can help you."

"This way," hissed the Raggedy Man. "You gotta ignore those who clutch."

Now there was an expression to fill you up with confidence. *Those who clutch?* What in hell had we gotten into here?

Henry didn't seem to have the same reservations that wriggled coldly through me and we followed the Raggedy Man as he swiveled and hobbled through a corridor leading off the main one. I went after them cautiously, my hands spread like fans, ready to simulate Bruce Lee at his lightning best. If anything had a mind to clutch me, I was about to repel all boarders.

I was glad of the dark as we squeezed through several corridors because things did try and make a grab for Henry and me. Soft, pulpy things, like big fat worms, slippery and smelling like rancid meat. I swept them aside, my hands slick with their juices, sticky and gelatinous. The Raggedy Man got us through and we came out into a wider chamber, the light barely fit to pick out its minimal details. At least there were none of the clutching horrors here.

"Where the hell is this place?" I growled, towering over our bizarre guide.

"It's where the broken things come to be mended," he whispered, almost whistling the words through the last of his crumbling teeth. Seemed like the place hadn't worked for him.

"What broken things?"

"Evil things. Dark powers that have been crippled by their betters. Things that serve the lords of the night, damaged things. Some can be healed through twisted magic. Others, like me, can only wander, searching for freedom."

"Who are you?" I asked.

"Can't remember my name. I had powers once, bestowed on me by servants of Satan. In conflict, I was bettered. I crawled here. Thought I was going to die, but a life of sorts still flickers within me. If I help you, will you take me back when you go?"

I would have weighed up my answer before entering any kind of bargain, but Henry's youth burned brightly again. "Sure," he said. "It's a deal."

"Why are you here?" said the Raggedy Man.

"Two young women were brought here recently," Henry said, evidently having tossed circumspection aside. "Singers. With great voices."

"There have been many such singers. The Cold Lady has them. She is grooming them. She had powers lately, but lost them. Now she uses the singers to act for her. She imbues them with dark gifts from the ones she serves. The Angels of Malice."

The air got much colder. I'd met one of these things before. In fact, with a little help from a bunch of very talented Hungarians, I'd trapped one of them and seen to its imprisonment. If the Angels of Malice got wind of me, they'd be out for a whole lot more than my blood. Blood which, right now, was running about as cold as it could get without actually coagulating in my veins.

"Where are the singers?" said Henry.

The Raggedy Man pointed up into the darkness. "In the upper halls of this edifice. They are well protected and besides, they would not welcome you."

"Two of them would," insisted Henry.

"I think not. They are changed. They are *her* creatures now."

Henry's expression soured, a mark of the grim determination that burned within him, a powerful drive that those who didn't know him would have been surprised at. He was erratic and more than a shade gung-ho, but he was no fool.

"I guess we'll just have to put that to the test." He looked at me and I nodded. We'd paid for the ticket, so we may as well see the show.

Somewhere in that endless maze, there were steps, a narrow, winding set that corkscrewed up into the shadows overhead. The Raggedy Man led the way, followed by Henry and his blue guitar, with me at the rear. My hands were itching. I really missed my guns.

We came to a level area, almost blanketed by darkness, although there were lights of some kind high up as if we'd come to the nave of a building the size of a cathedral. There were no dramatic gothic columns, but more great slabs of rock soared upwards, like no place I'd ever seen in my own world, or any other for that matter. Also, there were no sculptured motifs, or weird sigils, or carved monstrosities that looked like they'd been dredged up from the sea bottom.

But the place felt *wrong*. Alien, haunted, the air thick with the suggestion of pain, oppressive and soul-destroying. I'm getting a little melodramatic here, but I tell you, that was an evil place.

To top it, we heard singing, echoing from some nearby but invisible chasm, as if a pit into Hell itself had opened. The sounds, deep and seemingly male, were bass and disturbing, suggesting unspeakable things. Rising.

Things were moving in the dark spaces at the base of the stone pillars, flitting about like aerial spirits, or ghosts. The Raggedy Man watched them, apparently unmoved. "Some of the singers are here," he said.

"What does the Cold Lady use these things for?" said Henry.

"Spells," said our guide. "To trap the unwary. And also to control the Pullulating Tribe."

I never heard of this Tribe, but it sounded like bad news.

"The Tribe sleeps out in the great wastes that surround this labyrinth. The Cold Lady wants to rouse it and unleash it on the enemies of the Angels of Malice."

"Who would they be?" Henry asked I thought a little naively.

"Humanity," said the Raggedy Man. "The powers of darkness hunger for its enslavement. A time is coming—"

"Yeah," I cut in. "We've seen the trailers. Let's just cut to the chase. Where are the girls we're looking for? Are they among those things?"

The bundle of rags shook, nodding but drawing back. "Find them if you can. When you flee, take me out of this place."

Henry and I were conscious of a swirling movement around us. Whatever these spirit-things were, they had surrounded us and seemed to be closing in on us, like we were at the heart of a vortex. I looked upwards and in the vague light thought I could make out a balcony, or some kind of higher level, cut into the stone. And she was there, that extraordinarily beautiful creature I'd tangled with once before—Carmella Cadenza, now going by the handle of the Cold Lady. I had a brief glimpse of her face— unmasked here—before the shadows covered her. She had been smiling, but there was no warmth in it. Her undeniable beauty couldn't make up for the maliciousness that fuelled her.

It would have washed over me. I've had more than a few withering glances from disgruntled dames in my time. What poured the ice back into my veins was the other shadow I'd seen up there. I'd only had a brief glimpse—a shape that was as hunched over and obscure as the Raggedy Man. Pure darkness, congealed and imbued with warped life, and with an unhealthy spread of limbs, jointed and elongated, as if a man had been fused with some other life form—a spider maybe. A particularly big spider.

This place was where broken things came to be mended. So I knew what that was up there, hugging the shadows beside the Cold Lady.

Spiderhead. An old nemesis of mine. Just as I'd fouled up Carmella's plans once, so had I put a big spoke in Spiderhead's wheel. I had a feeling at the time he'd limped away to fight another day. That being today by the look of it.

"They're here!" called Henry, snapping me out of my daze. He was indicating the faces that were glaring at us from the swirl of creatures around us. I peered into that human whirlpool and saw two faces I recognised from photos Ariadne had shown me. Suki Yosimoto and Maria Mozzari. They were smiling, idiotically, like part of their brain was on hold. That would be the work of the Cold Lady.

As the blurred crowd closed in, their arms reached out for us, slender and pale, making the whole thing look like one unified beast, intent on absorbing us. Which I didn't think would be a good idea. Their unholy singing had started up, shrill and discordant and definitely not the kind of thing that would go down well in any respectable night club.

"Now would be a good time for some accompanying riffs," I called to Henry.

"I'll do the music, you do the muscle," he said. "Grab the girls," he added when I gaped at him.

Grab the girls? Like this was a gentleman's 'excuse me.' Well, what else was I supposed to do?

Henry played a gentle riff on the guitar, the sound almost smothered by the banshee screech of the spinning creatures around us. I waited, trying to pick the right moment. I watched Suki Yosimoto's spinning face, her white arms reaching out in a blur and I tracked her. I let her get closer, closer then reached out myself and made a grab for her. I managed to get one hand fastened on a wrist and I yanked her towards me. It was like pulling something out of a pool of muck, or quicksand.

I could feel the resistance of the powers fuelling that concentrated energy, but the protective charms I was wearing, coupled with the stuff I'd smeared over my flesh so painstakingly exerted its own power. I felt myself boiling, my hapless torso a battlefield for energies that buzzed and fizzed like shorting electricity. Fortunately, the whirling motion of the singers worked in my favour and with a final jerk, I tore the girl free so that she tumbled into me. I wrapped my free arm around her, aware that her mouth, and more significantly her *teeth*, were inches from my neck.

She did shriek even louder, but her shriek was worse than her bite— that is, she didn't bite me. She just sagged down as if she'd been slugged, and curled up into a ball. As the others closed in, hands—claws now—still tearing at the air, I singled out Maria Mozzari. Again I struck while Henry played. It took me a couple of goes, but then I had her and drew her in. Steam emanated from me as if I'd got out of a baking oven.

The noise had become deafening and Henry strummed out some stronger chords. The effect was startling. His music went out in waves and it was like two tides clashing head on. In that maelstrom of sound, everything churned and broke like waves on invisible rocks. I gripped both of the fallen girls, while the others started to break apart, flying this way and that like foaming surf, slowly dissipating, their singing melting away.

I couldn't see the Cold Lady and her companion for the grey fog that palled around us, but I knew they'd both be in a real funk over my antics. Hell knew what they'd try next. I didn't want to hang around to find out.

"Time to beat it," I called to Henry.

Carefully holding the guitar, he nodded and followed me as I hoisted up the two girls, one under each arm. They acted like they'd been drugged, which was a relief and I made for the exit to the chamber. The Raggedy Man was in the shadows, waving us toward him. I let him lead the way back through the narrow defiles towards wherever the main exit was. My guess was, we'd have to stop for a time at least, while Henry sorted out his repertoire and played the right tune to open the way back home.

That wasn't going to be so easy—already the Cold Lady had set about closing her net. The stone walls were moving, like huge doors on hidden rollers. If we took the wrong turning, we were going to be crushed to bloody pulp or pinned helplessly. The Raggedy Man led the way, hopping like a huge flea, and at least he seemed to keep one jump ahead of the closing stone.

There was an eerie light ahead, high up like a weak moon, hidden among dense clouds. We seemed to be out of the labyrinth, but wherever we were, it was obscured. The Raggedy Man pointed ahead into the near darkness.

"Bridges," he said. "They criss-cross this place. Keep to them. Don't fall into the mire. It festers with the Pullulating Tribe and they will suck you in and drag the very soul from your bones."

I didn't relish that prospect, especially as I could see the many pools of this mire, disturbed by things below their sticky surfaces. On either side of the narrow bridges—which seemed to be some kind of twisted root, interlinked and tangled, slick with moisture—the foul sinks bubbled and frothed.

"Play the exit tune!" I yelled at Henry.

"I need more time," he yelled back. "If I stop here now, they'll overrun us."

That meant we had to get out on to those contorted root-things. The moonlight—or whatever the hell it was—brightened a tad and I could see that the landscape stretched away indefinitely, another maze. From out of the stone defile, the swirling spirit creatures, now re-grouped, came tumbling. They had the look of harpies on Benzedrine, intent on mayhem.

The Raggedy Man moved a whole lot quicker than I would have expected, doubtless prompted by the prospect of being shredded and fed to the pool-dwellers. So our little company moved on to and across the root maze as quickly as we could without slipping off and plunging into what would have been a revolting bath. Writhing tongues slapped at us as we passed, thick greasy fingers, green and stinking. Mercifully the two girls remained in a stupor, so I was able to keep them moving, their eyes glazed, their expressions empty.

Miraculously we reached a wider expanse of root, like a flattish area of trunk, slightly raised up, a kind of crossroads. Several paths led away from it, though they all seemed to head into an even more dismal mire. Fog billowed, shutting us in. We looked back and saw that the aerial creatures had again pulled up as if something in this place deterred them.

As we studied the marsh, things began to ooze up from it like bloated plants, vaguely human shaped, dripping with muck, emanating tendrils of vapour and exuding a stench that curdled the blood. They clawed their way out on to the root paths, slithering, snake-like along them. My guess was there were scores of the things, mud-beasts, shaped like fat slugs, unfinished and ungainly.

We were surrounded. "Henry, it really is time for that exit tune," I told him. "Either that or the last post."

He shrugged. "I was hoping to avoid this," he said, "but I think maybe I'm going to have to give it the old Entropy Chord. You might want to block your ears."

I told you he was an impulsive lad. With Henry, you didn't always get a chance to deliberate with him. This was one such time.

He gripped the guitar firmly, fingers of his left hand fixing its strings tightly to the frets, and ran his right hand down dramatically. The chord that erupted—oh, yes, *erupted*—from the instrument was like the crack of doom. It thundered outwards around us like a miniature tsunami. Well, maybe not that small. As the sound waves hit the things that were gathering in their disgusting multitudes, they burst like ripe fruit, showering the mire—and us—in filthy, sizzling gobbets of muck.

The whole structure under us shook as if it would crumble. I could vaguely see shapes back at the mouth of the stone labyrinth exploding, turned into a white cloud. I was getting a bad feeling about this. Like everywhere was about to disintegrate. That Entropy Chord was the trumpet of doom, a real world-ender.

"Henry," I called above the din, "I'll say it one last time—you really need to play the exit tune. It's time to go home."

He steadied himself, grinned like an idiot, and thankfully did as I asked. The two girls had partially come round, no doubt shaken awake by the apocalyptic events around us. I took hold of each of them as the new chords and riffs rippled from the blue guitar. It pulsed with life, the air about us went abruptly very still and for a moment everything stopped as darkness closed in.

When light seeped back into our little bubble, we seemed to be in another old building, not unlike the one Henry and I had first entered. The five of us moved through its dusty corridors and out through a broken door to stand on a sidewalk, where dim light splashed down from neon signs across the street. The two girls shook themselves, still dazed. I wondered if they'd remember anything of the bizarre events we'd all come through.

We didn't stay long enough to find out if anyone had followed us. My guess was, whatever chaos the Entropic Chord had unleashed, the Cold Lady and Spiderhead had survived it, one way or another.

Henry was still gripping the guitar like it was welded to his fingers.

"I think maybe it's time to put that goddam thing back in its case," I told him. I noticed that it had lost its blue glow and it looked like any other battered old guitar.

"It's okay, Nick. Once the Entropy Chord's been played, it takes a long time for the guitar to re-charge itself."

Suki turned to Henry, her face breaking out into a big smile. "Henry!" she chirped. "So nice to see you."

The kid looked embarrassed. Now, that was a first.

Maria also managed a smile, but the Raggedy Man had already beaten a hasty retreat into the night. What the hell, he'd earned his freedom.

"Come on, you guys," I said. "I know somewhere we can get a stiff drink and a clean-up. And I know who'll pick up the tab."

There were no objections.

* * * *

"Piece of cake," said Henry.

We were sitting in a late bar, the two girls almost asleep beside us, their drinks untouched on the table. I'd been that thirsty I'd sunk two bottles of beer and had a third in front of me. Henry didn't usually drink alcohol, but after our exhausting escapades had managed to down a bottle of beer himself.

"It bothers me," I said. "I know we had that crazy guitar to get us through, but don't you think it was a might…easy?"

He frowned. "One false step and we'd have been dragged into that mire."

"I know. I'm just saying." I let it go for now. "You get the girls somewhere safe and we'll talk about it when Ariadne gets back."

I left him to it. Outside, the night life buzzed, and there didn't seem like there would be any immediate moves from the mob we'd cheated. I reckoned Henry would take care of things for the time being.

* * * *

A few days later, after Ariadne had returned, I gave her a blow by blow account of the rescue of the two singers. Like me, she thought maybe we'd got off lightly, given the kind of powers we'd been up against.

"You smell a rat," she told me, knowing me well enough to read me and my murky mind. "What are you thinking?"

"The girls—are they okay? Anything out of order?" I'd had Henry deliver them to her. No one had tried to interfere. It was like the Cold Lady had given up on them. Maybe she had, but then again—

"They don't seem any the worse for their experiences," said Ariadne. "And it hasn't affected their singing. They're coming on fine. In fact, I'll be ready to give them their first night at the club soon. Warm up act for FiFi Cherie at the Big Jamboree I told you about. It'll be *the* place to be seen.

You'll be there, of course."

"Front row," I grinned. "But you'd better have the place well protected. There's a couple of things bugging me. For one, the Raggedy Man told us the girls were being groomed by Carmella Cadenza. To do the work of the Angels of Malice. Which was to unleash the Pullulating Tribe."

"What else?"

"Something Henry said the other day. He was wriggling with embarrassment like a teenager on his first date—which he is not—when he told me that Suki is not as hot as she was. Now, maybe she's cooled off toward him, or just needs a bit of private space after her little adventure. You know more about these things than me. Apparently, she don't kiss like she used to. Kind of dead, as Henry put it."

Ariadne gave me her thoughtful frown. "May be something in it."

* * * *

For the next few days, I chewed over the events in the stone world and our remarkable abduction of the two girls. Remarkable, yeah. The more I thought about it, the more it bothered me. With all the powers at their disposal, the Angels of Malice—who'd had us at their mercy—had let us slip through their clammy fingers. Sure, I'd been protected and we'd had the guitar, but it was their world, bulging at the seams with their teeming hordes. No, something was wrong. Why did I think we'd been suckered?

I thought about the guitar, going back to the auction. Now that I did think about it, that was odd. If the thing was such a goddam prize, why run the risk of losing it at an auction? If the Nasty Guys had wanted it that bad, they'd have raised Hell to get it, wouldn't they? So why the soft approach?

There could only be one reason. They *wanted* Henry to have it. Dressed up to look like he'd beaten them to it, albeit with my help. So that meant they'd wanted him to take it into their bizarre little world. But even then, they hadn't taken it off him. They must have known he would use it to win back the singers. And in doing so, blowing the Pullulating Tribe and its surroundings to smithereens.

And in so doing, exhausting the guitar! *It takes a long time for the guitar to re-charge itself*, Henry'd said. Which meant, right now, it was useless.

We'd brought the girls—the singers—into our world. Singers who had gifts bestowed on them by the Angels of Malice. Singers who, according to Henry, were not quite as they had been. Puppets.

It was an Oh my God moment.

They were going to sing in Ariadne's Big Jamboree at the night club and raise God alone knew what horrors, and there would be no blue guitar to blast them back to Hell. And when was this going to happen?

Tonight. In a few hours' time.

* * * *

If I thought I was going to leave my office, sprint out into the city, grab a taxi and hightail to Ariadne like a bolt from the blue, I must have been kidding. I had my armoury strapped in and I went down the stairs to the alley like a cat with its tail ablaze, but no sooner had I got out of the door than I knew I was not alone. I almost ran into a hail of lead.

They were at both ends of the alley. Luckily the street lights were on the fritz again, so I must have made a blurred target. I was able to duck back inside before they shredded my carcass. Something nicked my arm, and I felt something hit my chest like I'd been punched but not enough to slow me down. I tore back upstairs, locked the door and made for the fire exit out back. I tossed an old jacket out first, and sure enough, it was ripped apart in seconds by another crossfire.

They had me pinned down. I had to get hold of Ariadne and tell her what I'd figured out. I reached inside my coat and pulled out my cell phone—or what was left of it. It disintegrated in my hand. The punch I thought I'd felt was a bullet glancing off it. I was glad enough the damn thing had saved me what might have been a crippling hit, but now I had no way of warning Ariadne.

I had one last chance to get out of there. I went into my cunningly converted broom cupboard, dropped down a makeshift elevator and emerged in the darkness of the cellar. There was a hidden door and I opened and closed it cautiously. Beyond, in a dank, dripping tunnel that was originally dug here generations ago, I crept away, listening for anything other than the rats that frequented the place.

I was intending to head for the office block where I knew Ariadne would be making her last preparations before going to *Diamonds Are Forever*. We had to cancel tonight's show. On my way, however, it occurred to me that the block would be watched from all angles. Our enemies would be out in full force tonight. Divide and conquer. No doubt Henry and Stan would also be watched, not that Henry could do much damage without the blue guitar.

I got out of the cab and paid the driver, a block from Ariadne's offices. I usually entered through a private door, but I could only do it if I gave her notice. Maybe I could climb up a fire escape out back somewhere. There were phone booths, but they'd be watched for sure. My guess was, Carmella Cadenza had given orders for her people to rub me out on sight, no messing. I couldn't take that risk.

As I was sneaking my way towards an alley that I knew would take me to the back of the huge building, ducking and diving into every shadowy doorway I could en route, I felt an arm wrap around my neck and some-thing hard jam up against my spine. I allowed myself to be pulled into the darkness. Someone had got the drop on me and as I swore crudely, it was at my own stupidity.

"Take it easy, fellar. You're in good hands."

The voice, coupled with the faint whiff of very expensive perfume made me realise I hadn't been snared by one of Satan's children.

"Ariadne," I breathed.

She pulled me deeper into the shadows, released me and took me down the narrowest of alleys to a doorway, tapping on it with the gun she was toting. The door opened and we slipped inside.

"Sorry about that," she said, with a rueful grin. "The bad guys are out in force. Didn't want to be seen."

I was about to blurt out what I'd pieced together, but she put a slim finger over my lips. "I know what you're going to say. You realised what was really happening."

"You, too?"

"I had a tip off. There's someone I want you to meet. It'll come as a shock, but just stay cool, okay?"

I nodded, but I was feeling more than a little edgy as she took me through another door and up some stairs. We came to a room that was lit by a single bulb. Some of her people were there, dependable guys who I knew could handle themselves. It was a relief. What was less relaxing was the sight of the guy sitting in the middle of the room on an old chair, his head down, his hands folded in his lap.

He looked up at me and for a moment it seemed like he was shudder-ing. "Mt Stone," he said. "You know me."

Yeah, I knew that bastard, all right. Erik van Brazen. We'd crossed paths a few times, and if there was a man on this Earth I'd sworn I'd tear apart with my bare hands, it was him. He was responsible for more misery in my life than a whole shipload of Satan's sidekicks.

"This better be good, pal, because I am going to pull your head apart before I leave this room," I told him in a tone that does not get any nastier.

Ariadne put a restraining arm on mine and it's probably the only thing that prevented me from carrying out my threat.

"You're too late," he said and as he lifted his head, I saw now that he looked like he'd aged about a hundred years. His skin was waxy, lined and creased, and his hair was thinning, white and fading. I looked at his hands, and they were little more than bones. "You want to shoot me, I don't give a damn. Go ahead."

"What's he doing here?" I snapped at Ariadne.

"He's the Raggedy Man. The shaven, cleaned-up version. Before that, he was controlled by the creature who tried to abduct me, the thing you called Spiderhead. When you rescued me, Spiderhead fled. Licking its wounds, it rejected the human vessel it had used for its purposes and found somewhere to hole up. Just like Carmella Carnadine. You saw them, Nick, in that place where Henry took you."

Van Brazen was nodding. "Once that creature had dumped me, I was finished. It and that floozy abandoned me and let me crawl around in the dark. The only reason they didn't kill me was maybe I'd earned the right to live, even if it was a parody of life."

"We should have left you there to rot." I had no sympathy for the man.

"I became the Raggedy Man. My days are numbered now, Stone. If you don't kill me, it won't matter. I'll be done for soon enough. You don't want to worry about me—it's that thing you call Spiderhead you need to deal with." He shuddered again.

"Where is it?"

"Oh, it's here, not far away. It's gotten its filthy grip on some other sucker. In a coupla hours it'll make itself known, through those two girls you pulled out of the hole. They were bait if you didn't know it."

"So why were you so damn keen to tip Ariadne off?"

"Listen, pal, when you've had your brain clamped by that monster and had your every move controlled by it, your skin would crawl at the thought of it. I'm no saint. Maybe I'll burn in Hell. But if I can pay that creeping horror back for what it did to me, then fine."

"We're supposed to trust you?" I sneered.

"We may have no choice," said Ariadne.

"You made a deal with this creep?" I said to her, but she shook her head. "Okay, so make sure he stays put. If he moves an inch out of line," I told the heavy brigade, "put a bullet between his ears. And when we've done, give him to Police Chief Carter. That's the best deal you'll get from me, van Brazen."

"You're going soft, Mr. Nightmare," he said.

"If Miss Carnadine wasn't here, your brains would already be decorating the walls." I turned to Ariadne. "You got somewhere else we can talk?"

We quit the room and I felt myself slowly getting control of my fury. Ariadne gave me a quick hug.

"I don't like it anymore than you do," she said. "But it's all we've got."

"So what's the plan?"

* * * *

I had to wear a tuxedo, and worse than that, a bow tie and shoes that were so polished they dazzled the eye. I had to look the part for my appearance at the Big Jamboree. Ariadne told me we were to act as if the whole show was going to be fine and we had no idea that something sinister was going on. I knew her administrative machinery was ultra-slick, but the trick she pulled off with the guests was, to my mind, beyond belief. Somehow she'd gotten discreet word to every guest that the show was postponed for a few days, but that it would go ahead, very sorry, and no one would be disappointed once it did. No doubt it caused ripples throughout city society, especially as diaries had to be adjusted, but it had to be done. The dignitaries and celebrities did not want to miss this, so they'd do as asked.

Diamonds Are Forever, however, was about to have a dummy run. Ariadne was going to fill the place with hired guns, or at least, guys she could depend on to tackle whatever the Angels of Malice were lining up. I'd told her that by alerting her guests, she'd have simply been warning the enemy off, but she pointed out that the major servants of darkness would be keeping well out of things, given what they thought was going to happen.

The Pullulating Tribe. That's what was going to happen. I thought Henry had blown the whole mob to atoms, but Ariadne said van Brazen had told her we'd only gotten shot of a handful, sacrificed in the grand deceit. The main task force was all geared up and ready to roll.

"What the heck are these things going to do?" I'd asked her.

"They're parasites. Think of demonic possession."

"Do I have to?"

"Once they're summoned and unleashed, they'll attempt to possess everyone in the club. Can you imagine what that would have meant if it had been the original guests? New York city taken over by servants of Satan, big time."

"Right—so now it's just you, me and your private army that stand to be possessed."

"Forewarned is forearmed," she'd smiled. "We'll fight fire with fire. Magic with magic. When I was in Europe, I was warned that the forces of evil were stirring and I brought back a few goodies."

So once again I was wearing my special sigils and my bangles, baubles, and beads. They'd worked okay when I'd clashed with the Pullulating Tribe before, so maybe they'd protect me again. If I'd had any sense, I'd have been on a Greyhound bus heading far off into the West. But it was Ariadne.

When I entered the club and gave the doorman my invite card, the place was already humming. Everyone inside—and there was a huge crowd, very convincing—was giving a first class impression of having a good time, drinking, dancing, fooling around as any normal guest would do at such an occasion. I recognised a few faces—tough guys on Ariadne's team—and I marveled that she'd been able to gather so many together, like a private army. But I knew there was a lot more to her than met the eye.

She would enter separately, probably keeping out of the way until she made her appearance as FiFi Cherie, although if things went as expected, she'd not be needed to sing. Things were going to blow up before then.

On the wide stage, the regular band was playing, maybe with a tad less gusto than usual. Ariadne had told me she'd given them instructions to beat it once the two new singers were introduced. She'd brought in some special support for them. Van Brazen had told her that the girls were under a form of hypnosis and would speak and act as normal, oblivious to the fact that when they started to sing, the powers fused into them would be unlocked. They had no idea they were being used.

Ariadne put this to the test by gradually having the crowd dissipate. The two girls were backstage. As far as they knew, things were swinging along and they were getting tense and nervous about their debuts. Whatever had been implanted in them was waiting, like some kind of beasts about to pounce. As long as events around them panned out as expected, they wouldn't be warned off. Ariadne reckoned that Carmella Cadenza and her immediate confederates were watching events through the eyes of the girls. So, by the time the two of them slid out on to the stage, to perform a duet, most of the audience had left the building.

I was in the wings, watching. Ariadne knew her stuff—she'd had the lighting fixed so that the girls couldn't see beyond the glare off stage. As far as they knew, there was a full house out there. Whereas in fact there were now no more than a dozen people, all with a particular power placed there by Ariadne. Around the walls, tall curtains, heavy velvet stuff, had been hung in a wide circle, so the place was closed in, and would prevent sound echoing in a way that would suggest the place was empty. Ariadne had told me it would suit the enemy, who wouldn't want a single soul, literally, to escape the trap.

It was late when the moment came. The band, also reduced now to a few guys who were more than just straight members, again selected by Ariadne, struck up the chords that would prompt the two girls to take the stage. Lights flared, spotlights swiveled, as Maria Mozzari and Suki Yosimoto appeared and began to sing. It seemed like they were unaware of the change in the hall. They just sang.

It was weird stuff. Almost like it wasn't human, high-pitched beyond the normal vocal range and eerie. The girls interlocked the sounds. Maybe a free form jazz fan would have made something of it, but it was pure headache music to me. Ariadne was at my shoulder. I glanced at her. As far as the girls knew, she was due on stage as FiFi Cherie, but by now she'd changed into her black Ninja gear, complete with those two blades that could slice a human hair into a dozen pieces.

"Now we're cooking with gas," I whispered.

"Keep your mind on your job," she whispered back, jabbing me in the ribs, but she was right. This was a time to concentrate. The muck was about to hit the fan.

I shifted around the edge of the stage, easing down some wooden steps to the auditorium floor, to where I could see it clearly, my eyes no longer dazzled by the brilliant glare. I had my twin Berettas out, although when it comes to that old black magic, I'm never sure if they're going to be effective. I do like the feel-good factor, though.

It had already started. Enemy action. That dreadful singing was bearing fruit. Something was curling up through the floorboards, like a dawn miasma from a swamp. The air became foetid as the vapours thickened and coalesced. They had an unhealthy resemblance to the stuff that had steamed over the weird landscape Henry and I had visited before the Pullulating Tribe had materialised. Sure enough, it was happening again—the girls' voices rose and shrilled, conducting this bizarre summoning to the point where the first shapes solidified, quickly multiplying.

Dripping with ooze, these things were only vaguely humanoid in shape, but their purpose was clear—they were intent on assailing the remaining people in the hall. Ariadne had told me she'd chosen them carefully—they were adepts, all of them purporting to be masters of spiritual matters. Each of them carried a weapon, either a short sword-like instrument or a wand and as the air began to boil with the gathering Tribe, these weapons glowed with white light.

I watched from the side-lines, sweat dripping off me. A furious battle was taking off. Scores of the infestations from beyond were hurling themselves at the adepts, the clashing of power drowning out the girls' singing until two of Ariadne's remaining members of the band jabbed each of them with a needle and took them out of the scene altogether. It shut off the flowing arrival of more of the Pullulating Tribe, but there were enough of the monsters here now to choke the place.

Bedlam reigned. I would have used my guns, but Ariadne held me in check, as though she was expecting this whole farrago to work its way to a climax, without our interference. She was right. The adepts were banded together in the centre of the hall, the intruders swirling around them in a black vortex, filled with leering faces and claws as if Hell itself had discharged an entire army of demons. Somehow the adepts, hands and weapons raised like banners, were repelling the assault, although as it increased in ferocity, I wondered how long they could hold out.

The Pullulating Tribe was trying to surge forward, like a huge tidal wave that would not be restrained for much longer. Someone else entered the picture and I could just about make out its silhouette.

It was Henry Maclean.

And he was carrying the blue guitar. I gaped at Ariadne. Didn't she realise it wouldn't work? We'd drained it when Henry had played the Entropic Chord.

Henry tugged the instrument from its case and set it down on the floor. The adepts stood either side of it, making various passes with their weapons. Like some ravenous beast, the swirling horror that was the Pullulating Tribe, zoomed forward and down, breaking through the defence of the adepts, scattering them this way and that, sending them tumbling across the dance floor. Henry had skipped back towards the stage, out of immediate danger. As he did so, all the surrounding curtains dropped, like their supports had been severed, to reveal the walls. Walls, which had been daubed with cabbalistic designs and what must have been magical inscriptions.

The guitar glowed its familiar blue, though it was faint and didn't look to me like there was any power in it. The vortex poured down over it like a waterfall hitting a flat surface. Except that there was no explosion, no outward waves. All that fuming dark power drove into the guitar, and as it did so, the thing just got bluer and bluer, its light becoming too strong to look at.

I don't know how long it went on for, but I was practically on my knees by the time it had finished. There was an abrupt silence. Just the guitar, pulsing and humming, its strings vibrating.

"I'd say that thing is re-charged," said Ariadne beside me.

"You knew that would happen?"

"Sort of. It was worth a try."

I had no time to voice my views on that. Something else was manifesting itself out on the dance floor. The adepts had all been swept sideways in a rough circle by the implosion of the Pullulating Tribe and they were all flat on their backs, apparently exhausted by their efforts. The thing that drew itself up out of the floor twisted and stretched itself until it became a man. But this was no ordinary man.

It had elongated arms and legs, a weirdly bloated body and an oversized head. I knew immediately why the head was elongated. Something had attached itself to the mass of hair, burying its own legs into it.

Spiderhead.

This wasn't van Brazen, but a new host for the monster. He—it—stood there, feral eyes blazing like a demon, lips drawn back in a snarl that would have embarrassed a full grown tiger. Those eyes fixed on the stuff scrawled on the walls, *containing* spells. It howled like a caged wolf, or worse, stepping toward the guitar like it intended to snatch it up.

Ariadne was quicker than me to respond. She pulled out both her blades and ran across the floor with the clear intention of decapitating the creature. She had good cause to want to exterminate Spiderhead, having suffered the thing's evil attention once before. But the two swords whistled through the air, inches short of their target as the monster leapt sideways, incredibly agile. Ariadne was no slouch and moved with speed that almost defied the eye.

Time and again the creature weaved and bobbed out of reach. I thought it must be a matter of time before she nailed it. I had my guns up, ready to use them, but the movements on the centre of the dance floor were so rapid that I could have hit her. I stepped a little closer, waiting.

In the end, Spiderhead landed the first blow, one of those long arms swinging out and catching Ariadne off balance, sending her tumbling. She rolled, both blades upright in a defensive move, while the creature closed in over her. It swept both blades aside and I realised it was going to dip its disgusting head and close its teeth over her face.

There was no time to think. I used both guns, aiming as best I could in the faltering light for the elongated arms that were supporting the creature. My aim was good and the elbow joints both exploded in a welter of flesh, gore and matted hairs. Spiderhead was blown sideways by the impact, emitting a high pitched shriek, a mixture of fury and pain.

Ariadne moved twice as quickly, rolling over and up. She brought one of her blades down and severed the head of the monster, which tumbled end over end into the shadows. She used the other blade to drive down into the guts of body, pinning it to the floor, where it thrashed for long moments. I ran forward and emptied one of the Berettas into the shadows where the head—the enormous spider—had rolled. There were adepts near to it, but they all put some space between themselves and the spider-thing. Chances were it would try and take one of them over.

I got as close as I dared, preparing to fill the bristling monster with enough lead to sink a rhino. There was blood and other fluid pooling around it and I was careful not to step in any. As quickly as the thing had first materialised, it began to alter its shape, like some kind of thick, black gunk and found enough cracks in the floorboards to drain away. I fired again, unsure whether my bullets were having any effect.

By the time Ariadne had reached me, Spiderhead was gone. All that remained was a wide pool of viscous fluid.

"Do you think you killed it?"

I shook my head. "Damaged it, maybe. More damn lives than a cat."

Henry joined us, his arm around Suki Yosimoto. She seemed a little dazed like she'd just come out of a deep sleep. Chances were she and Maria were free of the powers that had used them. Henry stooped down and slid the blue guitar into its case, zipping it shut.

"This thing wants putting somewhere well out of reach," he said. "If anyone wants to play the Entropy Chord, there's going to be one hell of a blast. Thermonuclear stuff."

* * * *

It was long gone midnight by the time Police Chief Rizzie Carter had been to the club and arranged for his crew to dispose of the headless body. I explained to him what had happened. Only a cop who knew me and the kind of madness I got mixed up in would have taken it at face value. The dead man was known to him and Ariadne, an ambitious hoodlum by the name of Jed Rawls, who the Chief had been trying to nail for some time. Just the kind of creep that Spiderhead liked to use.

"We'll put this one down to a mob killing," Rizzie Carter said, grinning through a big mouthful of hot dog. No matter what time of the night it was, you could rely on the Chief to find himself a big, fat feast.

"And nice work getting hold of van Brazen," he said to Ariadne. "Your men handed him over to me earlier. Looks like all the fight's gone out of him. Tomorrow we'll send him back to the sanatorium. That's if he wakes up. He looked about ready for the big sleep when I left him."

Ariadne and I watched him leave.

"Nightcap?" she said.

"I think I'll just hit the sack."

"You do say the sweetest things."

A Queen of Carpathia

K.A. Opperman

*O my belovèd, in your loveliness
I trace the shadow of an ancient queen
Who ruled a proud, Carpathian demesne
From out a castle lost in wilderness.
Dead pomp and splendor haunt your sapphire eyes,
And in your visage rouged with eglantine,
I note refinement of a monarchess;
Your sable mane the baser comb belies.*

*I see you leaning from a moonlit tower,
To catch cruel winter's kiss upon your cheek,
But why so mournful, I cannot surmise,
Nor why you watch the forest at that hour.
I only know that on that night antique,
The wolves all serve you, howling as they scour
Those haunted mountains, barren, cold, and bleak.*

The Dead of Night
Christian Riley

We were against the storm for three days and three nights before our fishing vessel, the *Portland's Pride*, finally sank. Failed welds in the hull most likely. She took water in the engine room, tipped from a large wave, and then sank to the bottom of the Bering Sea. Except for me, everyone was trapped inside the galley, or the wheelhouse, and I'm sure that their deaths must have been horrifying.

Just before our vessel went down a wall of water swept me off the deck and threw me into the sea. I was wearing nothing but raingear. The waves handled me like a toy, tossing me every direction. The currents sucked on my body for what seemed like a lifetime. The icy water drank itself into my soul, tempting me with each passing minute to let go, let the sea take me away.

But then their ship appeared from out of nowhere: a golem of steel against the early morning horizon. The crew of the *Aleutian Whisper* plucked me out of the water just in time, and then I blacked out shortly afterward.

I woke the next morning in a bunk, wrapped in a warm blanket. I lay there for a while, glad to be alive. I felt vibrations from the diesel engine below, pushing us through the mild seas. The storm had broken sometime while I slept, and now the crew was out on deck, fishing for crab. I heard the occasional shout, a laugh, and then the unmistakable pounding of the hydraulic crane swinging crab pots against the rail. Taking a deep breath, I wondered—*was it all just a horrible nightmare?*

When I looked around the stateroom, I realized that no, it wasn't a nightmare at all. And then a chill crept back into my skin. I thought about my friends who had lost their lives and of where their bodies now resided—at the bottom of the sea. I said a prayer for them, and then I said another prayer, thanking God for my rescue.

Fortunately, the cold water hadn't robbed me of any appendages or digits. I discovered this when I climbed off the bunk and made a quick inspection of my body. Although comfortable, I still felt the lingering presence of a dampening cold deep within my bones. It was as if a dull current of sadness had nestled into my soul.

Again, the sounds from the working vessel rang in my ears, as I made my way toward the wheelhouse: the clank and reel of the hydraulic block outside, followed by a few curses from the deckhands; the churn, rattle, and hum from down below, in the engine room. Then, as if someone threw a switch, a loud stereo suddenly cranked through the cabin, playing *La Bamba*, by Richie Valens. Not the fishing vessel I was used to, but one all the same.

I climbed the stairs to the wheelhouse and there she was—the vast Bering Sea. My stomach turned into a ball of lead at the sight of her, knowing that just hours before, she had been toying with my life.

"Well, looky here!" The captain startled me. About fifty, he had a round face, and eyes that twinkled like fire. Thin strands of silver hair draped from his bald head, brushing his shoulders.

"Back from the dead, are we?" I missed the humor in his words. Seemed like a cruel response to someone who'd just lost a boatload of friends.

"Name's Bailey." And then he threw out an open hand. "Your name, son?"

"Jake Sanford," I replied, shaking his hand. "How long have I been out of it, sir?"

"Just a day, or so. We picked you up—was it yesterday? Shoot, I can't remember. You know how this crabbing thing works on a man's mind."

"Were there any other survivors?"

He shrugged his shoulders then turned back toward the sea. "Nah. Just you, I guess."

He guessed? I didn't know what to say in return, so I stumbled over and sat on the bench to the opposite side of the captain's chair. I looked out the windows, noticing that the *Aleutian Whisper* had a forward-facing wheelhouse.

"What's up with the Coast Guard?" I asked. The captain was staring into the horizon, and I saw that the side of his face went sullen, as if he had just had an unpleasant thought. "Captain?"

"Huh? Oh yeah, the Coast Guard. I ah…I alerted them. Yeah, that's what I did."

His last sentence came out as a mutter, and it snapped at my nerves like a rubber band. What he should have told me was that the Coast Guard was currently searching the ocean for survivors, dead bodies, debris. He should have told me that the Coast Guard had asked for my name and that he would relay it to them once he found out himself—which he wasn't doing.

"Go on down and make yourself some food, son. Get comfortable."

"Are we on our way to port?" I asked.

"All in good time, sailor." Then, in the blink of an eye, Captain Bailey was out the side door, his back to me and his eyes toward the gloomy sea. His actions were terribly awkward, in those fleeting seconds, it took him to step outside. There was the brisk manner in which he turned away from me, and how he slammed the door on his way out. And then, the swift glance in my direction before he faced the open water. I saw his eyes, and they had turned black as night and sharp as daggers.

Stop imagining things, sailor, I told myself. On the radio now, was Phil Phillip's, *Sea of Love*.

* * * *

Down below, there was a porthole in the ready-room door, overlooking the deck. I peeked out and watched as four deckhands in orange rain gear stumbled through the motions of hauling, and stacking pots. I hadn't noticed anything out of the ordinary, but I did see that they were pulling up blanks—no crab often makes for a cranky captain.

I turned and made my way down the hall and into the galley. A clock above a television was stuck on ten minutes after four. The digital clock on the microwave blinked "12:37." Not a big deal, as I thought about it. I knew that some crews ran gear without a working clock in the galley. It's tough to have Father Time stare back at you when you're cold, tired, and miserable.

Opening the fridge, I found a mishmash of leftovers and half-empty containers. Nothing looked appetizing, so I rummaged through the cabinets for a candy bar. I never heard the door from the ready-room open, and I jumped at the sound of the man's voice behind me.

"Hungry?"

"Yeah, I guess I am. I'm Jake, by the way." I reached out to shake his hand, but he ignored me. He walked over and closed the cabinet doors, then gave me a foul look.

"My name is Taylor. Taylor Bailey… And the food in here is for working crew only. Keep out of it unless you mean to put on some rain gear." He turned, facing the hall. "Follow me, I'll show you what you can eat."

A river of ice ran down my spine. How could this man treat me like this? Or the captain, for that matter? Nothing about the way both of these men acted seemed remotely normal. My boat went down, for Christ's sake! I lost friends. I barely survived, myself. And now, to be denied the comfort one would expect from fellow fishermen, after being pulled from the sea. To be denied *safe passage*.

I followed him down the hall and into the small storage compartment next to the bathroom. There were containers on the shelves with various dried goods, batteries, and miscellaneous tools. But at the bottom, and on the floor, sat a dilapidated cardboard box tucked into the darkness.

"You can eat what's in there," Taylor said, and then he swept past me, on his way to the wheelhouse.

Baffled, I pulled the box out from under the shelf. Inside was a head of wilted lettuce and some moldy cheese.

"This must be a joke," I said aloud. Captain Bailey and his brother Taylor—as I now presumed, since they both had the same last name—were just messing with me. *They're probably up there right now, busting their guts with laughter.*

When I reached the top of the stairs, I heard the two men cackling, which convinced me of my previous assumption.

"Very funny guys," I said, walking into the wheelhouse. "Moldy cheese?"

"Go on now, you don't need to be in here!" the captain shouted. "Didn't I tell you to get something to eat?"

I stared at the two men for a second, a long second. My thoughts were lost, and it felt as if someone had pressed a hot iron into my chest.

"But stay out of the galley," Taylor added, grimly.

"By the way, this here is my brother," said the captain, jerking his thumb, smiling proudly.

* * * *

Things only got worse as the day rolled on. I managed to talk to the rest of the crew, when they came in to use the bathroom, or get some coffee. They were all just as distant and remote as the captain and his brother had been. Some of them seemed cheerful enough, but when I asked them about heading for port, they just shrugged their shoulders and walked away. None of them invited me into the galley for a meal.

In what must have been the late afternoon, I went back to my bunk to rest. I thought about my predicament, still hoping that everything was just one big joke and that now, the entire crew was in on it. I thought this, in fact, moments before I fell asleep. But hours later, when I opened my eyes…

The stateroom was morbidly dark. There were no sounds other than the humming of the engine below. I climbed down and crept out of the room, thinking the crew was asleep. I walked down the hall toward the galley, famished, prepared to steal food. As I approached the ready-room, I saw a man lying on the floor, and my first assumption was that he had passed out after coming inside. But after close inspection, I realized he was dead.

It was Taylor, lying on his back, eyes and mouth stretched open, a face of death staring at the ceiling. I noticed streams of what looked like yellow earwax that had bubbled and oozed out of his ears. And there was a putrid smell lingering in the hall, like rancid milk.

Nerves now rattled, I stepped past the body and approached the galley. I wasn't sure what had happened to the man, and I certainly wasn't going to touch him. Briefly, I suspected a heart attack, and that nobody had found him yet since everyone must have been asleep. But then I thought about all that earwax and the smell.

My thoughts spun into a different direction after entering the galley. I found the rest of the deckhands, and all three of them were sprawled on the floor, eyes as vacant and vast as the Bering Sea. And each of them had that yellow goo dripping from their ears.

I choked on my breath and ran for the wheelhouse.

* * * *

Captain Bailey's head was drooping over the back of his chair. His scraggly hair swayed absently from the motions of the boat. His arms hung low. His eyes stared at the wooden paneling above. His mouth gaped crookedly as if the jaw had become unhinged. And from his left ear…a mound of goop the size of a tennis ball.

I had awoken into a nightmare—a gruesome death that had touched every man on the *Aleutian Whisper*, except for me. I was both chilled and mystified, and in the grip of this terror, I reacted.

I grabbed the captain's body and flung him to the floor, tenderness aside. Yes, the man had saved my life, but… But what?

Panic set in, and I quickly surveyed the instruments, the compass, looked for a map. My legs got the shakes, and my imagination got the best of me. I pictured some kind of monster on the ship—a yellow blob, searching for its next victim—so I flipped the mast light switch in response. A blink of the eye and the *Aleutian Whisper* turned white against the black hollows of the night.

"Some kind of monster," I told myself. Then I thought that that was just an irrational fear. But still—every man was now dead. Hadn't I been in this same situation only the night before? The lone survivor.

I reached for the radio, the word "Mayday" clinging to my lips, when suddenly…

"*Sissssss…*"

A turn of the head and he was there, standing, glaring—with those fire-lit eyes. The pale face of Death now leered at me in the form of Captain Bailey. I froze at the wheel, eyes locked with his. Then, with blinding speed, he grabbed me!

His hands wrapped around my throat, he snarled, his face contorted into a visage of lunacy. He squeezed at my neck with impossible strength. *Some kind of monster!* The horrific thought broke my initial shock, and then I punched the captain in his nose.

"*Haaaaaaa!*" The captain hissed, and his jaw dropped open, releasing a foul breath of air. His hands were successfully crushing my trachea, and he had me pressed up against the side-door. I clutched the strip of hair on his head and jammed my thumbs into his eyes. I tried to push him away, but he wouldn't let go. The captain was killing me.

"*Arrgghhh!!*" He roared, and again, that breath, stinging my eyes. I dropped my hands and reached for the door handle behind me. I turned it, and then the wind took over.

I collapsed with my back to the railing. The sweep of the black ocean struck instantly with a light mist, swathing across my face, clinging to my hair, while the creature known as Captain Bailey just stood there. He stood in the doorway, scowling, and for sure, I expected him to drop down on me and finish the job. But no; he simply turned and walked back into the wheelhouse!

The icy wind snapped me out of it. I stood and observed through the doorway, studying the captain. I couldn't believe my eyes. It was a nightmare, as there could be no other explanation. Or so I thought.

I left the dead man as he was, pacing the wheelhouse, and climbed down onto the deck amidship, via the side rail. My body screamed for warmth, I was freezing, my hands shook with fear, and my stomach churned. I needed to get back inside. But I wondered about the others. Would they be just like the captain?

The door into the ready-room gave an aged, metallic squeak as I opened it. I cringed, and carefully slid my way through. I walked toward the galley. They were still there, all four crewmembers, and I was careful not to touch any of them. It seemed my own hands had brought the captain back from the dead, and into the unwholesome state of a mindless sentinel. Obviously, I didn't dare reproduce this scenario with the others. But I needed to get warm. I needed extra clothing, possibly some raingear.

Like a mouse, I stole my way down the hall and into the nearest stateroom. Rummaging in the dark, I found a wool jacket and a cap. I put them on and crept back to the ready-room, avoiding Taylor's body. There was a set of raingear hanging on the wall, just above him. Carefully, I reached over his body and grabbed the gear. But as I pulled it away from the hook, a pair of gloves fell from within its bulk, and onto Taylor's face.

"*Muuaaaahhhhh....*"

I panicked, and threw myself out the door and onto the deck! I slipped and fell, but swiftly regained my footing then ran behind a stack of crab pots, where I promptly turned and looked back toward the door. The corpse I had just awoken was now sporadically breaking the light from the hall, and the galley, as it wandered the inside of the ship.

Taylor stayed put, however. He stayed in his "area," and so the hours passed. My stomach churned and toiled with an angry hunger. My mouth went dry. I put on the raingear and was mildly warm, but my body shivered endlessly from fear. Yet despite all this—the hunger, the thirst, or the ceaseless terror—my eyes also grew heavy.

* * * *

"Hey sailor!"

I woke with a start!

"What the hell are you doing back there?" It was Taylor, and he was wide-eyed, alive, breathing the cold ocean air without a moment's pause—as if the notion of being dead the night before would have seemed a preposterous one, had I brought it up.

"Found some raingear, eh?" He turned and walked back toward the galley. "Good! You can be our baiter then."

I felt the sudden urge to release my bowels. Had I become a madman? Was I insane? The ability to process this astounding, unending nightmare seemed an impossible task. My mind flailed. *"Their baiter?"* I whispered into the wind.

Minutes later, the others came out, and before long, the crewmembers were working the deck, getting ready to pick up pots.

"Hey, bait-boy!" Taylor shouted. "Get to work already! We're coming up on the gear!"

Unsure as to what the consequence for disobedience would entail, I stumbled out from my hide.

"That a boy," Taylor said, pointing to the bait table on the port side of the boat.

Walking past the man, I did a double take after spotting that yellow goo smeared across his right cheek. My hands trembled violently in response. *I must be going insane*, I thought.

At the bait table, I took a deep breath. I had done this job a thousand times before, and insane or not, I'd work on autopilot as I considered how to escape this hell. And I would stay out of their way in the process.

But now, and to my complete wonder, the bait table was empty. I turned and walked toward the engine room door. On a normal vessel, with a *normal* crew, there would be twenty-five-pound boxes of frozen herring stored in freezers down below. I found the freezers, but they too were empty.

Baffled, I went back up on deck. How could I be the baitboy if there wasn't any bait? I saw the bait jars—a few dozen or so hung on a wire across the bait table—but there appeared to be nothing to fill them with.

"Hey, where's the bait?" I asked one of the deckhands. And again, I got that dead response: the shrug of the shoulders, the broken eye contact.

A crab pot ascended onto the launching table with a clamor of noise, and two men grabbed it with dull weariness—as if they had been doing this task for all of eternity.

It was absent of crab, of course, but I did my job nonetheless. When the captain commanded us to 'put her back in,' I climbed into the pot and replaced the empty bait jar with a different empty bait jar. I climbed out, helped tie the door shut, and then watched as the pot went over the side once again. Then I looked at their faces—they were distant, remote. I looked at the immeasurable, gray sea. I looked up at the wheelhouse...

The purest form of madness was here for my taking.

* * * *

Twice, we dined on stale bread and strips of beef jerky in the course of the grim day. The crew consumed this food in silence, like dumb cattle, and then moved back outside with a mindless shuffle. And in the cold Alaskan air, we hauled our gear. I hung empty bait jars into pots. I coiled wayward rope and cleaned the boat to make myself look busy, as my mind wrestled for a means of salvation. I observed the crew as they bustled about on deck. And always, I looked out toward the sea. Without pause, I would have leapt into the icy waters and swam for any vessel or shoreline on the horizon. I would have killed for such an opportunity.

But to my anxious dread, the day slowly came to an end. It was the evening that lurked on the horizon now, and I wondered what this would mean. I thought about the night before. And as the first stars appeared in the amethyst sky above, I was quick to make myself a shadow amongst the outer edges of the boat. I hid.

And sure enough—they died.

* * * *

With soft footsteps, I skulked my way to the wheelhouse via the side railing. I avoided the main compartments—the galley, ready-room, and staterooms—where I knew the others lied in death, yet in wait. And when I reached the wheelhouse, I looked through the side door window and spotted the captain, once again in his chair. Like before, his eyes were staring at the paneling above.

My heart sank, as I had hoped to find him at best, dead on the floor. But he was in his chair, and because of this, it would be difficult, if not impossible for me to take control of the ship.

I went back down on deck and decided to brave the interior. I was hopelessly tired, hungry, and cold. My clothes were damp. My thoughts were floundering through depression, searching for a way to escape this hell. *Bait-boy for life?* Perhaps even for all of eternity, once I finally died myself.

I realized I needed a cohesive plan. I went down into the engine room, found a dark corner to hide in, and waited. I stirred over my situation and its incredible absurdity. I was a prisoner on an aberrant ship with a supply of aberrant men who slaved mindlessly throughout the day…only to die at night. Yet in their death, they could also wake.

At last, it would be a few more days of relentless hell before I put together a plan. And on the fifth night aboard the *Aleutian Whisper*, I was prepared to set this plan in motion. I thought hard about what I needed to do, and I prayed for the courage and strength to carry out my will the following day. I would begin during the lull of picking up and dropping gear. My timing would need to be perfect, of course.

* * * *

Gray, for as far as the eye could see. The boundless ocean that surrounded us was cast in this dull shade of maniacal terror. And the heavens above, sheets of muted silver as they were, only mocked my torment—a torment consisting of nothing but gray.

This was how it looked aboard the *Aleutian Whisper* the following afternoon when that lull I'd been waiting for finally presented itself. I had to be quick, while the men dawdled on deck, preparing for our next set of gear a few miles away.

"Gotta use the restroom," I said, passing Taylor on my way to the cabin. He nodded, and then I opened the door and crept into the ready-room. My knees were limp with fear, and my mouth dry with the taste of a rising conflict looming on the horizon. This was the hour—but could I go through with my plan?

From the wheelhouse, the radio was playing Elvis Presley's, *All Shook Up*. I found the irony unnerving, but took advantage of the radio volume to dampen my climb up the steps. Absently, my hand went to the pocket of my coat. It was still there.

Captain Bailey sat in his chair, as usual, staring at the open sea. From his peripheral vision, he could have spotted me. I was prepared for this, but to my enormous luck, he turned away starboard side.

I tiptoed up the final steps and took a position behind the man. I stood less than a foot away, holding my breath. Could I really do this?

I doubted myself, actually. I was on the verge of giving up, but then, amazingly, to the far horizon, I spotted land! It was all I needed, the final push up that hill of terror. Quietly, I reached into my pocket and pulled out the ice pick I'd found earlier. I stared at the back of Bailey's head. I took notice of his defectively thin hair, but more importantly, of his shiny, bald scalp. I took notice of the skin and skull, as it stared back at me, leering, laughing, whispering that forever more, I'll be a prisoner on this ship. *Bait-boy for life…*

"AAAHHHHH!" From the crux of my scream came a mighty blow to the back of that head! And with the sound of a crashing melon, Captain Bailey fell to the floor, blood spilling out of his punctured skull. I did it! I killed the man!

My heart ran wild. My entire body trembled as I made a quick sweep of the wheelhouse. It's common for a captain to keep a weapon of some sort near him. I had hoped for this to be the case and was thrilled when I found the revolver clamped underneath his chair.

I grabbed the gun, pausing only briefly to give Captain Bailey's fallen body a moment's notice before I made my way back down the stairs. I had others to kill.

* * * *

"Hey, Benny?" I shouted through the opened door of the readyroom. I had seen this guy go up to the wheelhouse on more than one occasion, so I hoped he would fall for my ploy. "Captain wants to see you." Then I shut the door and ran down the hall. I stepped into the shadows of an adjacent stateroom and waited anxiously. What if Benny went up to the wheelhouse via the side railing? It was unlikely, but possible all the same. Matters would turn profusely complicated if he did. I would be forced to use the gun sooner than expected.

But then I heard the creak of the door as it opened, and adrenaline shot down my spine like liquid fire. I heard the door shut. I heard Benny curse. I heard the movement of his body as he ambled down the hall toward the wheelhouse. Intuitively, I pulled myself further into the darkness, then I heard my own breathing, which seemed so loud. *My awful breathing*, I thought, just before I spotted Benny arrive at the steps.

It had to be swift and silent. It had to be—NOW!

In a blur, I moved out of the shadows and behind Benny. I raised my killing hand, ice pick dripping with blood. And with my other hand, I grabbed Benny's hood, twisted, pulled, and yanked back with tremendous violence.

He didn't even have a chance to gasp. I brought the pick into his head and chest a hundred times—or so it seemed. More than enough to kill the man, with all the blood pooling out of him, and the disfigurement of his face.

Left with a sudden urge to be sick, I ducked back into the stateroom and began to dry heave. My job was nowhere near finished. I needed desperately to compose myself, so I took a few minutes in the darkness, breathing deeply. Then I went to the sink in the bathroom and splashed cold water on my face, thinking about my next victim.

It was Stovich. The small guy, not too strong as I'd observed. I knew I could overwhelm him with my strength. And so I did, when he came down to the freezers to help me bring up more bait jars. With a three-foot length of rope, I wrung the last breath out of the man. I was amazed at how simple it was—like lifting a heavy box onto a shelf or climbing a short flight of stairs.

Finally, I was ready to use the gun and end my torment. I had seen the next step of my plan a hundred times, in the movies. It would begin with a casual stroll toward their proximity—the two men left on deck. I would make myself busy, perhaps find some rope to coil. And then, as smooth and swift as the hydraulic block used to pull crab pots up from the ocean, I would simply walk up to the first man and put a bullet in the back of his head. Then I'd unload the remaining cartridges into the last man before he realized what had just happened. I'd kill the last man—Taylor—before his stupid face would turn into the scowl I'd seen back in the storage room when he offered me moldy cheese.

* * * *

Seconds after the first man's brain blew out of his left eye, I stood on the deck and stared in dumb horror.

Click, click, click…!

Taylor's face twisted into more than a scowl, as there was something much heavier than anger in his eyes, his bent brows, his quivering lips.

Click, click, click…!

He came at me, a cannonball of fury. I fell with a *thump*, landing on the slick deck. My hand that held the revolver smacked into the base of a crab pot, and the gun slid down a scupper and into the sea.

Taylor cursed as he laid one fist after another into my gut. I gripped his hair and tried desperately to push him away.

"Think you're a killer, eh?" he shouted. "I'll show you how to kill!" He reached up and scratched at my eyes. I screamed, and then one of his fingers fell into my mouth. Clamping down, I bit, chewed and ripped away at it. I heard an awful snap, followed by a howl of pain.

"Son of a...!" Taylor cried, pulling away from me.

I got to my feet and searched the deck for a weapon, or place to run. But I was too late. Again, he was on me like a charging bull. He smashed me into a crab pot, against its ribbed siding. Then he reached for my throat. Terrified, I realized he meant to strangle me—and I knew from experience just how easy that would've been. I knew he'd kill me in seconds if he got his hands around my neck.

I made a quick shift of my hips and used the slick deck to my advantage, sliding between his legs. The void left behind caused Taylor to fall forward and smash his head into the steel girder of the crab pot.

When I stood, he was blinking and rolling his eyes, and there was a naked gash on his forehead, leaking blood. "I'll...kill...you." Those were his last words before I sent him unconscious to the deck with a smashing fist.

* * * *

The time it took to kill four men...

The time had transpired with some effort, but before I knew it, I was struggling with my greatest challenge yet: getting the dead into the crab pot before they woke again.

Taylor, now bound with rope, moaned as I shoved him in with the rest of the crew. Far to the horizon, the sun was a sliver of orange fire, sinking deep into the frozen sea.

"Why are you doing this?" he mumbled.

Running controls on the hydraulic crane, I spotted the shadows of night rising from the northeastern corner of the world.

"Let us out!"

A gull passed through the ship's rigging before circling back to perch high on the mast.

"We saved you, dammit! We pulled you from the ocean! You'd be dead if it weren't for us!"

I brought the pot onto the launch table then stepped away from the controls. For a long minute, I stared at Taylor's twisted body as it lay on top of the others. His back was to the ship, and he thrashed about in vain to turn around so that he could see me. He cursed, spat, and begged, but when I finally threw the control switch, he was the first one to go in.

And just when the pot crashed into the ocean, not surprisingly, I saw hands move. I saw fingers grab at the cage, and bodies wriggle against one another. I saw Captain Bailey look up from the mouth of his cold grave. I saw his eyes: beads of fire burning a hateful path straight to mine. And those dead eyes of his burned for a full fathom, before disappearing into the blackness of the Bering Sea.

My subsequent conflicts were long and arduous. Close to land, I hurried to gather gear, water, and food, then stowed everything into a motorized dingy. Once ready, I set the *Aleutian Whisper* on a westerly course then struck for land in my little boat. And as I drifted away, from the wheelhouse came the sounds of Elvis Presley's, *Don't Be Cruel*. At last, I was liberated from the ghostly terrors of that abominable ship and her abominable crew.

But was I, really?

* * * *

Thirty years later and I now live in the basement of a colonial-style house near Seattle, Washington. I'm known as the recluse of the town, the old man who keeps to himself. In the evening, I seal my door with three padlocks, fearful of what might happen if I don't. And always, in the small hours of night, I hear the dampening sound of a crab pot slamming into mud. I see squirming cadavers as they jerk, pull, and claw for a way out. I see them, in the darkness, in my mind's eye, in my terrible dream that has woken me each and every day since that awful night. And in my ruined thoughts, I picture the dead crewmen stagger to shore, at last, broken free of their grave at the bottom of the sea.

But in the end, none of these terrors compare to what I must cope with once I rise from my bed: my single horror, as spawned from the night before, and from the cold depths of my subconscious…the mound of yellow goo I must cleanse away each morning.

✗

Mother of My Children
Bruce L. Priddy

Annie woke me in a frantic attack on herself. She smacked at her arms and legs, clawed at her mouth and ears. Sweat soaked through her night-gown and the bedsheets. My boxers were wet from where we touched in our sleep. Arms around her, I pinned her against me to stop the night terror. A few of the blows found me, leaving welts and scratches.

She was a furnace. Never in our years together had she ever even men-tioned having a bad dream. I can't say I was as scared as she was, but we both shook.

Despite my hold on her, she rolled in my arms, mumbled against my chest. "It was horrible. We were caught in a giant spider web. You, me, the baby, everyone. Everyone in the world. And everyone was asleep. I woke up, and the spider was happy. Babies came off its back, and crawled over me, tried to get in my every opening."

She was sick, I told her, it was just a fever dream. She was asleep before I finished. Through her, the oncoming flu spoke in tongues as she slept. She didn't try to move away and I didn't let go.

Annie woke me again with a start, forced me on my back. She smashed herself to me, hips to mine, our first time since the baby came five weeks before. I did not have a chance to ask, or even want to if she was sure if she was feeling okay. She opened her eyes just once—in the pale light of our alarm clock, I could see her hazels were bloodshot. The act possessed her, my wife wasn't there. For those minutes she rode me, she existed only as animal motions. The only sound she made was a satisfied grunt when I finished. She tried to coax more, but one time exhausted me. I fell asleep beneath her, this time I was wrapped in her.

When the alarm went off in the morning, I found her in the half-bath at-tached to our bedroom, vomiting. Everything Annie ever ate fled her stom-ach in waves. The furnace still worked inside her.

I said I was calling into work, so I could stay home with her baby and her. Between volleys, she told me to go, she'd be fine. When I tried telling her that I refused to let her stubborn I-can-do-everything-by-myself atti-tude get in the way of good sense, she screamed at me to leave. Her words, voice, so vicious she bit at the air between us. If I had been any closer, a chunk of my boxer-clad thigh would have come away in my teeth.

I thought I'd prove a point, get ready and feign leaving and she'd be sure to ask me to stay. Alongside, and around, Annie's vomiting I showered, shaved and dressed. Before leaving the bedroom, I asked if she was sure she wanted me to go. She ignored me, clinging to the toilet, gazing into the fouled water. I never realized how long her arms were, managing to hug so much of the bowl to herself.

My goodbye with the baby lingered. I sat on the floor next to the crib, fingers through the slats, her tiny hand wrapped around them. Thankful she was already sleeping through the night, or at least most nights, I cooed at her to stay asleep a bit longer until mommy felt better.

Annie's hoarse voice screamed from the bathroom, demanding I leave. I had to force myself from yelling back at her, that she was going to wake the baby. Ridiculous, I know. Instead, I decided to call her bluff. I gave the baby a soft pat of her fat little tummy.

"Call me if you need anything, honey!" I stage-whispered in the sweetest, sincerest voice possible, as I walked out the front door.

On the way to the office, I called my mother-in-law. Explaining the situation, I asked if she could go over to the house, check on Annie and the baby. The "please?" and "you know how she is," and "call and let me know how they're doing," and "thank you so much!" came before she got a word in.

Annie wouldn't be happy, but it was a fight I'd be willing to have, for the baby. And I knew how this would go. It was a happy pattern throughout our relationship. We'd fight due to her pigheadedness, she'd fume, and a bit later tell me she was accepting my apology—one I never gave—and had forgiven me.

Noon came and no one had called. I started to worry. After my calls to both Annie and her mom went unanswered, I begged off work for the rest of the day.

My home was a house of silence and spiderwebs. White gossamer clung to everything I knew. From the doorway, I saw her—Annie's mom—stuck on a wall, desiccated face visible beneath a thin silk, hollow eyes and mouth gaping. I should have run, should have called someone. But who could have done anything? Panic pulled me in.

I called for Annie and the baby. Tried to run, but the strands grasped at me, pulled me down to hands and knees. They fought me the crawl to the nursery.

The crib was empty but not the room. Clung in the corner against the ceiling, a swaddle of webbing the size of an infant. Wiggling. I screamed and tried to pull myself up. The webs held me, wouldn't let me reach for my baby.

Annie crawled into the nursery on all fours, clinging to the ceiling. Another four legs, once ribs, erupted from her sides, wiggling impotent. She was swollen, disjointed. A black mass teemed across her shifted and bulged. The only part of her recognizable were those hazel eyes, now multiplied by three across her forehead and cheeks.

She dropped to the floor and thousands of our children spilled from her. Each of them had her eyes, my face, and cried for their daddy.

✗

Queen of the Bats
K.A. Opperman

Upon her moonlit tower,
All naked to the night,
A wan and wicked flower,
She bids the bats alight.

Proffering scarlet nectar,
She raises up her wrist;
The flapping bats collect her
Hot ichor as they list.

Her blood inside them beating,
The bats obey their queen;
They swarm in monstrous meeting
Above her wild demesne.

They feed on fairest women
Who brave the village gloam,
Till mortal lanterns dimmen
In shadow of her home.

The Man Who Murders Happiness
John R. Fultz

He drives a car just like yours, the one you polish and shine on Saturdays. Nondescript. You'd never notice him parked across the street.

His eyes are hidden behind a pair of square-rimmed glasses with mirror-bright panes. His hair is black and slick, heavy with Vitalis and cigarette smoke.

You'll never hear him coming. You might see him step from the shadows. Or watch the butt-end of his cigarette hover like a firefly in the night fog. He could be anybody, but you know who he is the moment he sets his eyes on you.

In the alley outside Big Pete's, two vagrants were torched to death last night. Six blocks away a police cordon surrounds the body of a girl who leaped from the roof of her apartment building. Somewhere in the big maze of post-war housing, someone is dying from a stab wound. Someone else waits patiently, watching the blood seep out.

The man shows up when you least expect him. You never realize it when you're having a good time. That's the danger. Suddenly your senses are more alive, your skin abuzz with electricity, your heart beating faster. Suddenly there's hope in the world and a reason to keep on going. At this point, most people ask themselves: "Is this happiness?"

Then they look up and the quiet man is standing there. The man and his gun, a black metal extension of his gloved fist. He's the man who murders happiness, and he's caught you red-handed. Blam. Your time is up. On to the next fool.

They say his job pays immensely well.

* * * *

On Tuesdays, the factory boys come pouring out of the industrial park, checks in hand. The dive bars and strip joints fill up for the weekend. Drink will flow and blood will spill, all the usual shit. Behind the truckstop, an aging prostitute buys smack to feed her habit for another day. Her hungry baby wails as she slides the needle into her arm. A drunkard with a bloody face sleeps in the gutter outside the liquor store. There's an amputated leg sticking out of the dumpster. It wears a thousand-dollar shoe.

* * * *

The man drives by in his nondescript automobile, unmarked and unnoticed, just another motorist. Directions come through on the radio. He hates the way it interrupts the music, but it's part of the job. Mostly he listens to rockabilly, sometimes jazz. But the music dies every time the hollow voice of authority blares from the speakers. Direct communication with the boys upstairs, the secret infrastructure behind the official infrastructure. The one that knows where all the happiness is, and the one tasked with eliminating it.

He usually gets a name and the name of a town. That's it. He drives, sometimes for days at a time. It's all flat farm country now, and not much else. He drinks hot black coffee at nameless diners and bottles of cold soda sprung from gas station automats.

* * * *

They say he can actually feel it as he gets closer to his mark. He feels the happiness like a bloodhound scents his prey. Drives into town like a shadow and finds the right neighborhood, parks his car somewhere nobody will ever notice it. Nobody ever does.

* * * *

He walks along a sidewalk littered with dead leaves. Autumn wind moves cool and damp through the lanes. Each little house is exactly like the one next to it, and so on, all the way to the end of the street. And all the other streets here are just like it. Tiny green lawns, covered porches, a single old oak or elm rising in the front yard. Old folks sat on porches nursing shotguns. Lazy dogs lay a their feet. Children dig worms from the ripe grass, collecting them in old jelly jars. The sounds of television cop show themes blare from open windows.

He feels the happiness like warmth now, the heat from a blazing conflagration. As if the fifth house on the right was an inferno. On fire with joy. Sheer, raging happiness that will ignite the houses on either side unless it's stopped. The doors are locked, and heavy curtains block the windows. He slips in through the back door. He carries tools for the opening of locks, and he's very good with them. His primary tool is the gun now back in his hand. The soft moans of a woman drift from a back room with roaring fireplace. He moves closer on noiseless feet.

At first, they're only shadows. Locked in a tight embrace on a shaggy rug by the fire. He watches them for a moment, removes his square glasses. His eyes are blank and colorless, like dead fish scales. But he sees the happiness. He watches it spill from their sweating bodies, rippling waves of color, invisible to the human eye but glaring to his own. Their naked joy mesmerizes him, and he cannot look away from the sheer beauty of it. The awesome beauty of the awful thing he was made to root out and destroy.

* * * *

Happiness. The man and woman have found it together somehow. The quiet man's fascination turns to outrage. He's never seen such an intense bliss. Suddenly he's ashamed of himself for watching. He pulls the trigger.

It's fear that makes him do it. Time and time again, he pulls the trigger out of sheer fear. He accepted that long ago. He imagines what it would be like to be happy, to lose himself in those blazing energies he's witnessed so many times. To spark like a comet and burn yourself to nothingness, existing as nothing but pure ecstasy.

* * * *

To be happy.

It is a horror he could never endure.

That's why the government has agents like him. To keep its people from the threat of bliss. To keep the entire population from being devoured by voracious joy. Happiness leads to oblivion. To keep mankind alive, he must keep it suffering. The next stop he makes is at the lakeside, where a man with long hair mediates by the water, coming perilously close to bliss. The quiet man approaches, making no sound in the wet grass, and shoots him in the back of the head. Nobody notices. They never do.

In a rust-eaten trailer park, three children play with a stray dog. Their faces are dirty, their clothing little more than rags. He shoots the dog and walks away while the children weep, poking at their dead friend with a stick. On the other side of the trailer park, a man hangs up the phone. He's going to meet someone later that night—someone he can't wait to see. His happiness is like a flare in the dark. It draws the quiet man toward him, and the gunshot echoes above the squalor.

* * * *

On his way out of the park, he shoots down an old lady feeding pigeons. The birds scatter as her blood stains the yellow grass to red. If her deep joy had spread any further than the pigeons, it might have infected the entire town. He considers shooting the birds, but they've already lost themselves in the gray sky. Not his problem anymore.

That night the radio calls him back into the city, where a young father celebrates the birth of his first child. Far too happy, especially for the urban district. Even with a permit for a birth celebration, the new father's happiness had been blazing in his heart for a week, exceeding his allotment. Too much happiness. Expired permit.

The quiet man intercepts the new father in a parking lot and shoots him in the leg. He doesn't always have to kill. Sometimes a maiming shot is enough to restore the balance, squelch the gout of happiness. Close the psychic wound. The father howls in pain, bleeding on the concrete until his co-workers drag him away. He doesn't thank the quiet man for sparing his life. He's no longer happy, but he'll be fine walking with a cane from now on.

* * * *

After midnight the quiet man sits at an all-night diner, drinking black coffee. Long day. He tries not to think about the couple on the rug, the vortex of ecstasy that almost smothered him. It had been close, but he'd pulled the trigger. Restored the balance. He would never understand how they could be so terribly happy, so insanely elated. Some cases weigh on his mind, and he realizes this will be one of them.

He doesn't see the girl come in and walk toward his booth. He's looking at the plastic menu, lost in thought. She slides into his booth with a rustle of her silk blouse, and before he knows it she's looking right into his eyes. Her face is exquisite.

It's a face he's seen in his most secret dreams, the ones he can't even admit to himself. Her eyes are dark with secrets, brighter than stars. Staring at her, he cannot reduce the magnificence of the moment to the stumbling weakness of words.

His heart beats madly and he smiles at her. It's all he can do.

She raises the gun.

"Is this happiness?" he asks.

She pulls the trigger.

A Handful of Dust
Tom English

...I will show you something different. ...
Your shadow at morning striding behind you
Or your shadow at evening rising to meet you;
I will show you fear in a handful of dust.

—T. S. Eliot
The Waste Land

All his life old man Brumstead had lived in fear. As a child, he had been terrified of the dark, and his overindulgent mother had allowed him to sleep with the light on in his room until he was a senior at Dinsmore High School, back in 1956.

When he was fourteen, three of his "friends" locked him up in a rotting tool shed behind Grady's Feed Store. It was typical of the pranks Mill Hurst boys were constantly pulling on each other. They stood by the door smoking cigarettes and repeating dirty jokes they'd heard in the locker room, all the while looking about nervously, as poor Brumstead, crouching amid a clutter of hanging harnesses, castoff tractor parts, busted barrels and hay forks, first yelled obscenities, then pleaded for mercy, then started screaming like a frightened girl.

By the time his hysterical cries finally got to them, and his friends dragged his limp, sweat-drenched body from the cluttered shed, Brumstead was sobbing uncontrollably. He'd been locked in that cramped shack for just a few minutes, but a fear of confined spaces stayed with him for the rest of his life.

Brunstead was afraid of heights and crowds, speaking in public and the opposite sex; running out of gas in the middle of nowhere, and being audited by the IRS. He once even told me that the drone of a Hoover vacuum cleaner gave him nightmares. Perhaps some of his fears were silly and unfounded. Obviously, others were not.

* * * *

"But there was one thing in particular he feared, which affected him more than all the others," I said. "Something caused by an extremely unpleasant experience he had the year his mother died. One of those stupid and unlikely things you often hear about but can never imagine happening to you."

I paused in my story just long enough to brush away an annoying little insect buzzing about my ear. The room was stuffy, the air musty with the smell of old fabric and mildew. I leaned forward in the overstuffed wing-chair and scanned the room where Brumstead had died late one Friday night nearly two months ago.

The old man had managed to dial 911 before going into respiratory arrest, but the fire department was located on the other side of the county and manned totally by volunteers. They had arrived too late to do anything but find Brumstead's dead body slumped against the front door. The coroner wrote the old man's death off as the result of a weakened physical condition: Brumstead had had a bout of flu a couple weeks before, and at seventy-seven he just seemed worn out.

Worn out, I imagined, from too many years spent dreading one thing or another.

My twelve-year-old daughter sat across from me, wide-eyed with anticipation. "What happened?" Beth asked, eager for me to finish the story of Brumstead's neuroses.

I stood up and walked to the window. Chuck Harper's kids were playing in the yard across the street. "Old man Brumstead had an accident," I continued, but then stopped again while I struggled to raise the window. The thing had been nailed shut—like all the other windows in the house.

When I was a teenager, Brumstead's airtight house had been one of the many peculiar things that fascinated me about the old man. When other kids had begun to shun his place, I became a frequent visitor; while other kids were mocking him, I was lending a respectful, sympathetic ear to all his fearful woes.

"Dad!" Beth whined. Like most kids, she loved a good story, and the weirder the better.

"It happened just outside this two-story farmhouse. Brumstead inherited the place when his mother died, in 1977."

"And now it's ours," Beth said in childish awe.

"Yes," I said slowly.

Evidently, the old man hadn't had anyone else to leave it to. So he left it the skinny kid who used to come by and drink the weak beer Brumstead brewed in his cellar. And listen to the horror stories of all the old man's fears.

I swiped at the buzzing sound near my ear again and continued: "Forty years ago, this house sat in the middle of a field—this was all farm land. After the accident, Brumstead began selling off the surrounding land. At first, a few homes were built. Then Hurst Street was extended through.

"Then this housing development sprang up," I said, gesturing to the row of almost uniform houses across the street. "Brumstead had always loved the farm...nature...walking through the fields. But after the accident, he didn't care about any of that. He was glad to see other people living nearby—relieved to see fields give way to asphalt, and trees to street lights."

"But *why*?" Beth asked impatiently. "What happened?"

"Shortly after the death of his mother, Brumstead went for a walk through a section of field that had lain fallow for two years and was now overgrown with thick weeds. This would have been behind the house," I added, "but still in plain view of it.

"He had been devastated by his mother's death. Brumstead was almost forty years old at the time, and he had still been living with her when she died. He couldn't remember a time when she hadn't been there for him. She'd been his shelter from the dangers of the world, and hers had been the voice that calmed all his fears.

"Wondering if he could ever live without his mother, Brumstead wandered across the field, lost in his thoughts, scuffing his feet over the dry crust. Never before in his life had he felt so alone. Never before had he been so overwhelmed with doubt, so sick with uncertainty. As he walked along he could feel the brittle ground crumbling beneath his shoes; and he gave no thought at all when a small section of the crust gave a bit more than usual, collapsing and caving in an inch or so, accompanied by an unsettling crunch.

"He took several more languorous paces through the rising cloud of dust he'd kicked up before looking down at his feet. They were covered with something black and yellow; something moving—something creeping up his trouser legs.

"A rush of horror surged through his chest. He felt several bursts of pain on his legs, which felt like they were on fire. He slapped at his trousers, stomping and shaking his feet to dislodge the angry mass swarming up his body. Out of the corner of his eye, he could see the dust cloud about his feet thicken, blacken—and quickly rise. He lurched backward, then sideways, his arms flailing violently as he ineffectually grabbed first at one, then another, stab of searing pain. He screamed like he'd never heard himself scream before, stopping just long enough to slap mercilessly at his own face and head, both of which felt like they were burning up.

"When he ran, at first blindly, mindlessly, the seething cloud moved with him, enveloping him—hundreds of winged furies seeking vengeance for their destroyed nest in the dry earth, and each one of them gifted with the ability to sting again and again and again. When at last—after an eternity of mere seconds—a voice inside Brumstead screamed 'Get inside!' and he ran toward the promised safety of the house, the boiling mass chased him.

"With every yard he covered, the number of aggressors dropped and the swarm thinned. But when Brumstead reached the back porch and slammed the screened door shut, there were still several crawling through his hair and clinging to his blue denim.

"His face was a red swollen mask of pain, his body barely better. He managed to drive himself to a doctor who practiced out of his home four or five miles from here."

Beth was starting to feel the itch of some imagined intruder creeping across the back of her neck, her legs, her scalp. As I was soon to learn, she had a particular aversion to crawling insects. "What happened then?" she asked, drawing the collar of her shirt up tight around her neck and shuddering.

"Brumstead was lucky. Some people have severe reactions to the venom of yellow jackets. Even one or two stings can trigger an allergic reaction that can swell the throat shut. Brumstead was *one* of those people. But he made it to the doctor in time.

"When he got there, he was in severe pain, and he could barely breathe. He passed out on the doctor's front porch, and Kearney had to drag him inside."

I sat down again, on an old trunk tucked in a corner of the room. Beth had moved to the overstuffed wingchair and was sitting with her bare feet on the edge of the cushion, hugging her knees to her chest.

"Which couldn't have been an easy task," I said. "I think Dr. Kearney was around seventy at the time—still making house calls, still x-raying broken bones on an old machine in the backroom of his two-story duplex.

"Anyway, as soon as he got Brumstead stabilized, the doctor phoned Drury County Rescue to send over an ambulance and had the poor man transported to the hospital. I think Brumstead stayed there a couple nights or so. Kearney told him, later, that if he'd delayed getting there, even a few minutes, he might have died. He also told Brumstead to avoid getting stung again, because his body was now 'sensitized' to the venom. Another dose could perhaps be fatal.

"Needless to say, Brumstead didn't need a new phobia to worry about. But he got one anyway. He stopped going for walks, started staying indoors. Other than driving to the courthouse, where he worked as a clerk, or to Haskin's Food-Mart, the old man hardly strayed from this house.

"He read up on yellow jackets: their life-cycle, their habits, their diet. He learned far more than he needed to know; too much for his own peace of mind. Like honeybees, yellow jackets are communal insects. When their nest is disturbed or even threatened, they attack as a well-coordinated army to defend the hive. But honeybees die after stinging once. Their stingers break off and become embedded in the flesh. Yellowjackets were not cursed with such a limitation. They're capable of repeatedly stinging an enemy, with no harm to themselves.

"And swatting one of them only incites their fury: a smashed yellow jacket releases a scent that alerts the other members of the communal nest. Sensing that one of their numbers has been killed, the others will attack with a vengeance. But that was an extremely painful experience Brumstead didn't need to learn from a book.

"Again, a little bit of knowledge is a dangerous thing. As Brumstead mulled over the facts and licked his wounds, he grew increasingly fearful of being stung again. Initially, he kept all the windows shut—no matter how stuffy the house got. But ultimately, he *nailed* them shut."

"I'm glad he had AC," Beth said, scratching hard at her scalp. "Do you think there's any still around here?"

"I doubt it. A few days after being released from the hospital, he paid Mike Fenton's sons to destroy the nest in the backyard. Yellow jackets are supposed to be least active at night, so the two boys waited till dusk after most of the hive had flown back to the nest. They crept up to a respectful distance of the nest and one of them threw a pail of kerosene on it. The other one flicked a match at it. And then they both ran like mad.

"The kerosene burned long and hot. By the light of the flames rising from the dust, the boys could see dark shapes flying into the heart of the inferno. It was the stragglers returning to the nest—driven by instinct to try and save the hive. Flying to their deaths.

"Standing at the kitchen window, Brumstead watched the glow of the burning nest until the last ember had disappeared against the blackness of night. Years later, he continued to recount the whole affair, each time rubbing his hands together somewhat fiendishly—peculiarly comforted that vengeance had been served."

I finished my tale in an appropriately solemn tone, but unlike other occasions when Beth would clap and ask for another story, she was unusually quiet. I watched her head tilt slowly back as her eyes rose to the corner above my head.

"Dad," she said in a low, *anxious* voice, "There's one in here!"

I stood and looked around. There was nothing flying about the room but Beth's overworked imagination. She loved a good scare, and my stories—even the more ghoulish ones—rarely caused her even a moment of unease. But perhaps this time, owing to the truth of Brumstead's story, I'd gone too far.

"We don't have to worry about yellow jackets in *this* house, Beth. All the windows are shut. And nothing flew in when we had the door open." I threw my arm around her and squeezed her tightly. Outside, the late summer day had faded, and flashes of heat lightning illuminated the darkening eastern sky.

"We had a long drive today. I bet you're tired," I said, and she nodded in agreement. "Enough excitement for one day. Why don't you go upstairs and get ready for bed. I'll come up in a bit and tuck you in."

She nodded again.

"Tomorrow we'll go treasure hunting. There's tons of neat junk in this old house."

She smiled, scratching her sides and neck. "Maybe I'll find some old skeleton keys for my collection," she said.

"Probably so. We'll go into town and get some pancakes first."

"Yes!"

"Go brush your teeth," I said.

"And Beth," I added before she left the room, "We don't need to tell mom about this story." She nodded in agreement.

I went to the window and studied the heads of the large nails driven into the sides of the frame. It wasn't going to be easy removing them. But it needed to be done soon. Old houses were firetraps and the idea of not being able to raise a single window wasn't exactly comforting.

The whole place would need repainting before I could put it on the market, and I had serious doubts the electrical wiring was up to code. I'd have to climb into the attic tomorrow and take a look at it. Joan would be driving down in a few days, and she'd help me clean the place out. Still, the amount of work involved....

I caught myself. How often do we dream of someone putting us in their will, let alone leaving us everything? It wasn't fair to treat this unexpected blessing from Brumstead as though it were a curse. So I quietly thanked him for my windfall and then began to wonder if the old man had feared banks as much as he'd feared just about everything else. Was he one of those eccentrics who'd hidden money behind a wall or under the floorboards? What treasures would I find for *my* collection?

I sat musing over this fanciful notion, and over Brumstead's cloistered way of life. He'd lived alone in this old house for close to four decades—with only his fears to occupy him. Not the healthy fear that keeps us from doing stupid things; not the entertaining scare you get from a rollercoaster ride or a really good horror movie; but the kind of fear that has the power to cripple and choke the life out of a man; a genuine and palpable fear.

I yawned and checked my watch. It was a little past ten and starting to rain. I could hear the soft clatter of the rain striking the house's tin roof, accompanied by occasional rumblings of distant thunder. I switched off the light and headed upstairs. When I reached the landing, I stopped at the first room, where Beth was staying, and gently turned the knob.

Her room was impenetrably dark. I had unthinkingly put her in a room at the back of the house, sheltered from the streetlights. The faint glow of a lamp in the corner of the landing did little to banish the darkness in her room. Neither was there a single shaft of moonlight in the storm-blackened sky.

I stood in the doorway, waiting for my eyes to adjust to the darkness, trying to perceive Beth's shape upon the bed. I stepped softly into the room and was swallowed up in its darkness. If Beth were asleep, I didn't want to awaken her, but I felt a foolish need to reassure myself of her presence in the room. I moved carefully across the room, feeling my way blindly, one hand gently searching for her sleeping form.

I felt something, like a feather, sweep lightly past my nose, my ear—got the impression of frantic movement in the room, of something not quite right in the thick, stale air.

I fumbled for the lamp on the night table, then switched it on. For a moment I thought the sudden brightness that flooded the room had me seeing spots before my eyes—spots that circled, dipped, shot past my head. The whole room was crawling with yellow jackets.

There were dozens swarming about Beth's bed, perhaps hundreds more seething across the walls and clinging to the ceiling above her. The surface of the night table was completely covered over with them, the lampshade crawling with them, the water glass bristling with their winged bodies. I have never had a fear of yellow jackets, knowing that they attack only when provoked; but the sheer multitude of their numbers—forced upon me without warning—combined with some natural revulsion at seeing the things clinging to every available surface and object, sent a rush of utter panic through me.

I lurched back, knocking something from the night table, and stirred up a cloud of moving bodies. Beth sprang up in her bed. She was disorientated from being jarred awake. She squinted at me, puzzled, and rubbed her eyes. Before I could think or speak—before I could warn her and lessen the shock—she saw them. She screamed repeatedly, her legs kicking violently at the sheets.

"Beth!" I said hoarsely, "Be still! They're swarming, not attacking."

Almost as if stimulated by the intensity of her horror, the numbers of black and yellow bodies swarming about the room increased significantly. As the cloud of flying insects swirled around us, moving as a single, intelligent entity, I saw one of them alight on Beth's arm. She flinched in revulsion.

"No, Beth!" I screamed, as her hand arced across her face, and she slapped at the spot, crushing the tiny insect beneath her palm.

I cringed at the sight, like a soldier who's had a grenade tossed at his feet, and knows it's too late to do anything but wait for the explosion.

Nothing happened. Nothing changed.

And then they were on her.

I jerked the sheet over her head and swept her from the bed. She was screaming and writhing in agony. I wrapped the flapping edges of the sheet about her twisting form and bundled her from the room, slamming the door shut behind me.

* * * *

Pacing outside the double doors marked EMERGENCY, I kept wondering: Why hadn't *I* been stung. There had been hundreds of them, and I had been at the heart of their fury.

When the doors parted, I hurried to intercept Dr. Sam Travis as he walked out. "How is she?" I asked.

"Her breathing is no longer constricted. She's resting now."

Sam and I had attended Pratt University together, and I was glad he was on duty. He studied me for a moment, then said, "Let's get some coffee."

It sounded more like a command than an invitation. I followed him into the staff lounge. "Grab a chair," he said, pointing to a table at the back of the room. He poured two cups, then sat down across from me. "Rob," he said, hesitating long enough to sip his coffee, "what the hell are you trying to pull here?"

It took a moment for the implication of his question to sink in. "What are you talking about?"

"You bring your daughter in with all the symptoms of envenomation. Yet there's not a mark on her."

"Are you kidding?" I said. "She was *covered* with swollen stings when I brought her in."

"Yeah, I know she was." He stared at the Styrofoam cup in his hand. "They're gone now; there's no trace of wasp stings."

"How.... Is that normal?"

He shook his head and leaned back in his chair.

"Sam," I said, "do you believe in the power of suggestion?"

"Why? What's that got to do with anything?"

"Beth went to bed tonight thinking about yellow jackets," I said. "We drove down today to work on the farmhouse I inherited from Ray Brumstead. Did you know him?"

"No. But I remember you talking about him. He was phobic."

"Phobic is putting it mildly. He was scared to death of just about everything."

"What's your point, Rob?"

"Brumstead stepped on a ground nest of yellow jackets, years ago, and had to be hospitalized. It was something that changed his life. He sold his fields, stopped going for walks. And he had all the windows in the house nailed shut. I wanted Beth to know why, so I told her the whole story—in all its macabre splendor, unfortunately."

I stood and started pacing about the table. "Could the power of suggestion—hearing the details, seeing the windows nailed shut, being in the very house where it happened—trigger her imagination?"

"You think she conjured up a swarm of wasps out of her head. Got stung," he said, "and her initial symptoms were all psychosomatic?"

"Imagination is a powerful force, Sam."

"Interesting. But that would take *some* imagination." He put his cup down and leaned back in his chair. "And you saw them, too. Were you seeing the phantoms of a child's overworked imagination?"

"Yeah, I know," I said, realizing how ridiculous the whole thing sounded once it was verbalized. "But Beth *had* seen something that wasn't there: earlier, before bed, right after hearing the story. She said there was a yellow jacket buzzing about my head. I *didn't* see it."

I leaned on the table and stared at his smug expression. "How else can you explain why *I* wasn't stung?"

"That's what I'm trying to find out," he said. He drummed his index finger against his empty cup. "It's possible. Emotional stress can induce a variety of illnesses, including an allergic reaction. There *are* precedents of psychosomatic injury in individuals who too closely identify with a particular situation or person. The wounds in the hands of stigmatics, for instance, may somehow be mentally induced by a close identification with the crucified Christ."

He shook his head. "But this would go way beyond anything I've ever read about psychophysiological disorders. There's so much we don't understand about the power of the mind—the power of human emotion."

He pushed himself up from his chair. "But you saw it, too." He tossed the Styrofoam cup at the trashcan but missed it. "This sounds more like a case of mass hysteria," he said. "In fact, the whole thing sounds like the weird stuff you used to write for the college journal."

"That was fiction," I said brusquely, "meant to entertain. I'm talking about my daughter now."

"Whose care you've entrusted to me. That's why we're having this conversation." He glanced at his watch. "It's an interesting theory, Rob, but if I were you, I'd call an exterminator—pronto. Old houses can harbor a lot of things. You could have a nest in the attic or behind a wall. They probably have a way to get inside, a crack or hole somewhere."

"Yeah," I nodded.

"Mack Loomis is an exterminator. Call *him*."

"*Slack* Mack? The guy who quit high school? Haven't seen him in ages."

"Yeah, well, he bummed around for awhile, but I stopped thumbing my nose at him several years ago. He owns his own company now, and he probably makes more money than I do."

"I guess this will give me a chance to see him, again," I said. "Can I take Beth home now?"

"I want to keep her for observation, at least overnight. Besides," he said, "if that house *has* triggered some emotional problems, she shouldn't go back there. And if you *do* have a wasp infestation, she shouldn't be there. Her body's now sensitized to the venom. Another sting, even one, could cause a severe allergic reaction."

I thanked Sam for his time and care and then hustled upstairs to Beth's room. She was sleeping peacefully. The night-duty nurse reassured me that she would be checking on Beth throughout the night and that the best thing for me to do was go home and get some rest.

I got back to the Brumstead place a little past midnight and walked about the empty house, examining the walls, ceiling and floors till almost one in the morning.

Nothing. No cracks, no holes, no hidden passages leading to secret rooms.

I fell asleep with my clothes on and woke up early with the sun blasting through a curtain-less window. At eight o'clock sharp, I called Loomis Pest Control. When Mack heard it was me, he said he'd come out personally, and less than an hour later he pulled into the gravel driveway.

Mack had gained a great deal of weight since high school—probably from lounging in the air-conditioned office where he dispatched his crew of "hard-working professionals." As he clambered up the stepladder he'd placed under the attic door, it wobbled and groaned under his not insignificant mass; and I started wondering if he'd even be able to fit through the narrow opening in the ceiling.

"Yeah, buddy-boy," he bellowed, squirming through the opening. "Business has been good. Mind handing me that flashlight?"

I passed the light to him, and he took another step up the ladder, wedging himself up to the waist. "You gotta dusty attic, buddy-boy," he said, shining the light into one corner of the roof beams. "Yessir, old and dusty. But if you got bugs up here—and I'm sure ya do—your old buddy Mack's gonna fix you up. Yessiree," he said, slowly twisting in the attic doorway as the beam of his flashlight stripped the darkness from each succeeding rafter. "You bastards can forget about Raid, 'cause there's a *new* sheriff in town. Nope. When I find you, you're in for a helluva lot more than a little raid—this is gonna be a full-scale *Mack Attack*."

He had almost completed a half-circle turn in the too-tight opening when his flashlight clattered to the floor. "Shit!" he yelled in a husky voice, and I heard the thud of his elbows against the doorframe as he yanked his upper torso from the attic. The stepladder rocked from side to side, and he almost kicked it over as he stumbled down the rungs, skipping the last two and landing heavily on the floor.

"Outside!" he said, pushing me out the door and onto the landing. "Go, go, go!" he yelled, urging me downstairs. He cleared the front door, leaped from the porch, and ran to the street.

I walked to the sidewalk, where he stood bent over, his hands resting on his thighs, his chest heaving as he gasped for breath. "You okay?" I asked.

He looked up and nodded, then straightened and walked slowly to the van at the end of the driveway. He pulled the rear doors open and sat down on the back of the truck. "Buddy-boy," he said, still breathing hard and wiping sweat from his reddened face, "you gotta big wasp nest up there."

"Yeah, well, isn't that what you're here for?"

"Listen, smartass, I've been doing this for over twelve years. I've gone into barns and silos and rotted-out warehouses, and I've never seen anything like what you got up there!"

He sat there at the back of the van, staring at the ground around his feet, while he caught his breath. "I'm sorry, Rob," he said finally, wiping his face on his sleeve. "I started out in this business because I needed the cash and I couldn't find anything else. But I *do not* like insects, Rob, I hate 'em!" He rubbed the back of his neck. "Maybe that's where my success comes from—I love killing 'em. It's a passion, you understand. But when I run across a bad infestation...." His voice trailed off as he scanned the roofline of the old farmhouse.

"Rob," he said, still looking up, "you got a nest up there the size of... Hell, it takes up two-thirds of the attic space." He looked me in the eye. "It must be home to thousands."

I finally convinced Mack to come back inside with me. He cautiously followed me back upstairs, no doubt motivated more by shame than courage, and then steadied the ladder as I climbed into the attic to see for myself.

I was glad he had prepared me for what I saw.

The beam of the flashlight moved across foot after foot, yard after yard, of dark gray, paper-like shell. The nest stretched from the attic floor to the highest point in the rafters, from the back of the house to the front; and it extended at least half the length of the hipped roof.

It looked like a bloated cocoon, anchored to the heavy beams by a muddy substance the same sickly gray color as the outer shell. Half of the end facing me was honeycombed with thousands of dark holes—tiny tunnels extending deep into the heart of the nest.

I eased myself into the attic and knelt on a joist a few feet from the swollen mass. "What's this thing made of," I called down to Mack.

"Uh, cellulose," he said. "It's pretty much just regurgitated paper. They make it out of plant debris. Old trash, wood shavings…and dust."

"It looks empty," I said.

A couple minutes later, Mack slowly put his head through the attic door. "There's a lot of stuff I may not know, but I *do* know about this," he said. "This thing has all the signs of being an active nest."

"Come on, Mack. There's no sign of them."

"You wanna see 'em?" he said hatefully. "Go rap on it with the flashlight—just gimme a chance to clear out first."

"No, I don't," I said in a wave of anger. "But I do need to know. My daughter was stung last night, repeatedly, by…something I can't explain."

"Well there you have it," he said, pointing to the gray mass.

"But where are they *now*?"

"They probably all left the nest to scavenge. They feed on garbage, you know. Me, I'm glad they're not here. We better clear out too before some of 'em fly back to the nest."

"Mack. I need to know if I've got a problem with wasps or if last night I was seeing something that wasn't there."

"Something that wasn't there? Are you crazy? Look at the size of this monster. You're lucky to be alive!"

"There's nothing here but an empty shell. What evidence do you have that this thing's inhabited?"

"Evidence?" Mack cried. "There's your evidence!"

"I can see the nest," I said hotly, "That doesn't mean the house is infested with yellow jackets."

"For God's sake, Rob, come on out. Let's shut the door. Do you hafta personally see everything before you believe it. Hell, didn't you ever go to Sunday school? Why can't you trust my judgment? I've been at this for years. I'm telling you the nest is active. Have a little faith in me, will ya?"

"Faith?" I said.

"Yeah, some things you just hafta take on faith."

I stared at the empty gray cocoon rising up before me, but my mind was somewhere else, searching through a jumble of memories for something I'd forgotten—something someone once told me. I felt an urgency to remember it. But *what* was it?

"Hold the ladder," I said, crawling from the attic.

"Now you're talking, buddy-boy," Mack said. "You need to decide what you're gonna do about this thing quick."

"Any suggestions?"

"We can saturate the thing with enough chemical to kill anything that returns to it for weeks. But you'll hafta leave the house. Give the fumes time to clear."

I nodded.

"That's the easy part. I wasn't sure if you noticed, but the damn thing runs down inside the walls. There's probably not a void space in the whole house that's not plugged with paper. And with the old copper wire running behind these walls, you have the potential for one hell of an electrical fire."

"Can it be removed?" I asked.

"If you have enough money you can do anything," Mack said. "But is it worth it?" He shrugged. "You definitely need to have someone pull the stuff outta the attic. But I doubt you can get to the crap behind the walls— not without tearing them out."

I told Mack I needed time to think about it. He said he'd enjoyed seeing me again, despite the circumstances, then warned me not to put off having the nest treated. I watched him back the van out of the drive, and speed away—back to his air-conditioned office, probably.

Then I drove to the hospital to visit Beth. She was sore and a bit sluggish from all the antihistamines, but otherwise she seemed in good spirits. To her delight, I promised her we'd go to the beach before summer vacation was over and that she could spend the whole day treasure hunting with her metal detector.

I also promised her she'd never have to go inside the old Brumstead house again. I could read the relief in her young eyes.

I walked down to the cafeteria and bought her a chocolate milkshake. When I got back to her room she was sitting up, watching television. I gave her a kiss, then left her happily sipping the shake and watching *Jeopardy*.

Heading back to the farmhouse, I kept replaying the events of the last couple days: that monstrosity in the attic; the terrifying scene in Beth's room; what Dr. Sam Travis had said about the power of human emotion; and the words Mack had bellowed at me through that narrow opening in the ceiling.

I thought about the wretchedness of Brumstead's existence in that lonely old house; how fear had been the old man's constant companion; how it had dominated his thoughts and haunted his dreams.

Suddenly the whole thing started to make sense.

I stopped at City Hall to pick up the permits I would need. I was sent from one office to the next and spent four hours filling out forms. It hadn't hurt being something of a celebrity: the Mill Hurst boy who'd made it in the big city, and had returned to rub elbows with the folks he'd grown up with.

But by the time I had filed my last form, it was too late to do anything but hire the work crew. I scheduled one to start promptly at 7:30 in the morning, then drove back to the Brumstead house.

I phoned Joan. She wouldn't have to drive down after all. Then I packed Beth's and my things and loaded up the SUV.

I didn't sleep that night. I sat in Brumstead's over-stuffed wingchair, staring at the walls, a constant stream of words and pictures swirling like flying insects through my brain. In fact, I was still pondering them when I heard the sound of a bulldozer cranking. I stepped from the house, gently closed the door behind me, and walked out to the street.

I stood on the sidewalk with the demolition crew and watched as the bulldozer raised its blade and approached the house. Twenty minutes later, accompanied by a symphony of cracklings, crunches, and hand-clapping, the old farmhouse splintered and collapsed upon itself.

Through the swirling dust, I saw the gray form of the nest protruding through the pile of broken boards and bits of insulation. The demolition crew walked around the ruins, pointing at the cracked shell and swearing in angry tones, but no one ventured near it. No one touched it.

When I was a boy I used to walk to the old Mill Hurst Baptist Church every week to attend Sunday school. Pastor Barnes taught me many interesting things, but the one I remember now—triggered by the impatient words of an old friend—had to do with faith.

Faith, the pastor had taught us kids, was the evidence of things we cannot see; it was the substance of things we hope for. He also told us that fear was the opposite of faith, and that dread held almost as much power as hope.

I thought about the power of raw human emotions. All his life, Brumstead had lived in fear. Fear had shaped his habits. Fear had forged his destiny. Fear and dust and the dread of something that otherwise might never have happened.

Was the gray nest lying amidst these ruins a physical manifestation of everything Brumstead had dreaded? Was this monstrosity the *material* substance of all his fears?

There were no signs of activity about the nest. No stirrings of life from within. Nothing to indicate this was an active hive. At least, nothing in the natural realm.

I left the site for several hours—to visit Beth—and to take care of one last thing. But a little before five, I returned to the pile of rubble that had defined Brumstead's life; to the hideous cocoon reposing beneath the old man's broken dreams.

At 5:30 p.m. a pumper truck from the local fire department arrived, without fanfare, and I was joined on the sidewalk by Steve Gaston, yet another friend from my youth. He had brought two other men with him, and after a few minutes of quietly conversing, the trio set fire to the pile of rubble.

We watched the flames as they licked and consumed the gray shell. It was the final episode in the long history of a lonely, frightened old man. His terrible legacy would soon return to a handful of dust.

The pile burned hot for three hours. We sat together on the truck, watching the flames, reminiscing as though we were simply gathered around the fireplace at Tall Timber Lodge.

Then, just before dusk, a black, swirling plume rose up from the flames. But it wasn't smoke.

It moved off into the darkening eastern sky, sweeping low over the rooftops of the houses across the street until it disappeared into the blackness on the horizon.

We had all seen it. But not one of us commented.

✗

Taken from the Tcho Tcho People's Holy Codex

GUMI-GAN-OK CHAEK ("Book of Cracked Jade")

translated by

Frederick J. Mayer

The Apophthegmata of Ancient Ones:
Lloigor/Zhar Saith: #4
"Flowers of Night"
Flowers are bane
For nightmares
And when to enter sanity
The realm inside sane
Flowers provide me.
#10 [Title unknow/untranslational]
Bestiality
Of the soul
Is glorious
In its efforescence
Of malignity
Shathak Saith: #4 "Saving Grace"
Better to die
Skinned alive
Than fade away
With a mere sigh...Elder Gods lie
Fear enter I
Intercourse way
Come where I lie
Sfatlicllp Saith: #4 [Her statements seem not to have titles]
Give Me your Heart
And ride the Beast
Soul is nothing
In the small least
Let your Soulling
So come Apart!

✗

Revolution à l'Orange
Paul Lubaczewski

"The Roman deserves more than lack of employ, I can tell you that!"

"Oh Hendrik, it doesn't concern you," his wife said patiently, "and we have guests. Enjoy your meal, and stop poisoning it with politics."

"Doesn't concern me? A papist who fancies himself a new Caesar almost get's the country overrun, I think it's the duty of all the Dutch to see he pays for what he's done to us!" Hendrik bellowed. There were a few "Here! Here!"'s scattered from the guests in agreement.

"Please dear, at least try to keep it down some, the neighbors complain. If you do, I'll promise to bring up a few bottles of Bols for you and your friends." She smiled winsomely.

* * * *

For all of his gruffness, Hendrik had a hard time resisting that facial expression, and relented, "As you wish dear, if we won't moderate the topic of conversation, for your sake, we shall make to moderate the volume." His wife smiled thankfully and disappeared into the house's kitchens to see about the promised liqueurs.

After she had left, one of the other men at the table turned to Hendrik,"So what would you have us do?"

"Go back to the old ways, take care of things like men!" he said firmly. The others stared at him for a moment, the young silversmith was a bit of a firebrand, but a good friend they generally agreed with. They suspected his Protestantism, a bit, they suspected that it had less to do with any love of Martin Luther and John Calvin and more a detestation of Catholics and foreigners. If the men around the table were pushed too hard, though, they might admit their feelings were similar, but the man was so obvious about it.

"Hendrik, that may be the will and the way of ending it, but if we're going to get the Orangists to forgive us our trespasses we might want to phrase it a bit differently," said one of them, a plump older man named Johann. His word was often considered final on these matters among those at the table, he had strong ties to Prince William through his Admiral brother. "Let's be honest with ourselves, they at least want the world to believe they alone are the defenders of the rights of protestant Kings. How it is done is a matter for the people, how it is portrayed to the rest of the world is equally important."

"I suppose that's true enough Johann. But are you with us?" asked Hendrik his lean features sharp.

"My dear friend, if the de Witts return to power, I don't think any protestations of 'But I was only listening to them' would save me from the noose do you?" Johann said with a chuckle his jowls shaking as he laughed. All the men at the table joined him in his laugh, thankful to have the tension in the room reduced.

* * * *

Later that evening a man sat in a darkened room inside a lavish house staring thoughtfully out the bay window on the second floor. His hair once dark and long was starting to gray in places. His face, while still firm, and handsome showed a tinge of droop from middle age. There was an open bottle of cognac on a table next to his chair, it wasn't noticeable in the dark but at least one other bottle was empty under the table itself.

The room only had two small candles burning. The candles themselves caused there to be a myriad of shadows in the large room. The furnishings were expensive, as could be seen even in this dim light, from the reflection of their well polished wooden arms.

There was a knock on the door, light and tentative.

"Come in Johann," the man said smiling.

* * * *

The door opened to reveal his brother, Johann. His jowls jiggled as he laughed lightly, "How you knew it was me I'll never know."

"I knew where you were, and what you were doing," he said, with a minor barely detectable slur to his voice, "and who else should I expect at this time of the evening?"

"True enough I suppose," Johann said cheerfully picking up the bottle of cognac and looking at the label as he walked to the other side of the room looking for a glass, "hmm, very good cognac, at least it's nice to know if you insist on getting soused, you're doing it with class and dignity.

"Very droll indeed Johann, very amusing. So, how goes the conspiracy business?" he asked holding up his half empty snifter and swirling it.

"Very well indeed my brother, I think I have most of my pieces on the board now," Johann said as he poured himself an obscene amount of cognac into a snifter of his own.

"Can you move soon? I don't know how much longer we can keep

Cornelius. His brother is screaming to all that will hear of his innocence in this," with that the man took a deep draught of brandy, "And bring the bottle back you pig, I'm liable to run dry."

"Of course dear brother," the portly man came back and brought up his own chair. "You know," he added, "we're still quite wealthy, I'm sure we could afford more candles than this."

"I find it helps me, to contemplate things. I have not your mind for conspiracies and find them tiresome, this at least prevents me from being distracted."

"And less chance of fire should you pass out as well," his brother chuckled.

"That too, of course," the man said with a sad smile.

"Well, trust me, I have almost everything I need now," said Johann with a smile.

"Lord I hope so, I just want to get back to sea, it is where I deserve to be. If we hand William this, he's promised me my return to command," said the man wistfully.

* * * *

"Ho! van Banchem!," Johann called out jovially stepping into a cramped looking building.

A furtive thin looking man at a desk at the back of the room looked up and smiled wanly, "Come in Vroedman Kievit, please, come back to my private office."

Once the door was closed, van Banchem walked behind a battered desk and sat down waving his hand at the rooms only other decoration, an equally battered chair, "Please, sit, and let's talk. What do I owe the pleasure of your company Johann?"

"Well, I'll be blunt with you, Verhoeff worries me," the plump man replied taking a seat across from his friend.

"Don't tell me, let me guess, it's all his talk of the 'old ways' isn't it?," smiled van Banchem.

"It certainly is! What does that even mean? He talks like he hates Catholics, but then talks about the 'old ways' all the time, what else could it mean? It's worrisome, especially when you consider, the rest of us that are doing the planning, have some favor we want from it. But not Hendrik, he's asked for nothing more than a chance to kill the 'catholic roman traitor,' but I'm sure he doesn't mean in the defense of Protestantism."

"Oh don't worry about it so, Kievit. I've known Hendrik since he was a boy. Now yes indeed, his family has always worshiped at altars that were here before any Catholic Jesus, but he's a good solid man. If anything his religion works in our favor, he doesn't despise Protestants, because at least he see's its roots in the Germanic and Scandinavian peoples. He see's Catholicism as some fatal poison brought here from the south. It's part of the oppression of the country in his eyes," explained van Banchem smiling the entire time.

"So, it's just racial pride and patriotism for him?" Kievit asked with a raised eyebrow.

"As far as anyone can tell. All he's demanded from anyone involved is that we celebrate with him in the way of our people from time immemorial after it's done. Considering our own prices for our participation are so, so much higher, it's the least we could do, don't you think? After we're done, we go to his house, get roaring drunk with the rest of the heathens, and start counting our bribes from our new secure positions," van Banchem said with a laugh.

* * * *

"He doesn't actually expect William himself to be there, does he?" Kievit asked suddenly.

"Thankfully no, he seems content just to have you and me there, and frankly, you can't ask for more of a reasonable request than that."

* * * *

"How goes things with the prisoner then?" asked Kievit.

"We've tortured him as much as we're able. He won't confess to the attempt on his brother, but then again we never expected him to, we knew he didn't have anything to do with it. But he did commit perjury in the middle of it, nothing major, his conviction certainly won't hold if we are unsuccessful tomorrow."

"And his brother?"

"We've sent word that we will only release Cornelius to him, so they should both be there tomorrow," van Banchem said with a serpentine smile.

Johann stood up from his chair, "Well, until tomorrow then, and may god have mercy on all of us if we fail."

Van Banchem got up to show him out saying, "We'll find out quickly enough if he will have mercy on our souls if we fail."

* * * *

Van Banchem's heart was in his throat as he strode up to the jail. The militia behind him was of small comfort now, this was the all or nothing part.

"Surround the jail!" he called out loudly and clearly for all to hear. "It has come to my attention that an escape is planned!"

A man in an army uniform rode up to him on a roan horse, "Ho! City man, what is this commotion that causes a need for the city militia in such force?"

"We have no quarrel Captain, nor do we intend to cause one," van Banchem called out in a loud voice intended to carry to any bystanders. "There is a rumor that the criminal would-be assassin, Cornelius de Witt, intends to make good his escape today. As a man of the law, I must take steps."

"It was my understanding that he was to be let go," the man on the horse said mildly, it was barely perceptible and invisible to any distant onlooker, but he clearly winked at van Banchem.

"This has not reached my ears sir or the ears of Vroedman Kievit who is with me, and first brought this to my attention, good sir," replied van Banchem trying hard not to smile.

* * * *

"If you would permit, I will inform those inside of the situation. But, we understand your need for certainty in any release. Please, wait here," with that the man turned his horse and walked it sedately back to the jail itself. There, he dismounted and walked to the door itself. He stood in the doorway clearly discussing something with someone inside, turned and remounted riding patiently back to van Banchem.

* * * *

"His brother, the former raadpensionaris Johan is with him. He swears that Cornelius is to be released today. I will send a runner to the town hall if you will but wait, and I'm sure we can have this all sorted out shortly," the Captain smiled.

"As you wish sir, I'm sure you understand my men would gladly be elsewhere today. So, the sooner this is all sorted out the best," van Banchem said loudly, smiling broadly at the crowd. There was some chuckling at his joke among the ranks of his men.

"You there!," the Captain called out to one of his men," Verhoeff, isn't it? I need you to ride to find me a judge. I need to confirm that Cornelius de Witt is to remain in custody or to be set free. Can you do that?"

* * * *

"Right away sir!" the cavalryman shouted and rode off the through the increasingly crowded city streets.

Moments after the young man rode off the door to jail slammed open.

Out strode a middle-aged man with long flowing hair, dressed in opulent clothing. He took one look at the increasing crowd, and the militia before stepping directly to the head of the cavalry, "What is the meaning of this Captain?"

"Some confusion on the orders for the prisoner Grand Pensioner, we've sent a runner, we should have it seen to shortly," the Captain said with a courteous nod of his head.

"Please hurry sir, my brother and I need to be away shortly," the man fumed.

* * * *

"Well, for now, my duty is to the law sir, speaking of which I would ask you to return inside, there may be Orangists in the crowd, and I consider myself concerned for your safety out here in the open, let us please avoid incident,"the Captain said loudly but cordially.

"I think there may be some closer than that," the man said glowering at van Banchem, but he did indeed turn on his heel and walk back to the jail. The door slammed with a booming echo.

* * * *

"He took it well, don't you think Captain," van Banchem said with a smile, that the Captain fought not to return.

"Lovely day for it," said the Captain looking up to the clear skies.

"Oh quite,"agreed van Banchem.

Both men turned as they heard hoofs pounding through the city streets. "Well we should soon get to the bottom of this," the Captain said spurring his horse to meet the rider.

"Sir!," the man gasped pulling his horse to a halt, "you must come at once! I've received word the granaries are being raided. Townspeople and country folk alike have broken down the doors and are taking all that they can carry! The cavalry's been ordered to put an end to it!"

The Captain considered it for a moment, then turned to van Bamchem, "Well Vroedman van Banchem. It would seem that I will have to leave you without this being resolved for now. I am sure the de Witts will not be happy with me, or you for that matter. But the law is the law, and civil unrest takes precedence over their inconvenience. My men and I will return as soon as we are able."

With that, he turned to the rest of the cavalry, "Well men, we have a riot to quell, let's ride."

* * * *

Van Banchem watched them ride away with a smile, and turned to his own men, "Well men, we will hold here, unless there is some further civil unrest that could cause us to withdraw."

He proceeded to ride to the rear of his men, where in the shadows of the buildings sat Kievit on a horse of his own, a long-suffering mare chosen for a gentle temperament. "So far so good," he said, "how goes the rest?"

"Hendrik is in the crowd, give the cavalry time to make good their withdrawal. Soon enough we'll have an angry mob on our hands," the fat man said with a smile.

"Tsk tsk," said van Banchem, "thank god that the Orangists are returning to power, it isn't even safe to walk the streets."

* * * *

They watched as the crowd that had been gathering started to press in on the militia. Weapons began to appear in the midst of the crowd, peasants, and working people are often considered unarmed by commanders far away but ask any soldier, and he'd say he'd rather face the heathen Spaniards on a battlefield, then an irate butcher with a cleaver. The militia themselves were still trying to hold the crowd back but were giving ground to them. Rocks began to fly landing harmlessly among the troops.

"I should do something about this immediately, nice to have seen you, Johann," van Banchem said spurring his horse back over to his increasingly hard-pressed troops. "Men! Fall back! Without the cavalry, we're sitting ducks here! I was ordered to prevent an escape not defend the de Witts from a bloody mob!"

One of the men called up,"But sir! Shouldn't we do something?"

"Do you want to die for a traitor like de Witt? Because that's likely to happen if we stay here man!"

"No sir, I suppose not," the man said his face looking down.

* * * *

"Good man. Men fall back slowly, try not to engage the mob, and hopefully we all get drunk tonight!," van Bencham yelled with a smile on his lips.

Soon and in an orderly manner, the militia themselves had pulled back down the two side streets on either side of the jail, leaving only an open path for the mob that seemed to be getting uglier all the time. Faces could be seen peering out the jail's window fearfully, first one, then another, looking out at the angry crowd.

The crowd parted slightly, and a group of men came up caring a large squared cross timber from some kind of housing project in the area. The men rushed the door of the jail, using the stout enormous timber as a battering ram, the sound of the collision was enormous and filled the square. They pulled back and walked backward, leaving a cloud of dust around the doorway, In a moment they were running forward again with the log and crashed into the door again, this time, they were rewarded by an enormous splintering noise, this brought a loud cheer from the crowd. Finally, on the third try, the door splintered apart leaving a gaping dust filled hole in its place.

* * * *

Men swarmed into the building, there was shouting from inside, but eventually, two men were drug out into the courtyard. Both had been abused considerably, there were bruises and blood on both of them. One was the man who had stormed out to confront the militia and cavalry earlier.

The crowd parted, and one man stepped forward, flanked by two men with large flintlocks, the man himself had two pistols tucked into his belt. It was Hendrik Verhoeff, silversmith, and for today, commander of the mob.

"Johan and Cornelius de Witt, it is customary to read the charges!" he called out. There were catcalls, cheers, and bows from the crowd in response.

* * * *

"This is a mockery!" yelled the other man, Cornelius, only to be punched viciously by one of the men holding him.

"To continue without interruption again," continued Hendrik with a vicious smile, "the citizens of the Hague have found you guilty of denying your rightful King, William, also with conspiring with Papists to return them to power here, for denying Calvinism, and for causing due to those conflicting loyalties the YEAR OF DISASTER!," the last part he bellowed causing the crowd to erupt.

He walked quickly over to Johan de Witt and leaned in, "On a personal note, you allowed any who would practice the old ways to be hounded and tormented, to be labeled witches. When you see my dear mother in the afterlife, you can begin working off your debt to her."

As he strode away de Witt called at him, "You'll do no better with the Calvinists!"

Hendrik stopped and turned. "Let them go and step away from them," he said to the guards holding the men. "This may be true, it most likely is," he said drawing both pistols, "but I'll make sure you'll have paid for what you have done." He fired, the crowd surged.

Van Banchem and Kievit sat back from the crowds in a darkened shadow watching. "Well that, would appear to be that," said van Banchem smiling.

* * * *

"Quite," replied Kievit his face also grinning.

* * * *

"See you later tonight at Hendrik's, I hear that he's laid on quite the spread for the celebration," he said.

* * * *

"Quite a spread you say? Well, an assassination and a meal, how charming. A promise is a promise of course."

"And, we both did promise to join them tonight."

"Quite."

* * * *

Both men now walked to the quarter of the city where Hendrik's family lived. The streets were alive with merrymakers all celebrating the news of the de Witts demise. "Well, I would almost say from the atmosphere, that we did a public service," said Kievit.

"After the last year or so, I don't think many will mourn their demise. But, to be sure, the level of joy surprises even me," agreed van Banchem.

As they approached his house, they saw that Hendrik himself was sitting in a chair that had been drug outside, with a large tankard in his hand, "Hello friends!" he called out,"we've been waiting for you both so that the festivities can truly begin!" He had a huge beaming smile on his face as he stood up to greet them.

He shook hands with both of them vigorously, then waved them inside, "My wife is just now putting down the feast, I'll unveil our meal as soon as we're all in. I was afraid you might not honor your promise to the old ways. But," he said with a laugh,"here you are as promised.

Johan Kievit and Johann van Banchem went through the front door that Hendrik held open wide for them. There was a large crowd already seated around the enormous table that filled the room. A huge serving tray made up the centerpiece, all eyes turned briefly to the new arrivals, but turned back to the tray with great anticipation. Kievit's eyes swept down the table length, finally resting on the mantle piece, upon which sat...

"Dear god!" gasped Kievit, "it's..."

"Their hearts!" said Hendrik clapping both of them on the shoulders from behind and gently pushing the two stunned men to their seats. "It is in the manner of the old ways to cut out the hearts of your enemy! A trophy to let others know the fate of all oppressors!"

"And now for a feast done in the old way!" he said striding to the covered serving dish. "I give you a meal fit for a King, served to the killers of a tyrant, as it has always been for us!"

With that, Hendrik lifted the lid on the dish. Both men gasped with horror at the sight before them. There was no mistaking it, despite the time it had spent being blackened in the oven. From thigh to toe, they were staring at the now fully cooked, human leg of Grand Pensionary Johan de Witt.

"Now gentlemen, let us be merry at our success, and most importantly, let us eat!"

* * * *

In the year 1672 Johan and Cornelius de Witt, former Grand Pensionary Of the Dutch Republic, and former ruwaard of Bierland respectively, were drug from a jail in the Hague and killed by an angry mob. The suspected conspirators who history accuses of instigating the attack were all rewarded, Johan Kievit became pensionary of Rotterdam, his brother Cornelius Tromp became Admiral General of the Dutch Navy, Johan van Blanchem was rewarded by becoming baljuw of the Hague itself. But perhaps most rewarded of all was William III, with his hated rival dead, he consolidated his power and became King. From there he went on to become King of England in 1689. No record exists of any rewards for the silversmith, Hendrik Verhoeff, but perhaps, some things, are their own reward.

✗

Fiends of the Southern Plains
Patrick Tumblety

A wisp of fog hovers over the glen, climbing green hills and pooling inside their warrens. The sun is losing its dominion to the moon, but before either lays claim on the sky an otherworldly blue hue bathes the plain. Altermen of the north believe that for those few minutes before nightfall the living world merges with the realm of the After, a remembrance that life and death are two sides of the same coin. Boatsmen to the east call it the "Breach," an omen for those who fish for serpents in Deeproot to be wary of the sea's uncompromising nature. Women pace the dock towns like phantoms waiting for their husbands who are long overdue. "She's breaching," someone would answer an inquirer, halting further inquiry.

To the people of the southern plains, the blue is a reminder to seek shelter. Death grazes the land the moment that light extinguishes.

Yellow light burst through the room by the flare of a match. A young boy's eyes widen, frightened by the sudden creation of fire. The man who brought it to life looks toward his wife who has been busy latching the north window. She pauses to regard the child, waiting for another type of reaction. The boy's head tilts slightly, cautious, but curious. She returns her husband's nervous glare, then proceeds toward the west window.

The man lights a hanging lamp on each wall of the cottage, watching gleefully as the boy is mesmerized by the shadows that dance throughout the room. He reaches out to grab them but the room is too small and the lighting of all four lamps dispels the lingering dark.

"No need to be upset," the man laughs and slides a chair from under the table. "There are many games to play that I will teach you." He pulls two coins from his breast pocket and places them on the wooden surface. Standing one up with his forefinger he flicks its edge with his thumb and sends the coin into a spin. He does the same with the other coin and soon the spinning pieces of copper orbit each other, threatening to collide. The boy is enthralled. The man, however, can't keep his eyes from the youthful joy across the boy's, his son's, face.

"G'brel," the man says softly, and the boy looks up in response for the first time since being given that name. "Can you say 'father'?"

G'brel opens his mouth and the man's heart skips a beat. Before the boy speaks the ting of metal on metal draws back his attention. A coin slides across the wood and teeters on the edge of the table while the other falls to the floor. The boy claps his hands together and cackles. Husband and wife show the other an expression they had not previously shared when concerning the child: hope.

A knock on the door startles the three. The husband and wife immediately panic.

The husband pushes the table aside and reaches under the handmade rug. From underneath he pulls out a tiny piece of rope and lifts it to the air, detaching a piece of flooring. He motions for his son to descend the steps but the boy only stares down into the darkness below.

"It's okay, we will be right here. Wait on the steps like we practiced and don't make a sound." He places a hand on G'brel's back and guides him down. The rope helps him guide the section of wood flooring back into place. He sticks the rope between the planks and returns the carpet and table to their original positions.

His wife strikes a match and lights the fire pit. She drops in the potatoes that she had skinned earlier in the day into the pot hanging above the kindling.

"La'han," she calls with a low yet sharp tone.

Her husband nods to reassure her and then pulls the iron handle of the heavy wooden door.

"Mr. Entler," La'han feigns pleasantries, "Didn't think you'd be stopping by today, or should I say, night, sir." He says the latter with urgency and takes a glance behind the visitor to further indicate his concern. Hopefully, the time of day is indicative of the short interval the unwanted guest will be able to stay.

The stocky man glances behind himself, fingers pinching the brim of his Scoutman's cap. "I'd be lying if I said I wasn't nervous, but Captain's orders an' all. No worries though, I'm chasing the sun 'til Garin's Gall and holding up there for the night."

The woman approaches and places a hand on her husband's shoulder, squeezing it just hard enough to indicate her fear.

The need for a night's shelter means that he had traveled from the Capital. Only the most important or devastating news was worth the risk of a Scoutsman's life. The sweat that drips from his brow tells of the hard ride he had endured that day.

"Merta, a glass of water for Mr. Entler, please."

She hurries to the back of the cottage toward the pump for the well. When she returns and hands the visitor the glass he eyes her belly carefully, but her apron covers any signs of growth.

"Still no word on your petition?" The visitor asks, and then aggressively gulps down the entirety of the glass.

La'han's heart beats faster. Has rumor led the Scoutsman here? They gave almost everything they had to ensure their concealment.

"We sent another letter, but again, we were not chosen." He lifts his hands in the air and tries not to sound too disappointed. "We thought maybe your arrival has carried the words we wait to hear."

"Unfortunately, I come with dire news. Marauders attacked the King's caravan on his way to Temple yesterday evening."

"My Lord," La'han feigns his reaction again. "Is His Highness dead?" If the rebels he had recently been in contact with were successful, royalty has switched hands to the Governor-in-Waiting and their predicament might not be a problem any longer.

"Thank the Realms, no. His Carriage Whip did his job and fled the scene. None of the Guardsmen have returned as of yet." At this, the Scoutsman lowers his eyes.

La'han places a hand on the man's shoulder. An action like this is usually forbidden between a commoner and one of the royal commune, but he knows the man well enough to know he would appreciate the showing of respect. Though privy to the attack, La'han, too, mourns the men and women that were only fulfilling their duty to guard their king. If only they could have died for a better man.

"The light is dying, my friend," La'han said. "See to it that you live to fulfill your charge."

The Scoutsman looks behind him and sees that the sun has begun to touch the horizon. He squints against the blue light and considers the time that remains before it is lost.

La'han clenches his fist. To refuse shelter to an employ of the Royal Guard is treason and he's already in treacherous dealings beyond the consent of the King. Besides, Dougan Entler is an honorable man, it would be a shame to have to kill him if he finds the boy in the basement.

"Thank you for your generosity." The Scoutsman hands the empty glass to La'han.

"Thank you for your call, sir."

The Scoutsman tips his hat and then walks toward his horse. La'han is about to shut the man out until he turns around.

La'han's might just have to kill the man on the spot.

"Do you believe the stories, La'han, that strange creatures walk these lands at night? Us city folk get quite a laugh at all the tall tales you plains folk conjure." The man chuckles, but the expression on his face shows a hint of fear.

Anger replaces his frustration, but La'han knows he has too much to lose.

"I can't say I've seen anything strange myself, but there is a reason you are worried about getting inside before nightfall, regardless of who, or what, is out there."

The Scoutsman laughs. "Quite a pragmatic answer." He laughs until he saddles his horse, then chases the sun. Hopefully, he can keep up.

"Do you think that was wise, goading him like that?" Merta asks once the door is shut and latched.

"We've lost too many friends to their denial." He is rough on the chairs and table as he skirts them across the floor.

"But we have another's safety to consider, now."

La'han nods. His wife is the better pragmatist.

He lifts the trapdoor, eager to see his boy's face. They had tried for years to have a baby, but when Kerond was pronounced as King he refused to allow the southern villagers to adopt from northern blood. Fellow plains folk paid money to smuggle orphans out of the northern cities but the Journeymen they dealt with either absconded with their payment or were caught by Scoutsmen and hanged.

When natural means became difficult, finding out the truth behind the land's folklore became their last resort.

Rumors had trickled down from the northern cities for years. Elixirs. Rituals. Strange foods. There was a tale of an eastern native settlement that housed a priestess of an ancient religion that could awaken the birthing abilities of any woman she touched.

One spring past, they procured a map from a trader and headed east.

They understood that they were most likely chasing a tall tale but had come to the agreement that the dream was worth chasing. Enough terrible magic existed in the world, why couldn't some be used for joy? Wasn't a woman's ability to create life proof of virtuous miracles?

La'han and Merta nearly starved to death.

Merta still holds contempt at her husband for not letting them starve. "What is the point of living," she had sighed, half-dead of malnutrition and too weak to take the horses reigns back from her husband. "If we can't leave a legacy?"

"Living well, and serving the gods virtuously."

That didn't seem to satisfy her, and the way in which their prayers had been answered made neither feel virtuous.

"G'brel, you can come out now. There's no longer need to fear." La'han searches the darkness. He steps onto the first plank, wood creaking beneath his weight. His eyes adjust to the lack of light but still can't suss where the boy is hiding.

"Are you playing a game, G'brel?"

The cavern extends several more yards through the earth and narrows farther from the cellar. The space is still wide enough for a boy to slip through, but La'han has to turn sideways and shimmy along for several feet.

"I must warn you, G'brel, your father is a master of hide and seek!"

The narrow passage opens up to a round stone space just big enough for him to move his arms. A sliver of blue slices through from ten feet above his head where there should be a stone slate covering what used to be a pumping well.

"G'brel!" His voice bounces against the stone. "Get inside the house, it's not safe out there. Do you hear me? Your father demands this!"

La'han counts exactly ten seconds before he panics. He yells his wife's name as he squeezes back through the narrow tunnel, the hard dirt tearing his clothes and skin.

"Latch the door behind me," he says as he emerges from the earth.

"You only have minutes, La'han."

"He couldn't have roamed far. I'll bring—"

Merta grabs his arm and pulls him away from the door.

La'han spins around and howls at his wife. "You would leave our son to those monsters?"

His anger and fear loosens her grip. "We can get another, La'han, but I can't get another you." Her eyes tear, knowing the blasphemy of her words.

Her husband spits on the ground before slamming the front door.

La'han rounds the tiny cottage and runs through the clearing as fast as he can toward the wood. His wife is correct; to watch the sun go down without being sheltered is the same as watching the Reaper approach you without running away. He frantically moves and screams for G'brel as he reaches the edge of the clearing and enters the forest, trunks thickening along with the flora and fauna that narrows his trail.

The environment is treacherous enough but does not compare to its denizens.

So many legends surrounded the woods that denying the reality of any of them could mean you were ill-prepared for survival within. The bloodhounds of Helen's Hills to the west used to be no more than a tall tale until nearly an entire town had gone missing and the dogs were all that were left. La'han had heard about River Wraiths since childhood, never believing in them until he had encountered one. Mothers washing their babies in the water would return to their husbands in hysterics, speaking of "water angels" that hovered from upstream and took their babies. As a teenager, La'han would wash his axe in the river after hunting, and once saw a leathery creature hovering past him downstream. He was so startled by its strange visage that he dropped his axe into the river, the powerful current taking it away. The Wraiths were real, but not the cause of the children's disappearances.

Wood nymphs. Violet fern. Lantern spirits. Whether or not they are a myth, the woods have several ways of killing.

The worst of them are the Pale Men.

La'han once scoffed at the tales until he was confronted with the disease that turned his neighbors and friends into not of that realm.

The snap of a twig turns La'han's attention. He doesn't dare yell out his son's name for fear that 'those that live in night' are already on the fringes of the remaining light, following the edge of the darkness like a tide over the shore. He whispers forcefully, "G'brel," and then walks toward the thick brush where the sound had originated.

Thick vines interlace and pile several feet above his head. He learned a hard lesson about their deadliness when he was a child. His friends used to spend all day under there during their summers when the sun was too bright to play without shade. After several near-death experiences, they wouldn't dare climb the living canopy. The vines are as hard as stone and as malleable as an orgy of snakes.

A childhood promise is broken as he uses all four limbs to climb on top and then crawl across, keeping him from losing one in the tangle. Several yards across, La'han hears a hum beneath the mingling roots. The sound is deliberate, rhythmic. The heavy whining of a frightened child.

La'han sees a dark spot where the vines are farther apart. Their roughness scrapes his cheeks and arms as he squeezes through. He has to be careful to hold onto sturdier vines to keep gravity from pulling him down too fast. When there is no more foliage to grab onto his body drops. Mud squishes out from under his shoes and he nearly falls into it. The temperature drops nearly twenty degrees, and the wetness sends him into shivers. He blocks out the physical pain and looks around. So little light is able to pierce the bramble that he has to rely more on his hearing to navigate. Carefully maneuvering through the squishing mud he finds G'brel sitting in the muck and hugging his legs. His eyes stare unblinking, but then widen as they discover La'han.

"It's okay, my child, your father is here." He extends a hand to his boy.

G'brel continues to stare, so La'han shimmies closer.

"The sun has fallen, we need to go now."

At this, the boy lifts his head and peeks through a teardrop shaped opening amongst the roots. Satisfied, he crawls toward La'han, who quickly scoops him up.

La'han struggles with one arm to pull them back up through the twining. He has to move swiftly and pays no attention to the brittle plant life prickling his skin. He hides his son's head with his hand as best as he can. La'han breaks through the canopy and sees the world painted so blue that he knows only minutes remain before the night returns.

The roots shake as though they're alive and consciously trying to throw La'han off kilter. He uses his empty hand to stabilize and needs to stop for a moment. Close to the edge of the brush his foot slips. The roots have a terrible grip on his ankle. He shifts his son's weight to his other arm and reaches behind to pull on the tangle. Around his ankle is not an intertwining of plant life, but a human hand as pale as a cloud. He screams and pulls on the fingers to pry them off, but another hand reaches from between a different opening and grabs his wrist. With a yell, he rears backward, and the force dislodges him from the cold hands. He rolls over the top of the tangle and then over its edge. He lands on leaves and grass with his boy on top of his chest, just outside the mouth of the root system.

Within the darkness under the canopy pinpoints of light burst to life. Several Pale Men step into the clearing, daylight losing its reach across the realm.

With his boy in his arms, La'han runs home as fast as he has ever tried. The creatures are much faster, especially with the weight of the boy, so La'han risks breaking his straight line toward the edge of the wood and turns west toward the faint light of the dying sun. The thin veneer is enough to caution the Pale Men and slow their pursuit. The sizzle of sunburnt skin and tiny squeals of pain fade behind as La'han runs. He turns back toward the direction of the clearing that surrounds his home. If they can get inside, there is still hope.

The Pale Men will not enter a home unless invited. The villagers speculated this was because something remained of the person they had been, and so they tried to keep their own horror away from their families. La'han had discussed this strange behavior with the band of anarchists that he conspired with, and they agreed that the feeling of guilt might be the reason why the creatures never went into houses. The plains folk were almost certain that the disease was unleashed by King Kerond to eradicate the lower class and not have to rely on them to run the farmlands.

What is left of the daylight shines across the clearing that surrounds the house. The blue colors the world and the moon his high, but La'han has returned home with enough time to traverse the long expanse of hay and grass. His skin grows cold as he notices that not even a hint of light reaches fully across the clearing.

Pale Men scream their sickening night-howl as they emerge from his home.

"Gods, no," he cries. Their entrance should not have been possible, and Merta would never have invited them in willingly. La'han places a hand on the back of his son's head to make sure it doesn't turn and see the horde.

A tall, angular Pale Man exits the house, and though La'han is far away, he can see that its body is nude. The others gather around it and drop to their knees, craning their necks and opening their mouths like dogs waiting to be fed. The tall one releases a high pitched shriek as it lifts an arm into the air. It holds a broken broom handle, and speared on the top of its splintered end is Merta's severed head. The creatures catch the blood in their mouths and lap up the spill from each other's bodies. They squeal like pigs in a bath of slop.

La'han screams.

The sun has been swallowed by the horizon, and the blue is gone. Night pervades the realm.

The tall Pale Man sees him and the boy in his arms. The scream it unleashes terrifies La'han to near paralysis. As though the scream was an order, the Pale Men forget their meal and race down the hillside. The man looks at his son's face, his young eyes wide and frantic even though he can't see the amount of horror he should be feeling. The look in the boy's eyes turns La'han's heels and sets him running west toward a sun he knows he won't be able to catch.

La'han searches his memory for one piece of helpful information about the Pale Men that he could use for escape. He had only once witnessed their supernatural brutality, so he would have to rely on conjecture and hope there is some truth to the folklore.

The only salvation that he can think of is getting to the lake.

He has the knowledge of the immediate land to his advantage. He reaches the edge of the wood before his pursuers are even halfway across the clearing. Once through the thin line of trees and into the thick of the forest, he kicks up stone on the path he had dug with his human hands.

Moonlight shines across the lake and paints his boat as it rests upon the surface of the still water. He hopes that the rumor of the creatures' aversion to water will keep them safe at the center of the lake.

"Rest here, son, you will be safe." Though he doesn't know if his plan will work, it is his duty as a father to ensure that his child feels protected, regardless of the truth.

His son, head still buried in his shoulder, squeezes around his arm as though he will never let go. He embraces the boy and then pulls him off with his other arm, placing him at the back of the tiny fishing boat.

"My son, look at me," he says, but the boy only continues to shake and cry, too afraid to acknowledge anything that is happening around him.

"I know you're afraid, but I promise I will get you to safety." He prays that he isn't lying.

He uncurls the rope that ties the boat to shore and leans into it to set it free from the embankment. Slowly but surely it starts to give, "see my son, we are almost free—"

Pain pierces through La'han's neck as he's pulled from the ground. He can see the bald head of a Pale Man at of the corner of his vision shaking violently, and with each pull, he feels the muscles in his neck and shoulder tear. He feels the teeth puncture the bone in his shoulder. He knows he will not survive. His only peace comes from the knowledge of his son's escape. Every bit of energy that remains in his body helps him lift his legs and kick forward, striking the back edge of the boat. Once, twice, just enough energy for a third time...

The boat frees from the embankment and bobs across the water.

La'han catches his boys eyes twinkling in the moonlight just before the creature rips his throat from his body. The last thing La'han hears is his son scream "father!" before he falls to the ground and dies.

The Pale Man paces at the edge of the lake, hissing and snapping like an animal at the water as though it can frighten the pain-inducing liquid away. It spots a tiny glimmer of hope; the rope that tied it to the shore still lies in the mud. The creature picks up the rope and winces through the pain caused by the dampness in its fibers.

The boy watches on, wide-eyed and unmoving.

Pull by pull the Pale Man brings the boat back to shore. It jerks when it hits the edge and sends the boy tumbling back inside. The creature grabs the boat and hauls it onto land enough for it to stay, and then hops inside.

Tears soak the boy's face, but his frightful shaking has stopped. The Pale Man lifts the boy into the air and brings the little one toward his bloody lips, and when they part, he pushes them against his son's cheek. The boy wraps his arms around his father's neck.

The Pale Man is to meet with his wife back at their new home, but will reluctantly inform her that he is still of the mind that they cannot stay. The southern realm has become as tainted with hatred as the north. Rumors have spread throughout the wood that most of the western land has remained unconquered by their human progenitors. A land free from human beliefs in the old gods and untainted by their kings whose false ideologies fuel their paranoia. The Pale Man has to find a home for his family where they can live in peace.

Peace is most likely just a myth, but myth is all they have left to believe.   ✗

The Pyrrhic Crusade
Stanley B. Webb

Sir Cain emerged from the woods, into a tomb-yard. Tattered mourning flags snapped in the breeze. The road went through, between rows of iron-caged granite mausoleums, before reentering the forest.

His mount balked, stamping uneasily.

"Steady, Thunder."

Fear-sweat sprang out inside his ebony battle-armor. Cain touched the pentacle emblazoned on his chest plate, and from it drew courage. His own urge was to skirt the yard, but Cain would not submit to this base instinct.

"A knight, and a knight's horse, must face fear. Onward!"

Even so, he kept to the center of the lane and thrust the Pyre sign—his left hand raised, with the thumb and middle digits folded, and pointer and pinky extended, at each crypt.

A twig snapped in the woods beyond the tomb-yard.

Cain halted, grasping his sword.

A mounted knight emerged from the far trees, armored in the blue and silver of Saint Lawrent Country, his shield emblazoned with the device of the Eternals, a vertical bar with a short lower crossbar.

The knight halted, putting a hand to his own sword. "What do you here, Pyrrhic?"

Cain released his sword and made the V sign of peace. "I am Cain, a courier of Oswaygo Country, bound for my embassy in Alexandra, and armored only against your Departed."

"I am Samuel, knight errant of Lord Grissel, whose burials are secure."

A muffled scream drifted out from the tomb-yard.

Samuel coughed embarrassedly, then insisted, "Our burials are secure. What is your message?"

"Sealed for Sir Reginild."

Samuel considered. "Will you submit to Eternal Law while here?"

"I obey the laws of men." *Except those which violate the laws of God.*

Samuel released his sword. "Then pass in peace, Sir Cain."

Samuel turned his horse and galloped whence he had come.

* * * *

The sun set.

Cain rode through the deepening twilight until he spied a hostel's welcome lamp. He would have ridden all night, rather than bivouac alone in the Country of Tombs. He tied Thunder's reins to the lamppost and approached the iron-bound door.

Cain discovered a mourning flag tied under the bell. He contemplated the warning, then rang.

A scrutiny panel opened. A woman asked, "Traveler, will you seek shelter with death?"

"I will, good Lady."

"Then, be welcome."

The door hinged outward.

Cain's hostess wore a black shift, and her hair combed to hide her face. She parted the dark tresses to regard his chest plate.

"You're a Pyrrhic! Will you help me burn my father?"

"Good Lady, are you not Eternals?"

"We're secret Pyrrhics."

Cain touched the mourning flag. "Do the Tomb-Monks know?"

"I had no heart to summon them, though I displayed the flag, as Grissel's law requires. Instead, I prayed for the great Fire-Keeper to send me aid, and you have come. What is your name?"

"Cain."

"I'm Argenta. Will you help me?"

"You're certain that no Eternal knows?"

"Only you have passed."

"Then I will, with gratitude that God sent me here."

"Thank you." Her voice choked. "I am a poor hostess, let me stable your horse."

"This is a poor day for you. I will tend to Thunder, then your Departed."

* * * *

Argenta lit a torch from the hearth, then led him through the scullery to the cellar stairs. Muted, animalistic screams rose from the black depths.

"Father died three days ago," she said. "Following a week of stomach turmoil."

"Appendix," Cain murmured.

"The pains ended, and he woke hale, or so we hoped, but then I saw the death stains upon his back."

"Livor mortis."

"Father refused to believe that he had died until the rigor took him. While he lay stiff and contorted, I dragged him down, and locked him in the wake vault."

For a moment, the dungeon screams gained a semblance of humanity. *"Argenta!"*

She sobbed. "Why did you abandon me, Father, how might I continue without your strength?"

Cain took the flambeau from her hand. "Bar the door behind me, and open it not until I call."

He clanked down the narrow steps, then crouched along beneath the cellar's low roof, following the Departed's cries to a thick, oaken door. Cain raised the torch before his eyes and prayed.

"Fire-Keeper, help me to release this tortured soul."

Cain lifted the vault's heavy bar.

The screaming paused.

Cain drew his sword, kicked open the door, and stepped back.

The Departed slouched forth, moaning, feet sliding with each step. It towered over Cain, and nearly equaled his armored weight. Its hands raised before its waxen face, fingers torn from struggling against the vault's door. Dead eyes did not contract against light; its pupils shone wide and red. Cain flared his torch. The Departed snarled, and struck out with a thick arm, missing widely. Cain braced his feet, cast the torch aside, then brought his sword back two-handed.

The Departed shied away from the flight of the torch, then blinked, its gesture poignantly life-like. It saw Cain, bellowed out necrotic gas, and charged.

Cain stepped aside and struck adroitly. The tip of his sword severed the body's thick neck, setting the head free, to crack on the floor. The body continued for two steps, then paused, awaiting a command from its absent brain.

From his fighting kit, Cain took a burlap bag. He lifted the gnashing head by its hair, tied it in, then yelled to Argenta.

"Have you laid a pyre?"

"Yes…in the kitchen midden."

"That's a good place," Cain said in reassurance. "Come and help me."

She descended to the foot of the stairs, then stopped, a hand rising to her concealed face in a gesture of horror.

Argenta retreated a step. "…I can't."

"Do not make this your father's last memory, help him ascend to the next life."

Two steps by two, they herded the body upstairs, nudging from behind when it paused, through the kitchen, and to the midden. A masonry wall circled the garbage pit. Cain tied the body's wrists, then tipped it over the wall, atop the gathered wood. He placed the head on the pile, then offered Argenta his flint. She stood woodenly.

"End his torment, good daughter."

She snatched Cain's fire kit and struck steel to stone until the sparks found their home in the pyre's tinder.

The flames grew slowly, spreading from tinder to kindling to stickwood until the pyre became engulfed. The Departed sizzled and writhed in its bonds. Argenta made a trembling noise, reaching forward. Cain drew her back from the roaring heat.

The burlap bag charred away, exposing her father's face. The dead man's expression eased.

"Goodbye!" cried his daughter.

The Departed smiled.

Said Cain, "We'll rejoin him in our own time, at the Original Pyre."

They tended the pyre well past midnight, consolidating the embers until naught but ashes remained, then quenched those, buried the mud in the garden, and refilled the midden with kitchen waste.

"Now," said Cain. "No Eternal will know that a pyre burned here."

Argenta drew her hair back from her face. Starlight glistened on her tears, but she smiled at Cain. "You've delivered my father from eternal entombment." She took his hand, placing it to her bosom. "I would reward your service."

Only her shift separated his palm from her skin. Cain felt her heart race. He was a young man, unknown to courting, and stammered in response.

"I did no service, merely duty, and what you offer is the reward of love."

"Then, let us make love."

* * * *

He greeted the dawn as a new man, his hopes, and dreams of the previous morning discarded. Cain turned beneath Argenta's sheets, cuddling his nude body against hers, and kissed her sleeping mouth. She opened her eyes and smiled.

The sun stood high when they finally rose.

"Must you go?" she asked.

"I must, but will fly back when my task is done."

Cain felt uneasy leaving Argenta, but his duty pressed: Oswaygo sought an alliance with Antario Country against the Eternals. Lady Argenta would be safe until he returned. She believed that no one else had seen her mourning flag, and she would know who passed on her road.

Thus self-assured, he departed.

* * * *

A huge, black mastiff stalked from the woods, intent on Cain's dwindling back. The dog showed its teeth and crouched to spring after him.

A Tomb-Monk emerged, his blue robe adorned with the Eternal's device, his hair cut into a top spike. "Still."

The mastiff sat.

Brother Abel stroked the dog's skull. "We owe thanks to Samuel for his news of the Pyrrhic's mourning flag and his warning that this foreign knight would lodge here." He raised his voice. "Brothers, let's discover if these Pyrrhics have respected God's law."

Six lesser monks in dingy white robes pushed a funeral cart out of the trees, a skeletal buckboard with six push-bars. Upon the cart rode a sarcophagus of polished cherry, equipped with iron bands and padlocks.

They went to Argenta's hostel.

Brother Abel scrutinized the grounds, paying special attention to the midden and garden, but he found no evidence of a Pyre. He took a fragment of charred bone from his pocket, and let the dog sniff.

The mastiff cast about the garden then began to dig.

* * * *

A gang of lesser monks, armored in mail and bearing swords, accosted Sir Cain in Alexandra's outskirts. They escorted him through the undefended slums and the fenced crop belt, to the city's outer wall. Successively higher walls rose within, culminating in Lord Grissel's keep, on the shores of the River Saint Lawrent.

Sir Reginild, a silver-haired knight, greeted Cain at the diplomatic enclave. Reginild summoned a Groom to install Thunder in the embassy's stables, little imagining that she would never again see her master.

Reginild ushered Cain into his chamber of office, broke open the courier scroll, and smiled grimly. "Antario Country has agreed to a treaty of mutual defense. Do you understand what this means?"

"I've heard rumors of crusades," said Cain.

"The rumors are right."

"Have we cause for aggression?"

"Grissel has done nothing overtly provocative, but, what do you know of the man?"

"He's undefeated in personal combat, in battle or tourney," said Cain. "And his stoicism is legendary; it's said that he feels no pain."

"Grissel *was* such a man, but he's aged, and has spent the past ten years hidden in his keep. I think he's gone senile, or even mad. Not only has he granted the Tomb-Monks martial authority, but he has halted the practice of entombment."

"Is that not good?" Cain asked.

"No, for neither does he burn his Departed. I have a spy among Grissel's masons, who reports that Grissel has stockpiled an army of corpses, with the intent of releasing them into the Pyrrhic countries."

Cain considered this and shuddered.

Reginild continued, "Unfortunately, our relations with Saint Lawrent are cordial and profitable. We must declare this crusade to thwart Grissel's plan, but we must first *provoke* some provocation on his part."

"That sounds less than chivalrous."

"It *is* less than chivalrous, it's diplomacy."

The Groom announced himself at the chamber's door. "Forgive the intrusion, but Sir Samuel awaits outside, requesting to parlay with Sir Cain."

Reginild raised an eyebrow toward Cain. "Do you know Samuel?"

"I met him yesterday, on the road."

"Was he civil?"

"Yes…but, I assisted at a Pyre afterward. Perhaps Samuel has learned?" A pang of fear struck Cain. "I request permission to return to the hostel."

Reginild waited pensively before replying. "No, parley with Samuel."

"But, the Lady Argenta—"

"Will be safe, I'm sure."

Despite his anxiety, Cain obeyed, following the Groom through a gate near the stables.

Samuel asked, "Sir Cain, did you commit cremation at the hostel south of Alexandra?"

Cain was a Knight of the Pyre and answered honorably. "The Departed was a Pyrrhic."

Samuel sighed. "You promised submission to our laws."

"I submit only to the Fire-Keeper's law."

Something growled behind Cain, and he turned sharply. A black mastiff crept up on him, its teeth bared to its gums. He drew his sword, and Samuel replied in kind. The dog crouched to spring.

Brother Abel appeared, leading a group of armed lesser monks.

"Still."

The dog sat. Samuel withheld his strike.

"I arrest you," said Abel. "For the Murder Eternal of the hostel-keeper, to whom you have denied God's gift of Eternal Life."

"His soul lives forever with the Fire-Keeper," said Cain. He sought to remain stoic, but could not stop himself from blurting a question. "What of Lady Argenta?"

Abel smiled nastily. "Your slut and accomplice in murder awaits her judgment in the sarcophagus we built for her father."

Cain lunged in anger.

Samuel struck down Cain's sword and body-slammed Cain against the wall. The lessers swarmed the Pyrrhic. Samuel held his blade to Cain's throat while the monks disarmed their captive.

"Drag him before the Lord," said Brother Abel.

* * * *

The Groom, who also served as Reginild's spy, hurried back to report Cain's capture.

Reginild responded with exhilaration. "This is the provocation needed to declare our crusade! Roust my knights, call out the men-at-arms-tell them to prepare the engine ram-alert the Antario Embassy, then don your mason's guise, and assist Sir Cain."

The Groom hurried away.

Within the hour, Sir Reginild led his army to Alexandra's outer gate. In the vanguard went the engine ram, a bull-like machine of wood and spring steel. Men-at-arms flanked the ram, their shields raised to defend its crew from the Alexandran wall-archers. Reginild himself locked the ram's wheels, then helped turn the crank which compressed the ram's springs. When he released the trigger, an iron-tipped log slammed forward and cracked the gate.

"Push!" Reginild cried. His back seized, but he ignored the pain for the heat of battle.

The armored warriors heaved against the back of the ram, forcing the log through the cracked gate. Men-at-arms kicked the broken pieces aside.

A phalanx of lesser monks awaited them.

"Onward," cried Reginild. "Avenge Sir Cain and Lady Argenta!"

* * * *

The gates Alexandra closed behind Cain, but the wall surrounding Grissel's keep had no gate. Entry was via a rickety, wooden staircase, rigged for demolition under siege.

Inside, the wall revealed a disused portcullis, the outer wall rising one cubit beyond. Moldering Departed haunted the in-between space.

Two structures dominated Grissel's enclave: the keep seemed more palace than fortress, but abandoned, while the Tomb-Monk's abbey swarmed with Nobles and functionaries. Strangely, a gigantic cauldron simmered on the abbey's roof, tended by a bucket train of monks.

Cain balked at the abbey's chill entrance. "Why here?"

Brother Abel replied, "Lord Grissel resides within."

Cain's escort forced him onward.

The chill deepened inside, becoming a deadly cold. Then, the frost-rimed stone masonry surrendered to walls of yellow river ice.

Although Cain did not comment on this change, Abel explained. "The ice comforts Lord Grissel's aging bones."

A burly man passed, dressed in winter clothes, and pushing a wheel-barrow full of ice blocks. Mason's tools dangled on his belt.

He muttered under his steaming breath, "I'll clout that lazy 'prentice when I find him."

The passage opened into a candle-lit Grand Hall of ice. Nobles waited in line, all of them bundled in deep-winter robes. Brother Abel pushed his way through, his cries emerging in clouds of smoke.

"Aside, aside!"

Grissel sat in shadows, on a throne carved from ice. The monks forced Cain to kneel, but he kept his head high.

Grissel's voice rasped like an ice saw. *"Beg for your life."* No fog issued from his lips.

"I beg for Lady Argenta, accepting her penalty, as well as my own."

The Lord chuckled. *"Your dooms are entwined. Make this Pyrrhic ours."*

Abel bowed, then led Cain down a long, icy passage, halting before a slot doorway. The Ice Mason awaited them.

Abel said, "Disrobe."

Cain's naked skin turned goose-pimples. Without waiting for Abel's next command, he stepped through the doorway, into a dark ice cell. A dozen hoary figures loomed before him; as his eyes adjusted to the dimness, he realized that they were corpses. Cain's nerve broke, and he turned to flee.

Samuel forced him back in at sword-point.

Abel grinned over Samuel's shoulder. "They wait here, and in a hundred other vaults, biding the day, may it be soon, when they are freed to have revenge upon the living, and transform the Earth using God's gift of Eternal Life."

The Groom appeared outside the cell. The Mason rounded on him.

"Lazy, stupid 'prentice, seal this door!"

The Groom beseeched the Mason, "We cannot do this!"

The Mason struck the Groom to the floor. The Groom arose, regarded the pitiless eyes surrounding him, and obeyed. His left hand snaked through the doorway, and secretly showed Cain the Sign of the Pyre.

* * * *

The battle ran hot through all the gates of Alexandra, but Reginild's blood cooled when he found the demolished stairway outside Grissel's enclave. His men-at-arms shielded his contemplations from the archers atop the wall, while his knights held off the lesser monks from their rear.

"We'll ram straight through the masonry," he decided.

Reginild helped to shove the ram against the wall, his back clenching with pain. He locked the wheels and cranked back the springs, each twist an agony.

The lesser monks suddenly abandoned the fight.

Reginild triggered the ram. The log's iron tip shattered the outer stones. Darkness and a hidden portcullis lay within.

Corpses screamed out from the darkness, their flesh mortuary wax. The men-at-arms lowered their shields against the unexpected attack, and the Alexandran archers felled them. While they writhed on the cobblestones, pulling at the arrows in their flesh, the Departed fell upon them, wasted fingers tearing their raiment, and black teeth gnawing their skins.

Reginild stood against the wall, below the archer's aim, and worked his sword arm, severing a Departed head with each blow. Reginild's injured back wanted him to stoop, and his aged muscles trembled.

He denied his infirmities, straightened his back, and cried, "Pyrrhics, to me!"

The knights battled forward, while more Departed emerged from the breached wall.

* * * *

The ice vault seemed lightless at first, but a dim glow penetrated the wall from a candle in the passage. Cain's Departed companions leered in the corner of his eye but turned to shadows when he faced them. He imagined that the corpses moved behind his sight.

Cain forced himself to be calm and considered his predicament. The wall was two feet thick, but the blocks sealing the doorway had just been ice-welded into place, and he might still be able to break out.

Wrenching free his cold-bound feet, he groped toward the wall but touched a dead face. Cain recoiled with an oath. He reached out again, found the doorway, and set his shoulder to the blocks, pushing until his feet skidded on the melting floor. The ice did not yield.

Dread possessed him. He screamed and beat against the blocks. A bone snapped in his left hand. The sudden pain restored Cain to his senses. He crouched on his toes and hugged his knees to his naked chest. Since he could not escape, his only chance was to conserve his body's heat and pray that the Fire-Keeper sent aid.

His shoulders and neck ached with tension. After a time, he knew not how long, he came to himself as if awakening from sleep. Hot water splattered on his feet, and a cloud of invisible warmth rose from the ice. Cain realized that he was pissing. He had been in a daze, and the sudden warmth had roused him.

His shivers became tremors.

His urine roused him a second time.

Cain roused yet again when he toppled. He had forgotten where he was. The memory returned slowly. He no longer shivered. The ice floor did not seem as cold. His extremities ached. Cain resumed his crouch. Rising exhausted him, and he had to put his hands down to prevent another fall.

He had crouched thus forever when he heard Argenta's voice. He raised his head, wincing at the spasm in his neck.

"Where are you?" Cain whispered.

She called again, from the vault's corner, where her arm beckoned through a hole in the floor. Escape had been there all along, and he had never seen it. He crawled across the dungeon, and reached for the opening, but found only shadow and ice. His mind cleared, and he realized that he had dreamed.

He fell onto his back and sank into the cold.

The Departed smiled welcomingly.

* * * *

A sharp noise pierced his frozen mind.

He could not remember his name.

From the corner of his eye, he saw the candle outside the vault, its flame blazing like a tiny sun. A shadow struck again, and a chunk of ice fell into the vault. Light exploded through the gap. He could not close his eyes against it, nor even glance away.

His name rose in his memory, like a thread of smoke from a dead fire. He was Cain.

The Groom chopped the last ice block from the doorway. The Mason peered in over his shoulder and nodded.

"He ain't so mighty now, is he?"

"Don't taunt him," begged the Groom. "Isn't it enough that he's dead?"

"Get him out, the Pyrrhic slut's a-waiting for her lover, and we have to get him thawed in time for their *assignation*."

The Groom hesitated, his expression terrified. The Ice-Mason shoved him into the vault.

"They can't hurt you!"

The Groom kept his eyes on the looming Departed as he tried to lift Cain.

"He's frozen down."

"So, chop him loose."

Cain's did not yet understand what had happened, but a great fear grew in him.

The Groom chopped Cain free and then lifted, but Cain's limbs were rigid. The Groom sprawled under the load. The Mason swore and came to help. They brought Cain out, balanced him across the wheelbarrow, and pushed him up the ice passage.

Cain discovered the name of his fear: Death.

They hauled Cain through the abbey, into a small room, and tilted him onto the stone floor. Cain fell with a wooden thud. The Mason retreated through the door.

The Groom paused, glanced forlornly at Cain, and asked, "Where is she?"

"In the bear pit," said the Mason. "And Abel's promised us good seats!"

The oak door slammed behind them, and the bolts shot home.

Cain's skin itched.

His lids twitched, then blinked. Cain rolled his gritty eyes, scanning the interior of a wake vault. He did not want to believe that he was dead. That very morning, he had found his true love. Argenta must bear his sons, and those sons give him grandsons, who would someday tend his old man's Pyre.

His itching increased.

A knight must face his fears. Cain tried to lift his arm. The limb quivered, then fell back.

The itching burned.

He tried again to lift his arm. The ice broke within him. His arm turned slowly, and he saw the livor mortis on the sag of his elbow.

The burning gnawed at his immortal soul.

Cain fought to keep his mind, but he had never understood, no one alive could understand, what drove the Departed mad. His body had been ruptured throughout by freezing, his skin torn by the Groom's pick, and his thawing flesh taken to rot. His suffering had only begun and would grow forever in an Eternal's tomb.

Agony it was that drove the dead into cannibalistic rage against the living.

Even against Argenta.

The ice broke in his throat, and he screamed.

He crawled across the vault, and clawed at the door, tearing his skin to pulp, and ripping his fingernails off, but those pains were lost amid the greater agony of death. His soul cowered into itself, as a frightened mouse cowers in a hole, letting his basest instincts possess his body. He clambered upright and raged about the vault.

The door slammed open. The animal Cain stifled his screams and crouched against the far wall. Brother Abel and two armed lessers stood in the passage, bearing pitch torches. Samuel stood behind them, wielding his sword.

The torch-flames cut like beacons through Cain's agony. His soul peered out of its cowering place, but the animal that possessed him raged with fear.

Samuel grinned mockery. "God's gift of Eternal Life."

"The Pyrrhics misunderstand the Original Pyre," said Abel. "Which was truly a war, fought with sorcerer's bombs, to the destruction of the world. Eternal Life is God's righteous curse upon the descendants of those who spoilt his works, a curse which the Pyrrhics' rites evade."

Abel and his minions entered the vault, brandishing their torches.

Cain fought his way through the engulfing torment, intent upon the torch. The firelight burned into his dilated eyes, searing through his nerves, and filling him with Pyrrhic fervor. He straightened his back.

Samuel regarded the change in Cain. "Something's wrong."

Abel hesitated, for the corpse met his eyes as if it were still a man. Then, he steeled his courage, gave a challenging cry, and flared his torch into Cain's face. Cain seized the torch's shaft and threw himself against Abel. Abel's cry became a startled scream, his skull bounced off the stone wall, and he toppled. Blood squirted from Abel's ear.

Cain turned, with the torch in his hand.

"One side!" Samuel cried at the lessers and moved to behead Cain.

The lessers, as unaccustomed to obeying knights as to fighting sentient Departed, stepped on Samuel's toes, lunging with their torches. The knight cursed.

Cain struck the flames aside with his free hand and clubbed the first lesser with his torch, singeing the man's top spike and knocking him senseless. Cain stooped and stole the lesser's sword. The second monk fled.

Samuel regained his composure and charged. Cain turned to meet him. Samuel's blade cut flat, aimed to sever Cain's neck. Cain raised his sword, parried, and found that the Departed lacked a living man's strength. He turned Samuel's blow but nearly lost his sword. Samuel moved as quickly as lightning, reversing his aim toward the undefended side of Cain's neck.

Cain threw his torch at Samuel's face, then thrust his sword with both hands. Samuel instinctively ducked the flames, and his sword faltered, only slashing Cain's shoulder. Cain put his dead weight behind his attack, transfixing Samuel's breadbasket.

Samuel backpedaled, tugging the hilt from Cain's dead grasp, and fell screaming, wrestling with the jutting pommel. Blood sprayed from his mouth. His eyes rolled.

Cain bent, took ahold of the sword, and placed a foot against Samuel's chest. The Eternal knight winced. With three vicious jerks, Cain dragged the weapon free, while Samuel's dead face contorted in agony.

A hand fell upon Cain's shoulder. He whirled and faced Brother Abel. The Departed monk, wobbly from brain trauma, beat ineffectually at him. Cain backhanded his sword against Abel's already fractured skull. Abel clutched his head, cried out in agony, and collapsed.

Cain dragged Abel's wriggling body into the vault, then returned to the passage for Samuel, who had risen to his fours. Cain knocked Samuel down again, dragged him into the vault with Abel, then barred the door.

Cain followed the passage to the arena.

The bleachers overflowed with gaily-dressed Noblemen and Noble-women, who chattered at each other in a festival spirit. He saw the misera-ble-faced Groom, seated next to the jolly Ice Mason at the pit's rim, near to where Lord Grissel's shadowy form sat enthroned in its icy balcony. They all went silent when the armed corpse entered.

Argenta lay nude, bound atop a wooden altar at the pit's center. She screamed, and writhed against her bonds, weeping blood under the bristly ropes.

Reassured by her fear, the Nobles murmured with anticipation.

Cain went to his lady. She pressed her eyes shut. He lifted his sword, and cut her free. Argenta's eyes flew wide; he looked into them, his still heart breaking with love.

New tears sprang from her. "Oh, Cain!"

The crowd went into an uproar.

Cain met the Groom's eyes and beckoned. The Groom, as startled as the Nobles, leapt from his seat, and vaulted to the pit's floor, but stopped at a wary distance.

"Sir Cain?"

Cain gestured at Argenta. He forced air down his throat to speak. *"Save her."* His larynx buzzed painfully.

The Groom scuttled near, his visage awe-struck, took her arm and hur-ried her out through the pit's gate.

Cain turned toward the bleachers, and raised his sword, voicing a war-cry which felt to rip his throat asunder.

"Crusade!"

The Nobles panicked, surging up from their benches, and fighting each other towards the exit. The Ice Mason attempted to force an especially large man from his path, but the Noble turned on him and pitched him into the pit. The Mason landed with a pained grunt, scrambling to his feet to face Cain.

"Back from me, cadaver!"

Cain poised to strike.

The Mason squealed and cowered. Cain chopped into the back of his neck, then used his fallen body as a step to climb into Lord Grissel's bal-cony.

There, he learned the truth.

A corpse, bearing a decade of rot, sat on the icy throne, the royal circlet upon its mangy scalp. The creature regarded Cain with tattered eye-holes.

It spoke to him: *"Are we alike? My physicians cannot explain me; Abel says that I am blessed, born immune to that which men call* pain *and* pleasure. *The time is now to declare the Crusade of the Dead."*

The creature's hand moved, shifting toward a velvet rope.

"I will release my Eternal army to devour those who test my defenses and then to carry God's Holy Will across the world. Be my general, Sir Cain, and lead the Departed to Eternal victory!"

Grissel's hand crept like a vine.

Cain struck. The Lord's neck parted with a dry snap, and his skull split upon the floor. Dust puffed out through the fissures. Grissel's finger brushed against the rope and halted.

Cain stood as inert as Grissel, his sword hung in follow-through. His thoughts seemed like a muddied stream. The agony of death waxed, driving his soul back toward hiding. If he remained still, he would lose his mind again, perhaps forever, if no good knight found him, and brought him to a pyre.

Cain needed a pyre.

This was his life's final intent, and he clung to it against the rising tide of pain. He must keep his mind until he returned to his embassy. With his sword in his death-grip, Cain teetered to the balcony's rear, walking like a man on stilts. He bumped Grissel as he passed, knocking the corpse a-clatter. Through a curtain and down a passage, he came to the uproarious Grand Hall. Nobles and monks scattered before him, but Cain gave them no heed. The Eternals could do naught to him.

Then, there came a thing which could.

Abel's mastiff charged out of the shimmery candlelight, its hackles raised into spikes, its lips peeled back, and foam spurting between its teeth. The Eternals fled from its path, but the dog ignored them, its scarlet-gleaming eyes fixed on Cain.

His dead muscles betrayed him, contracting late and loose. His sword failed to meet the dog's attacking leap. Cain turned aside to protect his throat, and the dog clamped its teeth into his shoulder, crushing, tearing, and shooting lightning through his nerves. He toppled. The mastiff yanked, towing him across the ice floor.

Cain dragged his sword forward, intending to pierce the dog's chest, but the blade, too long, only slapped against the mastiff's ribs. Cain probed down its flank, and the point lodged into the crease of the dog's pelvis. He thrust; the tough beast growled. Cain thrust harder, and the sword's point touched bone. The dog yelped, and let him go, but did not retreat.

Cain turned to face the circling dog, his sword dangling and unsteady. The mastiff feinted and charged anew. Cain lifted his sword to meet it, knowing that he was late, but the dog fell late, as well. It's injured leg buckled, making its leap low, and it impaled itself on Cain's sword.

He retrieved his weapon, drawing a whimper from the dying animal; blood poured from the open wound. The mastiff shuddered, then lay in the endless stillness of brute death.

Cain turned away. The Hall had emptied during the fight. His footsteps slapped the ice and echoed from the frozen walls. He felt wearier than he ever had in life, but the corpse-pain drove him on. He left the abbey, and walked across the courtyard to the surrounding wall. The stairs were fallen, but the wall beyond the old portcullis had smashed; an engine ram lay overturned in the rubble.

Cain pressed against the bars, peering out to where knights of Oswaygo and Antario labored, grappling and hewing loose Departed, and feeding the remains to a great pyre, while physicians worked to heal injured men-at-arms. Sir Reginild, bandage-bound, stood with his Groom, and Lady Argenta, who wore a horse blanket.

Cain experienced an agony greater than the pain of death, for there was a life no longer his.

He located the portcullis' winch, raised the gate, and shambled forth. Reginild strode to meet him, sword in hand, expression vexed. Cain dropped his sword and raised his right hand in the sign of peace. Reginild halted with mouth agape.

"Sir Cain?"

Cain drew in air. His lungs ruptured. He delivered his last speech. *"Grissel...is...dead."* Then, he raised his left hand the Sign of the Pyre.

Grievous tears fell from Reginild's eyes. He raised his sword in salute. "You are a true Knight, Sir Cain, and I am but a knave!"

Reginild led him to the pyre. He climbed in among the burning logs and sizzling Departed. For a moment, the flames seared him, but then his skin blackened, and all sensation vanished. He met Argenta's gaze from within the pyre and smiled. A moment later, the flames blinded him.

Sight returned but an instant afterward. Cain stepped unharmed from the pyre, and met a vast throng: men, women, and children, all were strangers, but they smiled in welcome.

Argenta's father, alive and grinning, emerged from the crowd. "My son, come and meet the Fire-Keeper!"

* * * *

This is my father's tale, as Argenta, my mother told it to me.

✗

The Migration of Memories
Charles Wilkinson

'Though dead, your husband is digitally active. That cannot be doubted.'

The man entrenched in the leather chair opposite Zania Flink peered at her over his oak desk. He wore a tie and a three-piece pin-striped suit, items of clothing she had previously come across only in custom dramas and the module in 21 st Century Cultural Studies she'd taken as an undergraduate. His office on the top story of a half-timbered building was imbued with the scent of ink bottles, box files, damp document wallets and yellowing paper.

'I'm glad you didn't say *alive*. After all, I have probate,' said Zania.

Harris Wryght pressed his hands together and held them to the point of his chin, before drawing the palms wide apart—as if to release a trapped butterfly. Nearby was a street of Victorian houses restored to its late nine-teenth and early twentieth-century state. Most of the owners were men with a predilection for vintage clothing: tweed jackets, blazers, brogues and even plus-fours. The women were said to favor Laura Ashley replicas. Was this where Harris lived?

'You were quite correct to say several more of his accounts have been reopened. And he's still trading. He bought some shares in a pharmaceuti-cal company only this morning.'

'Is that legal? His estate has been wound up.'

'True. But there's evidence to show that prior to his death your hus-band bought several complex insurance policies; these appear to have giv-en him the capacity…er…how shall put? *To take a few post-mortem fiscal initiatives.*'

When she had risen early to catch the train into the center city, the sky had been dawn-burnished to a matchless blue. Now it was filled with air buses, delivery drones and the spaghetti contrails of a new day's flight paths. On the other side of the courtyard, a tiny pilotless pink helicopter hovered above the medieval hall and its lantern roof and sundial. Sunlight glinted on the gnomon.

'A few?' she said, turning back towards him sharply.

'Well, it's hard to be sure exactly how many. The partner who was dealing with your late husband's affairs is not in his office at present.'

'Now that I certainly wouldn't disagree with. I've made repeated attempts to contact Mr. Tredicott. With no results. He disappeared shortly after my husband's death.'

Harris Wryght's skin was pink and unlined; his silver hair worn longer than was currently fashionable. Zania wondered if its healthy sheen was natural or manufactured at one of the many salons she had passed on the main road nearby. No computer was visible in the room. Perhaps it was hidden in the Jacobean cabinet. She'd no objection to antiquarianism as long as it was not allied to incompetence.

'We are investigating, I assure you. Since he was a member of the Ancient Guild of Actuaries, you may be certain that in the event of any impropriety you would receive compensation. As insurers,' he said with a faint, donnish smile, 'you may take it we are very well insured.' He put both hands on the armrests of his chair and, with a grimace, levered himself upright.

Once outside in the courtyard, as she was congratulating herself on having coped well with Harris Wryght and the aggressive retro-elegance of his suit, she remembered the questions she'd failed to ask. Since Leopold's death, she'd become more forgetful. Subconsciously did she believe this was a widow's prerogative? Forty-three was far too soon to let herself slide; especially now she was alone in the world.

The ground traffic was sluggish: a few brightly colored trams, a mini-train on an outside track transporting children to school and some permissible private cars and observation vehicles in the middle lane. Above her, delivery drones hummed in the lower lanes below the aerial taxis and remotely controlled security 'copters. The cafés and patisseries were empty. It was a bright day but no one was sitting outside, even though the parasols on the pavements had been unfurled by proprietors anxious to announce the advent of spring.

She had almost reached the entrance to the underground when she saw her husband for the fourth time since his death. Although he was in the guise of a ten-year-old, she recognized him without difficulty. Sitting on a high stool in the window seat of an ice cream parlor with an ornate black and gold façade, he wore a striped jersey and long shorts of a type once fashionable in France. His hair, which had darkened as he grew older, was now back to its best boyish coppery blond; it curled over his ears and collar. In front of him was a tall glass filled with vanilla ice cream and chocolate sauce, which was clearly for show as he was making no attempt to eat, even though he had a spoon. In his present afterlife, he was finding it hard to muster much in the way of an appetite. She had loved him unreservedly ever since she was five.

* * * *

When Zania reached the outer suburb where she lived, the street lights were on even though it was still light; their orange glow, just before dusk, was strange and mysterious, a portent of the mingling of separate hours. Leopold had insisted they move out to the edge of the city. He found a spacious apartment in a block designed by a famous architect. There was green space between the buildings, as well as trees and shrubs and a stream: everything carefully landscaped to give the impression they were in a park. In the summer, Zania sometimes expected to see exotic birds perched in the branches or find a menagerie tucked away behind a hedge. Leopold and she, the youngest residents in the block, had not socialized with their elderly neighbors. Their own company was sufficiently absorbing, as it had been since their first meeting when she was five and Leopold seven. To distract themselves with friends and children was out of the question. Now she was prematurely by herself.

There was nobody and nothing in the lobby, apart from a profusion of anonymous plants with green broad waxy leaves in terracotta pots. One was the size of a small tree and had poisonous looking berries. As she entered the lift, she sensed but did not see Leopold step in after her. The doors closed. She would not have been surprised to glimpse his face in the mirror opposite. Once out on the corridor, she could not recall pushing the button for her floor. It was something he did if they were together.

As she opened the door of the flat, she felt a sharp shock: she'd moved the furniture around after his death; so for an instant, there was the sensation of entering someone else's property—the jolt of finding herself a trespasser on what should have been safe territory. Then familiar armchairs and tables reasserted themselves as indelibly part of her past. The changes were a way of making a new start, but if she didn't get used to them soon she'd put everything back.

A ringing tone. The screen of her monitor lit up and a message appeared: a reminder that her distance therapy was due. After a couple of clicks, Dr. Ventrick appeared on the screen. Since Zania's case had been upgraded, her medical advisers no longer had the barely detectable robotic rigidity that indicated her problems were not sufficiently idiosyncratic to warrant one hundred per cent human intervention.

'Any improvement?' asked Dr. Ventrick.

'I saw him again. This time he was about ten years old.'

'And how was he dressed?'

'He was pretending to be a French boy.'

'And so you didn't recognize anything he was wearing?'

'No.'

'Then don't you think it possible he was a French boy who resembled your husband?'

Dr. Ventrick's theory of the month was that Zania could not accept Leopold was comprehensively dead because she had not been allowed to visit the body after the accident. Since he was barely recognizable as having been human, there was no point in her identifying him; that was what she had been told. But not seeing him allowed her to retain a subconscious belief he was still alive. She was superimposing her husband's features on anyone who looked like him.

'I'm afraid matters have progressed since I last spoke to you,' said Zania.

'Oh, in what way?'

'He's reopened several of his accounts. In the time it's taken me to come back from the city, he's turned a profit on equity he bought this morning.'

'This sounds more like identity theft than proof that he's electronically sentient. Have you contacted the police?'

'He took out a number of policies. They said he bought financial products that remain viable whatever his condition is 'corporeally speaking'.'

'Zania, I'm sorry, but I'm trained as a therapist and grief counselor.'

Later that night, Zania admitted there had been a change in the quality of her sorrows. Professional help had proved ineffective, but now she had a fresh preoccupation: her husband had transmuted his physical absence into an on-line presence capable of moving beyond the confines of cyberspace to take decisions and plant images of himself in the world. Before going to bed, she went into the office. The computer they once shared was on. Five searches had been made while she was away.

* * * *

Aided by a silver-topped cane engraved with his great-grandfather's initials, Harris Wryght inched his way across the Tennis Club terrace. The only concession he'd made to late afternoon informality was the removal of his pinstriped waistcoat. Members carrying rackets and tennis balls were coming out of the Clubhouse, a riot of faïence, a neo-Gothic fantasy of the late nineteenth century, its façade embellished by oriel windows and topped with assorted turrets and towers. Some of the men wore cricket whites and luxuriant mustaches.

Wryght was pleased that Stockdale Magnus, a spritely octogenarian stockbroker, with a shock of black and white hair as coarse as a badger's, was already seated at a table just inside the bar. The older members were reading newspapers or political journals: at the end of days spent staring at computer screens, print came as a relief to the elderly eye. As soon as he saw his great uncle lumbering in through the French windows, Stockdale rose solicitously, but the old man signaled to him to sit down.

'Not much steam left nowadays,' said Wryght, settling his bulk deep into an armchair.

'It's good of you to come, Uncle.'

'Not at all. An excellent choice for a late spring evening. I'd forgotten you were a member. I haven't been here since my hundred and fifth.'

Stockdale Magnus closed the magazine he'd been reading—*Vintage and Veteran Computer Equipment;* he had a fine collection of early mouses and modems, as well as a twentieth century PC in perfect working order.

'I hope little Tredicott's vanishing trick hasn't caused too much of stir.'

'Well, I have to admit she noticed.'

'I'm afraid there was no option. We simply couldn't risk losing Leopold. He was the most successful trader we've ever had at Magnus Stack Magnus. There was never the slightest chance of the firm letting go of a man with such flair.'

'But was it really necessary…'

'Absolutely! Tredicott was a man whose indiscretion you could depend upon. If we'd waited another forty-eight hours the entire world would have known what happened to Leopold.'

'And how is Leopold now?'

'Very small.'

'No, I meant in himself.'

'He's…adjusted,' said Stockdale. For a second, it was as if he had emerged from a sett and was sniffing the air cautiously. 'Of course, when he realized what had happened he was very upset. Understandably. Refused to trade at all. But now he's started to dip a toe in the market. The results have been encouraging, although we won't trust him with any big accounts until we're sure he's back to his best. And Zania?'

The puck-pock polyphony of racket on ball drifted in from the courts; the rallies were interspersed with the rattle of shots on the wire netting, the dull *thunk* of drives into the net, the sporadic cries of 'out' and 'let.' Waiters bearing wine in ice-buckets went out through the French windows. On the lawn, older men in striped blazers watched the tennis from wooden benches. A low-flying delivery drone circled above them before landing outside the club secretary's office.

Harris Wryght closed his eyes. His hands were folded over the brow of his mountainous stomach. The little-inverted hillocks of flesh hanging from his jaw trembled in time to his slow but regular breathing.

'Zania, Uncle Harris?'

Wryght opened one eye and then sighed. 'A little too comfortable, these armchairs.' Then he unlocked his hands and raised himself up so that his head was upright. 'Ah yes, the wife. Not quite as resigned to being a widow as one would have wished. I did tell you we managed to install one of our people as her therapist.'

'Ventrick?'

'That's the one. Well, apparently Zania's...having visions of Leopold. Imagines that she is seeing him at different stages of their life together.'

'Well, they were, by all accounts, unusually close: a childhood romance; married young; spent practically their whole lives together. You don't think that, at some level, she senses...what was done to her husband?'

'I don't see how she could. By the way, where is Leopold?'

'Oh, don't worry. I've got him. He's one person I definitely wouldn't leave lying around.'

* * * *

The air taxi flew over the river's glittering arm. As it hadn't rained for a week, the flood barriers were raised. Miniscule trams crossed the bridge to the financial quarter. From his seat next to the pilot, Stockdale caught a glimpse of a postage stamp quadrangle, the tiny green square where Great Uncle Harris had an office. Warplanes patrolled the zone above the air taxi lane.

There was no point in trying to persuade Zania that Leopold was electronically inert or even the victim of posthumous identify theft. She knew him too well not to recognize his fingerprint on the web, the arcs, loops and whorls of his posts on forums and threads; the pattern of his trades. What he must do was convince her she had found no more than the numerical after-echo of his life in finance. He survived only as data, whose values were designed to repeat after death. After the accident, Leopold's identity as anything more than mathematical had perished. The recent spree on the stock exchange was triggered by 'buy signals' put into the system before his death.

In five minutes, they left the city behind and were flying above a county that had, for security reasons, long been cleared of those below executive standard. Apart from a few agricultural maintenance operatives, who were bussed out from the suburbs on weekdays, there was scant chance of being introduced to anyone who hadn't reached a high level in business or one of the top professions. Leopold had been doing sufficiently well to apply for a residency permit, but he had chosen not to. Why was what? More than any trader Stockdale had ever met, Leopold was uninterested in what wealth could bring. He turned down Wryght's offer to put him up for membership of the Tennis Club, sold the flat in the Victorian quarter he'd inherited from his father and traveled by public transport, even disdaining the services of privately owned air taxis. He chose to live in what was, by all accounts, a perfectly pleasant but unremarkable outer suburb; he traveled into the City alongside the horde of commuters, not one of whom earned a tenth of the salary he commanded. His passion for trading appeared to be powered by purely theoretical concerns. A man enchanted by algorithms, complex financial models, and charts, he was indifferent to his rising personal wealth. He ignored lobbying, tip sheets, the fashions and fluctuation of markets, and bought and sold with disinterested expertise.

The air taxi hovered above Stockdale's estate, a place Leopold visited only once, although he was invited on many occasions. The master of the emollient excuse, he had finally agreed to accept, possibly in order to defer future invitations. Stockdale arranged both a driver and a one-day residential permit. Just after lunch, he found himself alone in the living-room with Leopold. His guest's unlined face and dark gold hair curling over his collar gave him a youthful appearance and an air of serenity rare amongst those who traded on the financial markets. Seated sumptuously in armchairs either side of the log fire, they held cut-glass tumblers of post-prandial malt. Stockdale had noticed Leopold rarely drank, even when offered vintage champagne or the curiosity of a glass of Chateau Petrus, a vineyard long since vanished. Perhaps an unaccustomed indulgence would make him more forthcoming.

'I'm sorry your wife couldn't make it,' said Stockdale.

'To be honest, she doesn't go out much. She has a busy job that brings her into contact with a great many people. In her own time, she prefers the pleasures of home. We both do.'

'She's an administrator?'

'That's right…at a university.'

The view through the window was of undulating green fields, small perfectly composed copses, a wedge of mature woodland and a lake. Apart from two temples, follies built in the classical style of the eighteenth century, there were no buildings in sight, not even a barn. In a paddock, two chestnut horses, whose coats almost matched the colors of late autumn leaves, stood quietly, browsing the long grass between the apple trees. It was hard to understand why Leopold wouldn't want to be somewhere near here, residing in the immemorial manner of the English gentleman.

'And how's Outer Estate 97? I can't say I've been there.'

'It suits us. Only elderly people in our block. There's no obligation to socialize.'

'But wouldn't you prefer to be out here? Living…with a little more… finesse.'

Leopold smiled, quite guilelessly, as if at that moment he was happy only for himself and her. 'Not really, he said. 'You see no one bothers us— and we have ourselves.'

Stockdale paid the air taxi and watched it ascend into a seamless blue sky, not unlike the one on the day of Leopold's visit, the sun shining on the afternoon of his death. Unlike so much that happened in the over-regulated world, it had been an accident: a tight bend and an unfortunately placed tree, only a mile or so down the road from Stockdale's estate; the passenger mortally injured but a driver with sufficient wits left to phone Stockdale. Then one of the insurance plans the firm had taken out for Leopold came into effect: a private clinic, the inescapable death of the body mitigated by cognitive survival—but clothed in a new form.

Stockdale took Leopold out of his pocket and plugged him in.

* * * *

Zania knew drinking a glass of wine alone would make her feel worse, but couldn't bring herself to put the bottle back in the fridge. Evening was the worst time: coming home after work to find the flat silent and with only the memory of his company as a consolation; cooking for one; solitary sleepless nights.

Going back to her job after the month's obligatory compassionate leave had been wise, yet there were too many hours to fill, and no friends to confide in. She started spending long hours in the cinema before taking a late train back to Outer Estate 97.

In the last month, she had seen him three times before spotting him in the ice-cream parlor. Once, coming out of an opera, she'd recognized the back of his head bobbing in a crowd at the bottom of the marble staircase. It had been impossible to push past the throng of elderly couples descending slowly with their arms linked. The second time he'd been on a train that was opposite hers outside a junction. He looked as if he were in his late thirties, years younger than at the time of his death. A week ago, he was a teenage boy roller-skating past her, his long hair lion-flamed in the wind, just as she came down the steps of an art gallery. But not once had she seen him at the flat. Perhaps their happiness had soaked into the walls; made the space unavailable for haunting.

Attempts to track down Tredicott were fruitless, which was unfortunate as there was much to discuss. All of Leopold's bank accounts had been reopened and once a month money was transferred into the one they had shared. Her husband could hardly be making her an allowance from beyond the grave, yet she felt certain it was nothing to do with the untraceable Tredicott. Was it a widow's pension paid by Magnus Stack Magnus? Certainly, its regularity hint ed at such an arrangement. It was strange no one had mentioned it. Only later did she conclude the funds must be connected with the insurance policies taken out by Leopold.

Zania was holding her third glass of wine when Dr. Ventrick appeared on the screen.

'That's not precisely what was prescribed.'

'No, but nothing else is working,' said Zania.

'Did you drink much when Leopold was with you?'

'Hardly ever. That's what makes it effective for an hour or two now. I'm still seeing him,' she added, sliding the wine glass round to the far side of the monitor.

'As an adult?'

'It varies. Sometimes I think he's reprising every stage of our lives together.'

'It's you that's doing that, Zania; he's not there. Remember?'

Dr. Ventrick had moved forward so that her face filled the whole screen. Her eyes appeared much larger than was usual for an adult. They were pale blue-grey mist. Nothing else about her was important. Not even her lips moving, controlling a now soft voice that sounded as if she were in the flat and felt like the audible equivalent of an arm round the shoulder.

'I've been thinking very carefully about you, Zania. And I know what will help.'

'Oh?'

'It's a very gentle procedure. Almost completely without pain.'

'What is it? Will I have to take more pills?'

'It's been thoroughly tested. There are no side effects. Only benefits. And apart from the anesthetic, no medication is needed.'

'So it's an operation.'

'An intervention. You wouldn't have to go into hospital. There's a very comfortable clinic; it's more like a hotel. You needn't stay overnight. Just come in first thing in the morning and the driver who fetched you will take you back to your own home by nightfall. It will cost you nothing.'

'I can pay.'

'But you won't have to. Do you remember the policies you mentioned that Leopold took out? Well, I've checked. You're covered.'

Zania rescued the wine glass from behind the monitor and took a sip. 'And what does it involve, this intervention.'

'It will be as non-invasive as such a procedure can possibly be. A very simple sub-cranial attachment. A tiny chip. You'll be left with a small scar that will heal very quickly. And afterward, you'll feel a great deal better. I promise you. Now how does that sound?'

* * * *

As he subsided onto the wooden chair and a cushion the width of the woolsack, Harris Wryght breathed heavily. Why had he bothered to come into chambers? He was finding the steep stairs difficult, but it was too much trouble to ask if he could move to a set downstairs. Besides he loved his view of the Hall with its lantern, sundial and weather vane. If he shuffled over to the window, he could look down on the court and the fountain, a neatly mown lawn and well kept graveled paths. But on his next birthday, he would be a hundred and ten, an age when men fitter than he considered retirement. But first, there was the problem of what do with Leopold Flink. Wryght's own portfolio had always been with Morgan Stack Morgan.

His desk was clear but for a square of blotting paper and three gold pens in a tray next to an antique inkstand. The sound of footsteps on the staircase reminded him why he was in his office: Stockdale, of course. A very capable man and they were related in some way. He could never remember how closely.

'Ah, good of you to drop in,' said Wryght.

'Not at all.'

'The Flink woman? Not proving too recalcitrant, I hope.'

'It's convenient she thinks it was her husband who took out the insurance policies. Ventrick has been a great help. Worth every penny.'

'And Leopold?'

'He's asking for a body.'

Harris Wryght leaned back, knitted his hands together and stared out of the window. He could hear the sparrows squabbling in the fountain, as they had done in the time of the lawyers, centuries ago. 'Well, I suppose that's reasonable.'

'Of course, some of the board would rather he confined himself to financial matters.

'But they forget the market does have a human dimension. We wouldn't want Leopold to become too...rarefied.'

'Quite. And is there anything I can do.'

'Zania is still trying to find Tredicott. If you could...'

'I'm afraid there's no way of bringing him back. Not even in virtual form.'

'Of course, but find a way of stalling her. In a week or so she won't care about Tredicott. She'll have other things to think about.' Stockdale Magnus put his hand into his pocket and smiled.

Everything degrades in time, thought Harris Wryght. The disputations of the barristers who had walked in the courtyard were forgotten, less permanent than the sparrows' songs. And where was the wool that had been weighed in the courtyard in the days of the staple, before cases were considered and moots heard in the hall? At least Leopold had been given an afterlife, his digital existence more certain than the paradise prayed for in the lawyers' chapel all those years before.

* * * *

'You'll need it for a little longer.'

'What?'

'Your body.'

'How could it have happened? I never consented to this.'

'You may be entitled to some compensation. But for now we must deal with the outcome, not with its possible origins.'

A week after the procedure, Zania saw the black dots for the first time. They were not always present and didn't float across her visual field like liver spots. Although there were moments she wasn't aware of them, she was viewing the world differently: the black dots were embedded in the very act of perception. A visit to an oculist had resulted in her returning to the clinic, where she was now seated in a white room with four consultants and Dr. Ventrick. They were speaking almost at once:

'Your memories must be given time to migrate.'

'Until they've all been replicated electronically, it's vital that full physical support is maintained.'

'In a sense, your memory is your identity.'

'It's bound to feel strange at first. Your experience of time is no longer dictated by the hands of a clock.'

'I know it's difficult to envisage. But try to understand yourself as perceiving the world digitally rather than analogically.'

'In the end, you won't need a body in the customary sense, yet there are ways of clothing the digital self.'

'It's expensive but the policies your husband took out...'

'You may find that some memories are enhanced.'

Afterward, Dr. Ventrick drove her back to Outer Estate 97. Everything appeared almost the same: the green spaces, the white cube of her apartment block, the trees, shrubs and the artificial lake. But something about the way the lawn sloped was different, if only by an inch; and as she glanced at her watch, the red seconds ticking, she knew the time between the numbers was missing.

'You're happier,' said Dr. Ventrick, unlocking the car door to let her out. 'And drinking less.'

Zania nodded and watched Dr. Ventrick drive away. On the main road, the orange street lamps were on even though it was still light, their equable glow endorsing a different space. She turned and ran up the steps and into the building. As usual, there was nobody in the lobby and she had the lift to herself. In the silence of the early evening apartments, the elderly moved towards the kind of death she would not share. She unlocked the door to her flat and then took a step back: the furniture in her flat had moved back to where it was before Leopold's death. There was a very faint noise coming from the office; the shuffling of fingers over the keyboard. She pushed the door wider. He was seated at the desk. As she came in, he turned around to greet her, smiling exactly as he had done the day before the accident. Now she knew she would no long see him as a series of apparitions of his vanished flesh, but like this, and they would remain digitally together until the degradation of the files when the wingtip of the last bird of memory faded into the unknowable sky.

✗

When Wolfsbane Blooms
K.A. Opperman

When wolfsbane blooms,
And coldly looms
The death-white winter moon,
The purest man
Carpathian
Dark spells will peril soon.

Who nears the wort
That leaves amort
The wolves that eat its leaves,
On certain nights
Will meet the wights
Of wolves the forest grieves.

They prowl around
The flower crowned
With baleful bluish hoods,
The wraiths of wolves,
Where mist convolves
With devil-haunted woods.

They will possess,
At one caress
Of wolfsbane's fatal flower,
Those foolish men
Who cannot ken
Carpathia's dark power.

And thus is born,
Ere come of morn,
The Werewolf—feared of all
Who dwell beneath
The savage teeth
Of eastern mountains tall.

When wolfsbane blooms,
And coldly looms
The death-white winter moon,
The wolf in man
Carpathian
Dark spells will waken soon.

Maquettes
Paul St John Mackintosh

A passerby in Stockholm's old town, the Gamla Stan, just after the middle of the 20th century, might have been surprised to see a tall, nautical-looking man, somehow unlike the Nordic locals despite his high square forehead and thick fair hair, stop before a low shop window displaying ship models as though transfixed in shock, and then lurch forward and bang both his fists violently against the panes. It being Sunday, the shop was closed and empty, and the heavy aged glass resisted his onslaught until the Stockholm police appeared and politely asked him to stop. The British sailor, as he proved to be, cooperated quite reasonably, but the patrolmen could see nothing in the display of brasswork, binnacles, riding lights and sextants to account for his reaction, unless it was a diorama of a fast motor launch with a large RAF roundel on the bow, apparently capturing another similar vessel flying the Nazi German naval flag, entitled (in Swedish) "Encounter at Sea." The shop had stood there for decades, and its owner was well known and eminently respectable.

At the police station house, the British sailor volunteered a statement that led the patrolmen to release him with a mild caution. He gave his name as Graham Crozier, second mate on the Lyle Shipping Company freighter Cape Pembroke, on shore leave at the Katarina Seamen's Club after the latest scrap metal run between Stockholm and the Clyde. A Scottish seaman of some education, he explained that a decade ago he had served in the Royal Air Force Marine Craft Section as second-class cox aboard an Air Sea Rescue launch. The little tableau in the window of the shop had recalled all too accurately an incident he had been involved in during the War, which had left his crewmates dead and himself the master of a derelict adrift for days in the cold waters of the North Sea until found by a Swedish Navy patrol.

During the War, he had been one of the nine-man crew aboard a 67-ft British Power Boat Type 2 High-Speed Launch, alongside the skipper, Flying Officer Lambert, the cox, the other second class cox, the wireless operator, the three deckhands, the two NCO fitters, and Collier the medical orderly. Their boat, number 2505 out of RAF Castletown, had been ordered to sea to search for a Motor Gun Boat, HMS Gay Viking, reported missing while running guns and munitions into occupied Denmark as part of Operation Moonshine, the campaign to resupply the Danish Resistance. They crossed the North Sea in fair but cold weather with fuel and rations for six days at sea. Enemy activity in the Skagerrak this late in the war was minimal, with fuel short and frequent Liberator patrols, but the skipper was taking no chances, and conducted the pattern of square searches under strict low light discipline, with both ball turrets and the aft Oerlikon manned, and the crew nervously scanning the horizon for German sea or air traffic, swaddled in their duffels and fortified by self-heating soup from the launch's spacious galley.

So it was that near dawn after their second night on station and close to their endurance limit, they spotted the E-boat emerging from an early fog bank, running slow and heavy in the water, its lean sharklike lines obscured by dark bulks under tarpaulins the length of its after deck. Usually, the bigger German craft could have outrun and outgunned them, but its massive deck cargo had clearly fouled its aft guns, and the skipper ordered the cox to put them alongside. Already less maneuverable than the lighter launch, the E-boat managed only the most basic evasive measures, and they soon overhauled it, the deck crew with Sten guns and Webley pistols at the ready, determined more than nervous. With news of Allied advances and Axis defeats multiplying daily, no one expected the Germans to put up more than token resistance. "They'll be happy enough to sit out the last rest of the war in a nice safe prison camp," Lambert predicted confidently.

Only when they drew alongside the floundering craft did Lambert observe through his night glasses that the German crew, instead of the gray sea dress and life vests of the Kriegsmarine, wore black uniforms and caps resembling SS issue. Lambert's first challenge over the loud hailer was answered before it ended by accurate bursts of small arms fire that swept Fitter Oakeshott and Second Cox Cummings off the forepeak and into the sea. Fortunately, the armored turrets and the sandbagged wheelhouse withstood the first fusillades, and the launch was still far enough astern of the E-boat to be out of the firing arc of its foredeck gun. The starboard turret opened up on the German with its twin .303 Brownings, joined by the aft Oerlikon and the Stens of the remaining deck crew, now crouching or prone along the gunwales, toppling many of the dark figures visible on her deck, and 20 mm cannon shells from the Oerlikon triggered bright fires between the humped mounds of her cargo. The E-boat's hull armor only increased the carnage, as Sten and .303 rounds ricocheted across her deck, catching more of the dark figures. By the time the launch hove alongside her, she had lost steering way, with fires building aft and nothing moving on her decks.

Lambert, his face drawn and lips white after the unexpected night action, ordered Crozier to stay by the wheel while he boarded the stricken E-boat with a prize crew to secure any valuable intelligence and look for survivors. No one was in any mood to take chances now, and the four crew in Lambert's boarding party were armored in life vests and flak helmets, slung about with grenades, boat hooks, and pistols, and cradling Stens and a Lewis gun. As they went across on the rescue steps, Crozier noticed by the light of the flickering fires that the deck cargo crates bore an unfamiliar insignia, a sword with bands around it within an inscribed oval. Lambert and his party moved forward warily along the deck, towards the E-boat's low armored bridge, out of sight of the launch wheelhouse. Then there were sudden flashes and explosions, more bursts of gunfire, shouts, and screams, and a sickening lurch as the E-boat's diesels managed one last spasmodic surge that drove her forward and against the launch's bows, almost breaking the mooring lines.

Acting without thought, Crozier gunned the throttles and brought them back alongside, yelling to Gaffney at the Oerlikon to stay alert. Lambert appeared at the E-boat's rail, face lurid in the firelight, dark blood glistening on his life vest. "Savages," he shouted to Crozier. "We had to kill them all. Gordon and Osgood are dead, Tanner needs medical attention. Send Collier across."

Collier stepped gingerly between the two vessels, his field kit in hand, and disappeared behind the deck cargo, while Crozier watched the low orange fires nervously. Then, before his eyes, one of those orange fires blossomed in a brighter flare, to the accompaniment of more screams. Further secondary explosions, perhaps from a flare locker or magazine, were erupting behind the stacked crates, themselves now burning steadily. Two figures came staggering to the rail, both on fire, beating at blue tongues of flame that seemed to crawl along and lick at their bodies.

"Cast off, get away," yelled Lambert, the skin of his face already sloughing off in strips. Then another stronger explosion blew him into burning pieces and drove the two boats apart. Crozier threw the engines into full astern, and the Triple Napier Sea Lions snapped the hawsers joining the two vessels. Before his eyes, the burning E-boat broke in two as a more powerful explosion snapped its 114-foot hull like a twig, and sank beneath the waves, illuminating them from below for a few last moments with lurid corpse-fires.

Once he had recovered himself, Crozier inspected the rest of the launch, to find Gaffney slumped over the Oerlikon, transfixed by a length of the E-boat's railings that had driven through his chest. Also, the last collision with the E-boat had knocked a hole in the launch's bow, putting it at risk of foundering in anything but the lightest swell. Now the sole survivor of both ships, he nursed the launch into Swedish waters by dead reckoning, to be picked up a couple of days later by a Royal Swedish Navy destroyer. He was the one who spent the last few months of the war a prisoner, in the relative comfort of Swedish interment, at a hotel near Falun, where he learned basic Swedish and began his acquaintance with the country. And that, he explained, was the drama he had seen reproduced in the window of the model maker's shop.

From his side, Crozier could see that the Swedish police had no intention of pursuing the matter any further, and anyway, he hadn't wanted to tell them the most unsettling thing about the whole encounter: the fact that the models had even borne the correct serial number of his own launch and, from what he remembered, the correct flags and even uniforms for the Germans. All that from an incident that, at least during wartime, had been classified, with unresolved questions over the identity of the German craft and its strange cargo. Obviously, some information had come to light since the war, and Crozier resolved to check it out, more discreetly this time.

* * * *

The Lyle Shipping Company's generous shore leave allowance gave him several weeks while the next cargo was assembled, and Crozier preferred to spend his time in Sweden alone, on the strength of his wartime acquaintance with the country and the language, rather than with the rest of the ship's crew. He had freedom to investigate as he chose. His first stop, naturally enough, in the narrow cobbled alleys of the Old Town was the nautical antiquities shop and ship chandler where he had seen the model. Among the coiled ropes, piled stores, brass fittings and outdated marine furniture behind the shop's windows, he found a low cluttered desk with a small bent figure behind it, evidently the model maker as well as the shop proprietor, who introduced himself as Mr. Kolehmainen.

"Kolehmainen? That doesn't sound like a Swedish name," Crozier remarked, struck not unpleasantly by the old man's gnomelike demeanor and spry poise.

"My people were Forest Finns, from Dalarna," Mr. Kolehmainen explained patiently. "My great-grandfather left the charcoal burning business behind him when he moved to Stockholm. Now, my young gentleman, what can I interest you in?"

"It's about that model in the side window there," Crozier replied, pointing. "You see, I served in one of those ships during the war. I wondered where you found your information for that scene."

The old man sat up a little straighter on his stool, looking more than ever like a perching owl. "I can tell you gladly, but I'm afraid you won't believe me," he replied, peering at Crozier through his thick glasses. "You see, I saw it all in a dream."

"A dream," Crozier echoed. "Then would you mind telling me where all the details on those models came from?"

"Oh, I won't deny I researched a lot of the superstructure and used plans to get the proportions right," the old man admitted. "But they only confirmed what I saw in my vision. It comes like that, you see: all at once. Then I have to look up the plans and check out all the details, but it turns out that they were there all along."

He fixed Crozier with a gimlet eye, as though inviting derision. Disconcerted, Crozier looked around the interior of the shop, at the many other models on display, both civilian and military, showing all kinds of scene and period: gun crews, life below decks, salvage, towing, manning the winches, piping the officer on board. "So all of these came to you in dreams too?" he asked the old man, indicating the maquettes.

"Ja," Mr. Kolehmainen nodded. "It's all right: I don't expect you to believe me. No one else does. But if it is of any help to you, I can give you the details of another man who was also interested in your ship, a Norwegian. I met him while I was making inquiries in the same department at the Krigsarkivet. Perhaps he can help satisfy your curiosity."

The wizened old man fingered through the cards and paper scraps wedged in the inkstand on his desk and passed over a cardstock oblong, pinched between long yellow nails. Crozier took it and read "Jan Dahlberg," together with an address in Oslo. "He wrote his hotel address on the back," Mr. Kolehmainen added, pointing at a pencil scrawl on the back of the card, with a name and street number in Ostermalm. Crozier noted down the address and left the little man hunched over his bench, working on his next model.

* * * *

Dahlberg proved to be a lean, lantern-jawed Norwegian, just a little older than Crozier himself and sharing that same indefinable air of a veteran, though probably not from one of the regular services. Crozier warmed to him immediately.

"So you met that odd little gnome Kolehmainen? And he spins you that same yarn about seeing things in dreams?" Dahlberg's English was fluent, effortless and indelibly American. "Yes, I ran into him at the Krigsarkivet, where he was delving into their naval records from the War. Looking for the same thing I was, as it turned out."

Dahlberg's ice-blue eyes gleamed brighter and his attention quickened when Crozier told him that he had been on one of the ships in Kolehmainen's diorama. "And you just ran across it in his shop window? That's one hell of a coincidence," he remarked, piercing gaze fixed on the Scot. "You may be able to help me clear up one or two things then."

"Do you mind if I ask first what all the interest is?" Crozier countered, not exactly suspicious of the tall Americanized Norseman, but slightly taken aback by the force of his curiosity.

Dahlberg drew back a little and looked up at the ceiling of the small pension lobby, his long fingers interwoven across one folded knee. "Well, I understand from the naval records that your launch caught that E-boat napping in the Skagerrak. You got lucky, or they got very unlucky. That wasn't a regular sortie, I don't need to tell you. It was a commandeered vessel running a very special cargo from occupied Norway back to the Reich."

"I rather worked that one out for myself already," Crozier remarked. "But what was it then? I never found out after the War, and no one said anything at my debrief after I was repatriated."

"Well, we're still trying to work that out fully, but to give you some idea, I'm working for the Federal Ministry of the Interior of Western Germany, helping them track down and recover art treasures and other cultural objects lost during the War. Kind of a freelance investigator, you could say. This isn't about treasure hunting, though: more archaeology. You see, we think that boat was running a cargo of sacred trees and sandstone pillars from Germany, and the Nazis' Scandinavian and Baltic conquests, supposed relics of the pagan Aryans."

Crozier cocked an eyebrow. "The stuff we saw on deck back then did look like that. But then why would they go to those lengths for some piles of stone and wood?"

"We don't know that either. But we do know that Himmler's Ahnenerbe, the archaeological and racial research division of the SS, gathered them together from all the supposed Aryan heartlands, from the Externsteine in Westphalia, the Sachsenhain in Verden, from Rügen, and from their expeditions to Sweden and Finland before the war. They had some kind of sacred significance in the Nazis' mystic racial cult. The Ahnenerbe collected the artifacts at some sacred site in southern Norway, then, as things got hairy towards the War's end, they decided to try to get them back home. And that was when you came in."

He pulled a gray patch of cloth from his pocket and passed it to Crozier, who recognized the same oval design he had seen on the crates on the lost E-boat during the War, part of a badge apparently torn from a bloodstained uniform. "That's their symbol. And you can see that design, painted very very small, on the model in Kolehmainen's shop. Now, where do you think he got that, eh?"

"In dreams, naturally," Crozier quipped, peering at the badge. "But if you don't believe that either, then you think something's going on, don't you?"

Dahlberg nodded emphatically. "I have no idea what. Yet. But I intend to find out. And as it happens, we're putting together a salvage expedition to the probable site of the original sinking. Now, since I understand you're a mariner, how's about coming along to find out, and maybe avenge some dead comrades as well? Sounds good, eh?"

* * * *

So it was that Crozier found himself master of the tender of the *Amelia*, a marine salvage vessel leased from a Stockholm ship broker under a bareboat charter by Dahlberg's employer, a representative of the West German government. The commission was only for a few weeks maximum, with regular runs back to Gothenburg, where Crozier could catch the train if recalled to his ship, and he decided to tell his current company no more than that he had taken a few days for a sailing holiday. His new command alarmed him when he first saw it, though: a converted RAF rescue launch with the bolts and fittings from its guns still visible on its decks, and the old turret mountings plated over. "It came with the charter," Dahlberg shrugged when he pointed this out. "Besides, it's a different class from your old boat, no? A Fairmile D, while you had a Thorneycroft. Bigger and more seaworthy-all round." Crozier was more worried by the coincidence than by the craft itself, but he said nothing more.

Anyway, he had few nautical worries, at least outbound from Stockholm. His first mate on his small command was a seasoned local mariner who looked able to navigate the channels of the Stockholm Archipelago blindfold, and Crozier left the first legs of the voyage to him, content to watch the evening light on the passing skerries from his low bridge. Once out at sea, they picked up a tow line from their parent vessel to save fuel, and Crozier had even less to do. The handful of Swedish sailors under his nominal authority were quiet, polite, respectful, and too formidably competent to need any intervention from him, and the tricky course through the maze of islands, shoals, and channels in the Kattegat was the responsibility of the local pilots aboard the *Amelia*.

At anchor on the fourth night of the voyage off Karlskrona, Dahlberg called him over to the *Amelia* for a meal from the ship's galley and a few glasses of akavit with him and the representative of the West German government, a round-headed individual called Kaufmann who spoke entirely in German and almost exclusively to Dahlberg, who in turn bore him with grim amusement. Out at sea, Dahlberg seemed to undergo some kind of atavistic regression towards his seagoing forebears, ever more the quintessential sailor in his roll neck jersey and pea jacket.

"We'll be diving onto sand and shallow silt," he explained, spreading a chart of the Skagerrak over the mess table. "It's even money we won't find anything, with all the currents and drift over the past ten years, but the government is footing the bill, so what the hell. Brodman the diver is experienced enough to find something if anyone can, and if he does, we can haul it up." He waved his hands fore and aft, alluding to the two crane jibs hinged from the *Amelia*'s two short, substantial masts. "If we don't find anything, we just pack up and go home: easy money." Kaufmann nodded, although otherwise, he gave no sign of understanding. the English dialogue at all.

"You know these are treacherous waters," Crozier replied, pressing his finger on the penciled cross marking their destination. "Fine, it's shallow enough to be diveable, but that just means reefs and shoals. Not to mention the risks from the shifting silt and the weather. Many dangers. There could be any number of mines left over from the War, either drifting or on the bottom."

"We'll take our chances." Dahlberg shrugged carelessly, unsettling Crozier all the more. The War had given him his fill of devil-may-care buccaneers, and Dahlberg was growing into the mold day by day. "The Germans are paying us well enough." He winked at Kaufmann, who gazed back impassively. "You as well, eh. And it's Brodman who'll catch it worst. That's why he gets the biggest share. You'll be okay, trust me."

* * * *

They cleared Helsingborg and finally left the Kattegat behind for the Skaggerak proper, making for the grid reference off the northeastern tip of Denmark where the Swedish naval records said the original encounter had occurred. As Crozier had forecast, the footing was shifting and treacherous when they dropped anchor in the silt, but finally, they found firm enough purchase to remain more or less on station. The coast had been clear of sea ice since the previous month, but the weather was gray and gusty, with occasional fierce squalls. The distant glimmer of the Pater-Noster Lighthouse was just visible at dusk far to the east, but otherwise, there was nothing around them but gray sea in every direction and the occasional riding lights of passing ships.

"The sea seems unusually flat here," remarked Lund the cox, as they huddled together against the stiff breeze on the launch's little bridge the second day after dropping anchor, watching the *Amelia*'s aft jib lower Brodman into the water on a diving platform in her lee. "It's almost as though someone put oil on the waves."

"We're over sand," Crozier replied, pointing towards Brodman, who seemed oddly reluctant to step into the gray water. "Even he can go down to the bottom, like that. Surely that's the reason."

"Sand wouldn't do this," Lund countered. "We're looking for a wreck, no? Could some oil be leaking from it?"

"After nearly ten years?" Crozier answered. "Seems rather too long, no? Unless you think it started just for our arrival."

Lund looked at him strangely but said nothing more. Together they watched Brodman lower himself down the steps from the platform into the swell until only the rising bubbles from his helmet broke the surface.

* * * *

Two days of diving and dragging the bottom confirmed that there was something down there: in pieces and half buried by silt, but the wreckage of the E-boat nonetheless. To clear the silt off and start lifting the cargo, if any, would need heavier equipment than the *Amelia* had on board, Dahlberg said, and after telegraphing ashore, he arranged for a run into Gothenburg with the launch to take some extra cables worth of chain and a dredge on board. Crozier, as skipper of the tender, ferried him, with Lund at the helm, and was struck all through the voyage by his jaunty air as he stood on the bridge, exposing himself carelessly to the wind and waves. Dahlberg seemed to brim with barely suppressed excitement.

"I don't trust him," confided Lund, as they drank together in a dockside tavern, waiting for Dahlberg to finish whatever errand had taken him into the streets and alleys of the port. "He has something going on that he's not telling us about."

"This isn't the usual Swedish thing about Norwegians, is it?" Crozier responded, referring to the longstanding suspicion and hostility between the two neighbors.

Lund took another sip of Mariestads. "No, it's nothing like that. There's something else about him. I mean, just to give you one example, I complimented him on his English. He told me worked with the Americans during the War. Now, how is a Norseman going to do that, unless he's a commando, or doing something else very fishy? And now here he is, still fishing around, for something left over from the War, that he calls historical relics, or art treasures, with a hired crew? Whatever he was up to during the War, I think he's still doing it. And it scares me. I'm very glad Gothenburg is here, just a few hours sailing away. Just in case we have to, you know, run for it."

"If you're that worried, I'll talk to him about it," Crozier chuckled, nowhere near as confident underneath. He had liked, even admired Dahlberg from the start: he had never stopped to ask himself whether he could trust him. Now he wondered if the tall Norwegian had sensed that assumption, fostered it, used it. He excused himself to take a walk and scoured the stony quays until he found Dahlberg on his way back from the chandler, both hands jammed in his pockets, a toothpick poised between his teeth.

"Can we have a moment?" he asked, not exactly blocking Dahlberg's path, but not quite leaving him room to pass freely. "While we're away from the others?"

"Sure," Dahlberg nodded, grinning wolfishly. "What's on your mind?"

"Just what are we doing here? Is this really some kind of treasure hunt? Because what I see with that German, and what I hear about your war record, just doesn't add up."

"Ah, I wondered when you might work it out," the bigger man chuckled. "Well, you see, back in the War, I was working with the Americans, their Counter Intelligence Corps, attached to the Alsos Mission. And in a way, I still am."

Crozier blinked. Sure of his audience, Dahlberg went on.

"We were chasing down the scientific and other secrets of the Nazis. And with Telemark and all that, you know they had quite a bit going on in occupied Norway. The Americans wanted a Norwegian commando who could work with them on running down the scientists and assets in the German military research programs and go behind enemy lines where necessary to retrieve them, and I drew the short straw. Those were fun times. We captured all kinds of stuff: scientists, uranium, cyclotrons, even an early nuclear reactor. And since then, the CIC has kind of kept me on retainer to track down anything we might have missed, especially since we reckon there are still Nazi war criminals knocking around, looking for the same leftovers."

"So we're not here to dredge up ancient relics," Crozier responded.

"Well, yeah, we are, kind of," Dahlberg continued. "You see, our German pen-pusher Kaufmann is a mole. Yeah, fine, I know he looks like one, but it's more than skin deep with him. We know he's plugged into the ratlines of ex-Nazis who ran to South America and the Middle East, and we know they might have access to some hidden secrets. Now, we also know that Kaufmann is here looking for exactly what it says on the tin, but for his own purposes too, to make sure those Nazi cult objects are there for his own people as well as for the West German government, just in case, ya know, one day they might want to stage a comeback."

"Fine, then assuming that I believe you, why are we helping him?" Crozier pressed.

"Well," Dahlberg drawled, "We suspect there could be more to it than that. You see, late in the War, the Ahnenerbe started sending internal communique across the Reich about some war-winning weapon they were working on. Now, why they were the ones to be in on this, we don't know. There was some crazy Nazi theory that all those sacred trees and boughs were symbols of Yggdrasill, the original World-Tree that was the axis of Creation, and were linked to it by some kind of occult sympathy. The Nazi theorist Alfred Rosenberg wrote that the Germans were descendants of some kind of Aryan supermen from Atlantis and that Jesus was some kind of blood brother instead of a Jew. Apparently, the Ahnenerbe reckoned that they could use those artifacts to trigger some kind of chain reaction and bring about the second sinking of Atlantis. Meaning this time, the whole of Europe."

"And you organized all this because of that cock-and-bull story?" Crozier shook his head. "You don't actually believe it, do you?"

"Do I look like a chump to you? Besides, it's no more ludicrous than that little Finnish shopkeeper's story of seeing everything in dreams. We suspected he might be involved somehow: that's why I left my card with him, in case he could lead us to anyone else in the picture. For a while I even suspected you."

He stopped and coolly contemplated Crozier, who became all too aware of the dark water lapping at the quayside just a few steps away, and the easy, loose-limbed stance of the big Norwegian. His basic combat training from the War was long past, and he had been anything but the dockside brawler during his time as a merchant seaman. Dahlberg would comfortably outmatch him in a straight fight.

"Then after a few days with you, and reading some of Kaufmann's cables, I decided you must be innocent," Dahlberg went on, taking some of the tension out of the air. "After all, you looked puzzled enough. And I figured you'd want to be along to see what really was behind the whole story."

"And so what do you think is behind the whole story?" Crozier persisted.

"We think it's plutonium," Dahlberg breathed, finally looking just a little worried. "If the relics are down there, then, in any case, we want to know about it, in case the ex-Nazis can use them as some kind of future rallying point. But after what happened with your crewmates on that boat, we think that the Nazis could have got hold of plutonium somehow, God knows how, and were running it back to the heartland for some last hurrah. And if there is plutonium down there, we definitely want it, before the Nazis get their hands on it, or the Russians, or anyone else. Now you get the picture?"

"Plutonium: something to do with atomic bombs, right?" Crozier remarked hesitantly, searching his memory.

Dahlberg nodded. "Nasty stuff: nasty enough to account for what happened to your crewmates during the War. Unless it was poison gas or something else equally deadly."

Crozier stood silently for a moment with the lapping of the ripples against the dockside filling his ears. "So what do you want me to do now?"

he asked at length.

"Keep quiet about all this, do nothing, wait for my word," Dahlberg urged. "Oh, and one other thing: don't kill Kaufmann. I know this is all kind of hard to swallow, and will take a while to digest, but once you realize that this is the man whose friends killed your friends, just remember, we need him alive to get to his people and the others behind it."

"I couldn't kill anyone," Crozier said aghast.

"Right." Dahlberg appraised him coolly. "Okay, let's get back to the boat."

Crozier concentrated on the tasks at hand during the short run to the chandler's dock to take on board the extra equipment, and the voyage back to the *Amelia*. There was enough to do with the chains and the dredge (an improvised scallop dredge woven from chain to form a mesh bag) strapped down on the launch's after deck, exacerbating its tendency to roll, and his boat was already running on a skeleton crew split with the *Amelia*. Also, he honestly did not want to face the implications of what Dahlberg had told him and preferred to let them work themselves out at the back of his mind. Only, once the gear had been transferred to the mothership and his launch had taken up its usual station to leeward, he gazed at the open sea around him under a darkening sky, and felt as alone and exposed as an ant on a sheet of glass.

* * * *

Work with the new dredge had to wait until a squall that blew up early next day exhausted itself, and Dahlberg, director of operations on the *Amelia* despite the captain's nominal rank, spent the afternoon going over the plans for the operation with the deck crew and salvage hands, outlining how he planned to drag the bottom with the oyster dredge and crane winch while moving the *Amelia* as little as possible. He called Crozier across for the briefing, as he was requisitioning most of the launch's already minimal complement to help on board the *Amelia*.

"Brodman will position the net, then everyone else will help manage the drag," he explained, overlooking the *Amelia*'s crowded foredeck from her starboard bridge wing. "I'm hoping to fish up a lot with the first haul, from what Brodman says he's seen down there. Too big and heavy for him to bring up, though, and too deeply buried in the silt to rig a sling round."

"And if it is what you think it is, are we in any danger?" Crozier asked in a low voice.

Dahlberg sucked his teeth speculatively. "Could be. I'll keep an eye on it, though, never worry. And on him."

He nodded forwards towards the small trim figure of Kaufmann, incongruous in a dark greatcoat, who was watching proceedings from the forecastle, his elbows on the railing. Following his gaze, Crozier felt a sudden uncontrollable rush of anger that left him shaking and white-lipped.

"Just do what you have to," he snapped. The sea around had resumed its unnatural calm, and a coppery sunset loured from under the low cloud deck, plating the waves.

"Get back to your boat and get some sleep," Dahlberg urged him, with a cautious sidelong glance. "We dive first thing."

Brodman went down in the morning, followed by the oyster dredge, swinging and clanking from the *Amelia*'s foremast jib crane. Crozier and Lund watched the scene from the bridge of the launch, standing off to leave the *Amelia*'s sides clear. For an hour or two they watched, drinking coffee from thermoses in the Skaggerak's chill spring, as the *Amelia* rode at anchor and the deck crew fussed around the winches, and the hawsers tautened, then slackened, then tautened again. Finally, Brodman surfaced in a flurry of bubbles and climbed up on deck, to be followed soon after by the dredge, which was hauled dripping over the gunwales and deposited on the foredeck. From the launch, all Crozier and Lund could see was a gray mound of silt incongruously wrapped in chainmail.

Brodman, his helmet undogged, drank tea and ate sandwiches as his servitors bustled around him. Others pulled at the dredge's mesh bag and sifted through its haul. Through his binoculars, Crozier could see Dahlberg on the bridge, brooding over the scene and occasionally shouting an order. He turned aside for a moment and spoke to a sailor, who swung an Aldis lamp towards the launch and morsed a terse "Nothing."

"I guess they'll go down again?" Crozier shrugged to Lund, who looked back equally bemused. They watched as Brodman donned his helmet again and stepped down the side ladder into the water, the top of the brass dome taking forever to disappear under the gentle ripples in the lee of the *Amelia*. Down went the dredge again. An hour or so later, the *Amelia* paid out more anchor chain and got up steering way, the winches and the ship's engines pulling at the hawsers to give the dredge more bite. Crozier signaled to Lund, who followed suit, pushing the engines a little more to pace the parent ship. They watched the *Amelia* heel slightly in the water and tug at her hidden quarry under the waves, a fisher angling for a specially difficult catch. The light of the short spring day started to fail, and her riding lights came on. Finally, close to sunset, there was another visible lurch, and the *Amelia* settled in the water, with whatever she had been hauling against now obviously dredged up and rising.

Crozier and Lund watched intently to see what would emerge from the water. First came another froth of bubbles, which grew and spread, and became more and more violent, until Brodman broke surface once again, but this time hauled up by the safety line, limp as any fish, visible tears in his suit. The deck crew dragged him up the side, unmoving, deposited him on the deck and pulled off his helmet. Through his binoculars, Crozier could see what looked like blood on his livid, fishbelly white skin. Then the dredge surfaced, this time with dark objects protruding through the mesh, shedding their coating of silt.

"What is that?" Crozier sighed, mostly to himself.

The mesh net swung inboard and slowly subsided onto the *Amelia*'s foredeck, the dark nubbed objects obtruding and tilting as the crane deposited them on the deck plates. In the lurid sunset, Crozier thought he could make out a faint blue fluorescent halo around them. The deck crew seemed in no hurry to dig through the haul this time, and stood back in a circle round the dripping net, those not occupied in vain efforts to revive Brodman. Dahlberg too seemed in no hurry to order them forward.

Then Crozier saw a dark figure walk along the side gangway to the forecastle and take its place at the railing above the foredeck. Kaufmann raised his dark arms against the lowering sky and started a rolling chant that Crozier could hear in snatches carried on the wind over the lapping of the waves and the noise of the winches. Unless it was the fading light, it seemed as if the blue glow from the objects on deck grew stronger in response to his evocation. Everyone stood motionless watching him, except for Dahlberg. Crozier turned the glasses on him and saw him lower his head between his shoulders and extend both arms stiff and straight towards Kaufmann, resting on the bridge railing for a good shot, a big black automatic in his hands. The shot, when it came, carried over the waves too, and Kaufmann's body slumped forward over the railing. Then the entire foredeck erupted a massive plume of orange flame that blew straight through the bottom of the *Amelia*, breaking her in two. Within seconds she was foundering, both halves sinking into the dark maelstrom where most of her foredeck had been, but Crozier had only an instant to care for the fate of her crew before a hail of debris smashed down on the deck of the launch, driving her down into the water. He ducked and cowered in the little shelter that the launch's bridge offered as burning metal clanged down around him and hissed into the water, and once the fiery hail was over, jumped to his feet and grabbed the small fire extinguisher clipped under the bridge instruments. For minutes he fought the fires starting on the bridge, then looked around him to find that Lund had simply gone, perhaps knocked into the water by the first fall of shrapnel that had left gaping holes in the launch's deck. Crozier took a few seconds to make sure that his crippled craft was not actually sinking, and by the time he was able to look towards the *Amelia*, she was already gone, with only an ugly oily spiral on the surface of the calm waters to mark her passing.

And who else saw her go down? Why, I did, of course, with the same visionary eye that sees Crozier on his boat, lost at sea once again, drifting helpless into the sea lanes of the Skaggerak, the sole survivor once more; the same visionary eye that sees the eventual conclusion of the court of enquiry on the loss of the *Amelia*, attributed to a leftover mine from the War; the same eye that eavesdropped on Crozier's first encounter with the shop window and his conversations with Dahlberg. The eye that sees, or the hand that moves. Where is the cause and effect in this? If the little model boat that I built and sail now on a plaster sea across my miniature Skaggerak captures him so accurately, did I bring Crozier full circle, or did I simply follow him around? If I move my maquettes and figurines where the ships and men will be moments later, does this really show that it is I who moves them? Or simply that I know where fate or destiny will place them? And if I am the puppet master, manipulating them, then who directs me? If I move them, invisible strings pull me. Puppeting each other, we are all puppets.

✗

In the Shadows
J.S. Watts

The fierce sunlight made the shadows seem that much harder and darker. Not that it mattered. Nothing had mattered since the death. Not to her, anyway. James had seemingly got over it, the callous bastard. He denied it and said it was a normal fading of emotions, just part of the natural healing process, but three years on and she had not healed; didn't know if she ever could.

It was James who had made her sit out in the garden; said the fresh air and the sunlight would do her good after so long skulking indoors in the shadows. She wasn't skulking though, she was mourning, as he should still be. Indoors she could draw the curtains and wrap herself in the resultant gray vagueness like a soft, dull, comforter. Things were less definite, less certain, less hurtful in the half-light.

Out here, nature was growing, scuttling, moving on. The sunshine made things clearer and sharper. There were fewer places to hide. Even the shadows were flint-edged and wouldn't absorb her loss. It didn't help that James had thoughtlessly put her chair and cushions in direct sunlight. As soon as he went indoors she would move them into the shaded part of the garden.

* * * *

From the kitchen window, he watched as she dragged the chair and the cushions he had painstakingly set up for her in the sunshine down to the end of the garden where the large shrubs and trees grew, fighting one another for a place in the light. Once there, she wrapped herself defensively in the blanket and glared at the world through unnecessarily dark sunglasses. He sighed. Things weren't working out: again. It was beginning to feel as if they never would. He went into the shadowy interior of the house to phone Annette. When he came back to the kitchen, Clare had apparently fallen asleep in her shady bower.

* * * *

She was dreaming. It was a chiaroscuro dusk and she was watching a small boy of two or three playing in the garden. He was chasing shadows up and down the grass, faster and faster. Then he fell over and automatically she was up and out of her seat and running towards him, only the blanket was still wrapped around her legs and it was she who now fell over, waking up with a start. She hadn't actually fallen out of the chair, but she had slid down and sideways and the blanket was a big tangled knot of thick woolen material around her ankles. As she struggled to right herself, the chair tipped and she ended up on the grass in a mottled patch of afternoon sunlight and shade. It was then she saw the shadow.

* * * *

James found her, still lying on the grass, over an hour later. He rushed out thinking she had collapsed, only to find her contentedly staring into a pool of shadow and cooing at it the way you would a newborn, but he didn't want to go there. He wanted to phone Annette, but he knew he couldn't, so he scooped Clare up and took her protesting back to the house. It would soon be dusk anyway and maybe she was right, maybe she was better in the house than out of it, although she herself no longer appeared to think so.

* * * *

The next day, as soon as James had left the house, Clare was out in the garden. She took the chair, a book and the blanket, but really all she wanted to do was try to find that particular spot of shadow again. The sun was only hazy today, so it wasn't easy, but eventually, after much repositioning on the blanket, she had given up on the chair, she found it: a baby shaped shadow where the shade of the shrubbery started to melt into the sun of the lawn. So small; just like he had been.

It was just as well it was a hazy day or she would have been severely sunburnt. As it was, when James came home that afternoon she, for the first time in three years, had a healthy outdoors sort of glow about her. James was both pleased and concerned. The change had happened so fast. Was this an amazing recovery or the development of a new phase of the problem? Clare for once noticed James' discomfort and recognizing he would never understand what she was up to, particularly as she herself was not that certain what she was doing, or why, come to that, decided that a plausible excuse for her sudden interest in outdoors was called for.

The following day she took a book on gardening outside with her and the day after, she alternated sitting and resting with digging out a new flower bed, just where the shade of the shrubs met the sunlight of the lawn. The day after that, it was raining, but she carried on with her digging, arguing that the damp soil was better for forking over. James discussed this sudden burst of activity with Annette, but neither could work out what had wrought such a startling change in Clare.

* * * *

The new flowerbed was starting to take shape. She had even taken herself out to a garden center to buy some new plants. James was pleasantly surprised, if still somehow disbelieving of the change in her.

The planting pattern of the new bed was distinctive, if unusual. What no one but Clare understood was that she had bought and positioned the plants according to the shadows they cast, ensuring one pre-existing shadow remained unaltered and framed by the others, however the light fell. For a while, she was concerned about what was going to happen when the plants grew, but it seemed as if all the shadows grew in accordance with the original design, including the one significant one. It was now about the size of a healthy one-year-old child; a size he had never achieved.

* * * *

James still didn't know what to make of Clare's new found obsession with outdoors. In some ways, it made no difference to him. Before she had been withdrawn and isolated in the darkened house, now she was wrapped up in her gardening and withdrawn from him amongst her plants and the apparently rejuvenating light of day. At least the garden was benefitting and not just the new flowerbed, although that was the main focus of her attention. Clare herself was clearly growing fitter and healthier; plumping out, her muscles firming, her color returning with a vengeance, but James, James was without her attention; a stranger to both Clare and her new found passion. He had plenty of opportunities to discuss the matter with Annette, but neither could work out what, exactly, was happening to Clare, or why.

* * * *

Weeks passed. The shadows started lengthening and *the* shadow now looked to be the size of a two year old. Clare never actually saw it grow, but somehow, just like the plants, it became bigger and it carried on developing even as the plants around it started to die back down and give up their shadows. The weaker they became, the bigger and, it seemed to Clare, the darker it grew.

* * * *

James did not know what, if anything, to do. During the summer he could explain away Clare's new found obsession with the need to sort out their long neglected garden. Even in the early autumn there had been many things in need of attention, but it was getting colder now, the nights were drawing in and yet Clare was still spending as many daylight hours as possible out in the garden, particularly in the area by the flower bed she had put in earlier in the year. She had swept and tidied, pruned everything to within an inch of its life, filled the new bed with plump bulbs for the forth-coming spring and still she stayed out there every day until dusk. Annette said to leave her be; at least she was happy in her new obsession, but James was not so sure. Under the remains of her summer tan, she was starting to look pale and drawn. He thought she was losing weight.

* * * *

Clare had given up crafting excuses for her presence by the flowerbed. Occasionally she would half-heartedly snip another microscopic piece off a nearby bush, but mostly she stood staring at the shadow. It had moved. She was sure of it, and not with a random movement like the swaying of a branch or the flickering of wintry sunlight: there was little or no sun-shine today, anyway. The rain and the clouds had seen to that. No, she was convinced the shadow had moved of its own volition; had stretched out towards her. If she stood still for long enough and reached out towards him, perhaps he would move again.

* * * *

When James came home that evening he found the house cold, dark and apparently deserted. Entering the kitchen, he was alarmed to find the back door wide open and, when he switched both the kitchen and the out-side lights on, he could just make out Clare standing in the cold and the wet by the flowerbed. She seemed surprised to see him and after he had brought her in, for once unprotesting, it had taken a hot bath and a bed full of blankets and hot water bottles to warm her up properly. She submitted to his attentions willingly enough, but it was as if one of them wasn't there. Finally, she said, but not necessarily to him, "He touched my shadow like he was holding my hand. I was waiting for him to do it again." Then she went to sleep. He felt her head. She didn't seem feverish, but there were large dark circles under her eyes.

The next morning he left her sleeping, wrapped up snugly in their warm bed. Earlier, she had woken up long enough to convince him she was well and would not do any gardening that day, but when he came home early that afternoon to check on her, she was standing outside in exactly the same spot as the night before, her hand held out in front of her and, if anything, she was colder than previously. He tried to talk to her about it, but she just raised her vague gray eyes to a focal point well below his own and said nothing in response. Annette advised him to leave her to her own devices. He couldn't decide if this was sound advice, or not.

* * * *

He made up his mind to stay home the next day and take Clare to the doctors, but eventually, she spoke and assured him she was only out of it because she had caught a chill. She realized that gardening in this state was stupid and she would stay indoors and in bed. He wasn't sure he believed her, but he went off to work in the morning, as usual, with a guilty sense of relief at being out of the house and away from the direct worry of her.

He did ring her at several points during the day and if she seemed distant, it was no worse than normal.

On his return that evening, he was pleased to find her wrapped up in bed in a darkened, shadow-filled bedroom. The irony of it struck him. Less than nine months before he would have seen Clare staying indoors all day as a bad thing, not a good one, but things evolve and black and white had shaded into occluded gray. This time it seemed to be physical ill health keeping her house-bound. He noted the deepening shadows spreading below her eyes. They seemed even darker in the light of the following morning and he suggested she spend another day in bed. She acquiesced willingly enough, asking him to draw the curtains shut again before he left for work. She called out goodbye as he was going and, as he glanced back, he could barely make out her small pale form amongst the gloom and shadow.

* * * *

On the way back from Annette's that evening, James was kicking himself. How had he managed to forget today's date? Today was the day they celebrated a longed-for birth and mourned a small death within the same heartbeat. For the last three years he had never risked leaving Clare on her own on this date, but here he was out for the whole day as if it was just like any other, and God knew they were often bad enough. This year she hadn't even mentioned the anniversary slouching towards them and somehow he had chosen to let it slip his mind. Any subconscious relief this had given him was now swamped by guilt and an uneasy sense of alarm. She had seemed better this year, hadn't she? At least the gardening, however obsessional, had been healthier than lurking indoors in darkened rooms. Perhaps this year's anniversary had crept from her mind too? Perhaps it wouldn't matter that he had left her on her own today?

She was still in bed when he got home; sitting hunched in the dark like she used to. Her eyes didn't blink when he turned on the bedroom light and for a moment he thought the smile on her lips and the hand lying outstretched on the bedcovers were for him. Then he felt the coldness of her skin and the rigidity of her arm and knew different. He reached for the phone. In the shadows behind him, something scuttled.

✗

The Dinner Fly

James Matthew Byers

Oh, Widow, Widow on the wall,
How does your webbing weave?
Why is it said your belly, red,
Can stealthily deceive?

How is it that your hourglass
Does not sift endless sand,
And yet it flies in silent cries
When life ends in your hands?

* * * *

Where are you in the dead of night,
As nightmares follow suit
In luscious boons of silk cocoons,
Intended to dilute?

What can you do to comfort me?
I'm tangled in the strand,
Awaiting fangs and toothy pangs,
Unleashed at your command!

When will the feast be done at last?
My body cannot wait,
So hiss and spin as you dive in,
And leave me to my fate!

"Have patience, dear," the Widow sneers,
"My lips will calm you so.
Enjoy your last as ends my fast;
I will not let you go.

Your questions will not matter by
The time our deal is done.
Indeed, relax, my tummy tax,
For mealtime has begun!"

A dreadful feeling passes by,!
I close my eyes to die.
Oh that I was the Widow and
Not me, the dinner fly...

The Spot
C.R. Langille

Grey clouds the color of wet ash grumbled across the afternoon sky in a slow shuffle. Thunder boomed in the distance. Graham's buckskin let out a shrill whinny, but he patted the horse's neck until it calmed.

The dull clouds contrasted with the bright colors of the leaves. Pockets of pumpkin orange, warm buttery yellow, and blood red dotted the mountainside.

Graham navigated to the side of the road and waited for Emmett to catch up. Two older plow horses pulled an old Ford pick-up bed which Emmett turned into a wagon. With every bump and rock in the road, the old wagon screamed something violent.

"How much longer," Graham asked.

"Another hour or so. No need to piss your britches," Emmett said.

The wagon squeaked by, and the Emmett pulled a tattered wool scarf down from his face to reveal a beard the same color as the storm-laden sky. The old man spits a wad of tobacco in Graham's general direction before he adjusted his wide brim hat and shot him a toothless smile.

Graham returned the smile and adjusted his coat. With summer gone, the air had turned crisp and cold. He was thankful that Theresa had fixed up his wool coat before he left. Graham hoped that she would be okay while he was gone. It was only a week, but a week was too much. They were engaged and planned to marry when he returned.

He rode ahead to escape the squeak and squeal of Emmett's wagon. After a moment, the wagon's cry faded into the background and only the clip-clop of his horse's hooves on the broken asphalt graced his ears. A large building made of brick stood at a T intersection in the road. All the windows were broken, and an ivy plant crawled up the front of the dilapidated structure and covered it like moss on a log. Like everything else in the city, the only residents were half-forgotten memories, and dust—lots and lots of dust.

A young horse with a black leather saddle was hitched to an old gas pump and snorted when it saw Graham. Graham cursed under his breath and nudged his buckskin into a gallop. They weren't supposed to enter the buildings alone. As he neared the building he cupped his hands and bellowed.

"Randall! You there?"

His voice echoed through the building and caused a nearby murder of crows to take flight. They cawed their annoyance as they flew away.

"Randall, stop messing around," Graham said.

Graham tightened his grip on the reins until his knuckles were whiter than the nearby snow-capped peaks. He steered the horse next to Randall's and hopped off. The building stared at him with murderous intent. The town elder told them all stories of what some unsuspecting child would find in the dark and blasted buildings of the city.

"Randall?"

Graham's voiced cracked ever so slightly as doubt crept into his spine. He wanted to just leave him be and let Fate decide what she had in store for the boy. Graham had known the boy would be trouble the moment they started training together. But, he couldn't bring himself to leave Randall behind. Besides, it would mean longer shifts during the watch without him.

"Savior's light, Randall, come out, please!"

Graham took a step toward the building but stopped when the sound of brick against concrete scraped from inside. The tell-tale squeak of Emmett's wagon bolstered his confidence, but not by much. The wind picked up and carried the fetid stench of the Dead Lake to his nose. The lake was supposedly saltier than the vast oceans Graham heard about but never seen. The Dead Lake was impressive, but the stink reminded him of chicken eggs gone rotten. Some folk told stories, saying they saw all sorts of fancy things near and in the lake. The most common tale was that something big lived underneath the briny water, and if you watched on a blood moon, you could see its colossal body roll beneath the moonlight. But those were just tales.

"He in there?" Emmett asked.

Graham nodded and kept his eyes glued to the building. A shadow flitted across the ivy-covered doorway.

"Randall! Come on out, we've got miles yet to go, boy!" Emmett said.

The old man's voice was barely more than a wheeze on the wind. Graham dismounted his horse and hitched the reins to the same gas pump as Randall's. He started toward the building when Emmett whistled from behind.

Graham turned just in time to catch a worn tomahawk.

"You've got five minutes, boy. Then I'm leaving. At least one of us needs to take the watch."

Graham nodded and tightened his grip on the weapon. It wasn't much and had seen better days, but it was better than nothing.

"Five minutes," Emmett reiterated.

The old man lit a pipe and looked to the sky. It was getting late, and the rain would fall at any moment. If they didn't make it to their destination before the rain, it would be miserably cold.

Graham stepped through the ivy gateway and into the building. There was a different smell inside. Unlike the dry, dust-strewn scent of the valley, the building was musty and wet. This gas station was bigger than others he'd seen, and surrounded by an empty sea of asphalt. Emmett said it used to be a truck stop.

The odd drip-drip-drip of water echoed through the empty shell and played at Graham's nerves. It sounded too much like one of the big grand-daddy clocks he'd seen in the town square, constantly ticking until it drove a man insane.

"Randall," Graham said as loud as he dared. His words raced through the old pump station until they returned to him, out of breath.

The inside of the building was just as decrepit and time-worn as the outside. The drip-drip-drip of the water lulled Graham in further.

"You there? Come on out! We got to get on down the road or we're going to get rained on!" Graham said, a little louder this time.

The drips stopped, and so did Graham. There was a scrape of metal against brick from further in the building and something moved through the shadows.

"Randall?"

The sound of tearing fabric crept through the room and up Graham's spine. He wanted to turn tail and run, but he didn't want to leave Randall behind.

The tearing stopped and then there was a splash of water. Then a giggle. Then nothing.

"Randall?" Graham asked.

He took a couple of nervous steps toward the shadows. That's when the whispers caressed his ears. Graham couldn't tell what the voice was saying, but it made him want to throw up. When he looked up, he was just at the shadow's edge, and he didn't remember walking so close to the darkness.

Randall was crouched in front of him, poking the water with an old branch. The drip-drip-drip echoed through the room, but Graham couldn't see where the noise came from.

"Randall?" Graham said.

The boy kept his back turned toward Graham and continued to poke the water's edge.

"Come on now, we have to get a move on," Graham said.

The whispers picked up in intensity, and his vision blurred for a moment. He almost caught a word or two in the insane murmurs. Randall continued to poke at the water, so Graham reached down and shook the boy's shoulder. All at once the whispers stopped and the drip-drip-drip died away.

Randall dropped the stick and turned toward Graham. The boy's face was pale and covered in sweat. Randall's eyes were glazed over and unfocused, but when Graham shook him once more, the boy's eyes found their clarity and snapped on Graham.

"Graham?" Randall asked.

"Yeah, it's me. Come on. Emmett is waiting on us."

Randall looked around and stood.

"Where are we?" Randall asked.

"An old fill'em'up station. Come on."

The village elders warned them not to go playing around in the old buildings by themselves. Strange things happen when the living step foot in a dead building they said. Strange things. They were probably just stories to scare children, but Graham was starting to think perhaps there was a smidgen of truth to the tall tales.

Graham started to lead Randall out, hoping that some fresh air would do the boy some good. It wouldn't do if they had to babysit Randall and watch the spot. Maybe they could send the boy back with the other team if he was still in a stupor.

As they turned to leave, Randall threw the stick into the darkened room. It hit the water and sank without a sound.

Emmett was in the process of turning the wagon around when they stepped outside. Graham's ears popped as if he had just come off the mountain and into the valley. The fresh air, while tinged with the Dead Lake's stench, still felt nice across his cheeks.

Emmett noticed the pair and stopped the wagon. He motioned them over with a free hand. Graham helped Randall over to the wagon, but with each step, it seemed the boy got his strength back. By the time they reached Emmett, Randall was walking unassisted. The pair stopped short when Emmett leveled a sawed-off shotgun toward their faces.

"Let me see," he said.

"I'm fine, Emmett. I promise," Randall said.

"Quit your bellyaching. It's your fault anyway," Graham said.

Graham slapped Randall across the back of the head and inched as close as he dared to Emmett. The shotgun followed his movement and didn't waver a bit. When he couldn't get any closer, Graham held an eyelid open with his fingers and rolled his eye around in the socket, exposing all the whites to the old man. Then, he followed suit with the other eye.

Emmett nodded and then motioned Graham to the side before he aimed the gun back at Randall.

"Come on, boy. Your turn," Emmett said.

"This is ridiculous! Ain't nothing happened in that old building. I swear," Randall said.

The old man pulled the hammers back on the shotgun.

"I could blast you right now and be within my rights. Better safe than sorry, you know. Plus, you'd rather die this way than if you're infected," the old man said.

Randall looked to Graham for support, but Graham only motioned him toward Emmett. The old man was right if Randall was infected, better to die by being shot than let the infection run its course. Safer for everyone involved.

The boy sighed and stepped closer. He opened one eye, then the other.

"There, just like I told you, no infection."

Emmett eased the hammers back into place on the gun. Then he pulled his scarf up over his mouth and started the wagon rolling again with the whip of the reins.

Graham kicked his horse into motion and pushed past the wagon. He made sure Randall stayed between him and Emmett, and constantly checked back to ensure the boy didn't wander off again. Randall didn't pay as much attention to their training, and it was showing now.

As they made their way through the abandoned city, the ambient noise of life died away. The birds no longer chirped, and the bugs no longer buzzed. It was as if the city itself had stopped breathing. Off in the distance, a giant sinkhole pock-marked the city. Even at a distance, the hole seemed massive as it stretched across several city blocks. The townsfolk who had been out this far, nicknamed it The Pit. Some people came back telling stories of strange orange lights that danced in the pit during the witching hour. Graham was just happy that they weren't going anywhere near the thing. Their destination was something else, something more important than abandoned holes.

The temperature dropped as they navigated through empty streets. The remnants of cars and trucks lay in rusted heaps along the road. Others had cleared a path to their destination long before Graham had been born. Randall looked down the side streets, and it was easy enough to tell that travel with the wagon would have been impossible otherwise.

They moved closer to their destination. The sun began to set behind the mountains and cast the evening sky with a darker gloom. Graham's father used to talk about the magnificent Fall sunsets that would light up the heavens. Graham supposed there was a lot of beauty in the world back before.

They rounded the corner to find kerosene torches lining the sidewalks on either side of the road. The flames in each torch were steady and danced in what little breeze there was. The squeak of Emmett's wagon told him the old man was close, and that's when Graham noticed he had stopped his horse at the edge of the torches.

The light from each torch cut through the shadows and provided enough illumination to the keep the street lit in the darkness. The torches led the way and ended near a large building. An asphalt lot full of rusted and empty cars stood between them and a hotel—their destination.

The hotel was five stories tall. Dozens of windows lined the outer wall facing them. Most of the windows were broken, and the wind moved tattered curtains making it look as if people moved about and watched them from darkened rooms. A wagon, similar to Emmett's, was stationed out front, with a team of horses hitched nearby.

Emmett brought the wagon to a stop next to the two and then climbed down. The old man let out a groan and popped his back.

"Getting too old for these trips. I think this will be my last one boys," he said. "You wait here. If I don't come back, you know what to do."

Emmett double-checked to make sure the shotgun was loaded, then walked down the street. Graham watched him go until the old man disappeared into the hotel. Working the fields started to look like it was perhaps the better option. Theresa didn't want him to come on this trip, and she had said they could wait for him to make enough chits in the fields. Graham didn't want to wait, though.

"What do we do if he doesn't come back?" Randall asked.

Graham sighed and turned his attention to the younger man. Hadn't the boy listened during the training? It had been a mistake to bring two new watchers on the trip, but at least Graham had excelled during the instruction—much to Theresa's chagrin.

"If he doesn't come back, then we go in after him. We can't leave the watch unattended for any reason."

"But what if something killed him, or he's infected?' Randall asked.

"Any reason," Graham replied and turned his gaze back to the house. He checked his belt for the tomahawk Emmett had given him and found comfort in its weight.

* * * *

He didn't have a watch, so he was unsure of how long the old man was gone. Graham was about to head in when Emmett appeared at the doorway of the abandoned house. The old man stepped out into the street and headed back to the wagon.

"Everything okay?" Graham asked.

The old man shot him a look. The cold sentiment behind Emmett's eyes said everything. Graham lowered his head.

"All of them?" Graham asked.

"Almost."

"What? What's wrong?" Randall asked.

A slight tremor shook the boy's words. It was definitely a bad idea to bring him along. Why did the town council allow such a green crew to accompany the old man on the trip?

"They lost two," Emmett said.

Graham stopped. Two, dead. They hadn't lost a person in more than three seasons, and now they just lost two.

Emmett whipped the reins and sent the wagon moving again. A moment later, Graham and Randall followed behind.

They entered through the front of the hotel. The original doors, long broken and gone were replaced with heavy wooden ones. The doors screamed and creaked when opened and Graham flinched as the noise echoed down the street.

* * * *

"Don't worry, sound doesn't attract anything here. Not anymore at least," Emmett said.

Warm air caressed Graham's cold face as he stepped over the threshold. It came as such a shock he stopped and looked around. It wasn't just the warmth of being indoors, it was something else. The air inside was humid and heavy, not what he was used to in the arid mountains.

"I don't like it in here," Randall said.

Graham shared the boy's sentiments but kept his mouth shut. Emmett ushered them into the lobby where empty boxes of supplies sat in various states of disarray. The old man pointed to a corner.

"Bring our stuff and put it there," Emmett said.

Graham nodded and turned to Randall. Emmett walked down the hall and disappeared.

"Let's get it done," Graham said.

They spent the next ten minutes unloading the wagon. As they brought the last load into the lobby, Emmett returned with another man. Graham recognized the man from the village; it was Bartholomew, the town's apprentice blacksmith. He was older than Graham and Randall, but younger than Emmett. Bartholomew wore a long, stringy beard on his face. For some reason, the man still had on heavy leather blacksmithing apron and carried a large steel hammer which glistened red in the flickering candlelight.

"You should stay until morning, a storm's coming," Emmett said.

Bartholomew didn't say anything at first. He just stared at the ground with his hand gripped the hammer so hard his knuckles turned white.

"Can't stay here anymore," Bartholomew said.

Emmett didn't say anything. He clapped Bartholomew's shoulder once, then turned toward us.

"Help him bring up the others," Emmett said.

Bartholomew didn't go with them, merely pointed in the direction they needed to go. Emmett sighed and led them to the stairwell.

"Go down the stairs and take a right when you exit. You'll see it. We need to hurry this up because we can't leave the spot unattended for too much longer. Don't you boys go looking at it either, not until it's your shift. You hear me?"

"Okay," Graham said.

Randall didn't respond, seemed lost in the darkness of the stairwell, like when he was at the gas station earlier. They shouldn't have brought the boy.

"Randall!" Emmett said. "You understand?"

"Yes, sir," Randall said.

"Good. Now go."

They walked down and their footfalls echoed through the stairwell. There were more candles and torches lining the walls, but the further down the stairs they went, the darker it became. The humidity increased, and by the time they arrived in the basement, Graham wanted to pull his coat off.

Graham turned right as they went through the doors, not only because it was the way Emmett told him to go, it was the only way to go. The floors above had caved in years ago and blocked off any other direction.

Skeletons of the dead and forgotten were trapped within the rubble. Graham wondered why nobody had ever dug them out and gave them proper burials, but as he got closer to the pile of debris, he understood. A sense of utter sadness rolled through his guts, and he lost the will to do anything. Despair crawled through his body and doused his insides with and icy cold that had a bite much more bitter than the mountain streams. Lost in the cloud of depression, Graham thought of Theresa. She was right—he should never have come here. The infection would burrow into his body, then they would never be together, or worse he would carry the infection back to her.

He wanted to leave, and go back to Theresa, but they'd come this far and he had a duty to uphold now. Graham sighed.

"Come on," Graham said.

They entered the room to the right of the stairs.

It was an old laundry room. Graham recognized the giant machines from the stories his parents had told him. They talked about the machines with a sense of longing. Candles lined every flat surface other than the floor. The dance of candlelight was nearly maddening as the light and shadow constantly played tag along the walls.

A large, grimy white sheet, held up by heavy duty rope, cut the room into two sections. Graham knew that the spot was on the other side of the sheet. The spot they were supposed to watch when it was their time.

Randall pointed to the corner by one of the washing machines. Two bodies wrapped in the same dirty linen as the hanging sheet lay on the floor. Graham didn't know who the two were, and he didn't want to know.

They went to work and hauled the first body up the stairs. Sweat poured down Graham's face and stung his eyes as he ascended the stairs, and the cool autumn air kissed his skin as they hauled the body to the Bartholomew's wagon. The chill air was a nice relief, and he didn't want to go back for the second body, but he knew Emmett would get after them for dilly-dallying.

The blacksmith was in the wagon and ready by the time they loaded the second body into the rusted truck bed. Bartholomew cracked the reins and set the wagon into motion. Somehow, his wagon was even squeakier than Emmett's.

After they unpacked all the supplies, Emmett walked up with three small sticks in his hand. He held the three sticks so that they appeared to be the same length, although Graham knew that one of them would be shorter than the other two.

"Go on, pull a stick."

Graham reached out and pulled one. He didn't have to see the other sticks to know the truth—he would be first.

Emmett led Graham down the stairs. Neither of them said a word until they arrived at the room. The sheet still split the room into two halves, but this time, everything seemed a little darker, and Graham hesitated at room's threshold.

Emmett handed Graham a pack full of supplies and placed a hand on his shoulder.

"Remember, you don't have to watch it all the time. Just make sure to keep an eye on it at least once or twice an hour," Emmett said.

Graham nodded. This would be his first watch. They trained him, but this was the real deal.

"If it grows bigger, you come get us, okay?"

"Okay."

Emmett started up the stairs but called back down.

"Randall will be down to relieve you in eight hours," Emmett said. "Don't fall asleep."

Don't fall asleep. Graham didn't think it would be a problem. The room made his skin crawl, and there was a horrible sense of someone watching him. Graham wished he had more than the old tomahawk with him. Emmett was the only one with a gun. The elders didn't give out many guns due to the ammo shortage. Besides, the last time anyone used a gun on watch was years ago. What good would a gun do against the spot?

Graham stepped up next to the sheet and reached out to pull the cloth aside with a shaky hand. He took a deep breath to steady himself, then opened the curtain and stepped on through to the other side.

A plain wooden chair sat in the middle of the room facing a wall of red brick. The wall was undecorated and in a poor state of health. A large crack started at the floor and branched off into three different directions, but that wasn't the most significant feature of the wall.

In the middle of the brick wall, was a dark spot, blacker than Emmett's coffee, and no bigger than the size of one of Theresa's red apples. Other than some lit candles, an old tape measure, a wind-up clock, and a pad of paper, nothing else was in the room. At least, nothing Graham could see.

He still couldn't shake the feeling that someone or something watched him. There wasn't anyone else, though, at least not on that side of the sheet.

Graham set his supplies down and picked up the notebook. Each page was full of dates, times, and measurements. Occasionally there were observations or unreadable scribbles. Graham flipped to the last page with writing on it. The final entry was logged two hours ago. It read: *Sunday, Hour 19, 2 & 1/4 inches.*

He put the notebook down and picked up the tape measure. Graham took a couple of steps toward the spot but stopped short. He didn't want to go near it. Theresa told him not to touch it. She said that he would definitely become infected. Graham wasn't sure if that was the truth, and in his training, they didn't confirm or deny that aspect. However, they did say not to touch it if it could be avoided.

Graham pulled a length of tape from the measure. The old device groaned and squealed as he pulled. Then, he held it up next to the spot and looked. 2 & 1/2 inches. It had grown.

He almost dropped the tape measure and ran back up the stairs, but he stopped himself. The training took over. Three times, his instructor said. Always measure three times for an accurate reading.

Graham held the measure up again. 2 & 1/4. He held his breath and held it up one more time. 2 & 3/8. Graham let the air rush from his lungs in a contented sigh. While the measurement was larger than the previous entry, it didn't meet the threshold for growth. His instructor said there would be human error, and not to worry if the measurement was off by a couple sixteenths.

He returned to the chair and wound up the clock. It would ring an alarm in two hours and would notify him it was time to measure the spot again. Until then, he just had to keep an eye on it, and not fall asleep.

Graham watched the wall focused on the inky blotch. It seemed to move under the candlelight as if ate the light itself. He resisted the urge to measure it again, even though it looked somewhat bigger. Only when the alarm sounds, that's what they said in his training. It would still be over an hour before the alarm—

The bells of the clock started to ring and Graham almost fell out of the chair. It couldn't be time yet, he'd just set the danged thing. Yet, when he looked down, the clock read true. It had been two hours. The state of the candles confirmed his suspicion, as they had burned lower.

He measured the spot again. 2 & 3/8, 2 & 7/16, 2 & 7/16. It was larger than before, but not by enough to worry. Graham set the clock once again and took care to ensure he did it correctly. He grabbed his bag of supplies and looked for something to eat.

The bag held the usual rations, enough to get someone by for eight hours: half a loaf of bread, some cheese, and a sack of jerky. He also had his waterskin, and it was at that moment he realized just how thirsty he was.

Graham lifted the skin up to his lips and tipped it back, but nothing came out. He tipped it back further, but still, empty. It wasn't right. He wasn't a rookie when it came to the outdoors, and he knew what a full waterskin felt like versus an empty one; this one was heavy enough to be half full. Theresa always reminded him to keep it half full, because she didn't want him dying of thirst out in the fields.

Graham lifted it to his lips once again, but nothing came out. He growled and tipped it over, and was surprised when all the liquid gushed out onto the concrete floor. Graham just stared at the water, unsure of what to think. His instructor at training said the spot would play tricks on him. That it would try to get him to fall asleep or leave. That's all this was, was a trick—a costly trick, but a trick nonetheless.

"Emmett! Randall! Can you hear me?"

Nothing but silence. In fact, the air was thicker than before. His shouts were muted and Graham knew the others wouldn't hear him. He would just have to wait it out. It was only six more hours, and Randall would take over. Graham could wait six hours.

The fields were starting to look like a good option at this point. Theresa would understand. She'd probably be happy with his choice. The fields were hard work, and had their own dangers, but nothing like the watch. Most people didn't last too many seasons on watch. The majority quit and returned to the fields, while others ended up like the Bartholomew's teammates, or insane.

Graham looked at the clock, and his face scrunched up with confusion. He picked it up and listened to ensure the tick-tock of the internal mechanism still sounded. Then, he watched to make sure the hands still moved as they were supposed to move. Everything looked to be in order, which was why he couldn't fathom that it had only been one minute since he set it last.

"I'm here," Randall said.

Graham let out a scream and dropped the clock. It hit the ground and the alarm sent the bells ringing.

"Savior's light, you scared me," Graham said.

His breath came in ragged waves and it felt as if his heart would stop at any moment. Randall just smiled and let out a little laugh.

"Sorry. How's it going?" Randall asked.

"Strange. I swear I've lost time down here. I've only measured the spot twice."

Randall's smile disappeared and he picked up the notebook. The boy stared at the water for a moment.

"What's with the puddle?" Randall asked.

"I spilled my water," Graham said.

He didn't want to explain what happened. It would only make the boy nervous.

"According to this, you met all your measurements," Randall said.

Impossible. He'd only measured twice.

"Give me that."

Graham took the book from him and opened it to the last entry. He wanted to leave. He wanted to get on his horse and go back to the village. As Randall stated, all the measurements were filled out, and in Graham's handwriting. He didn't remember taking the measurements or writing anything down. Graham had trouble recalling anything past the waterskin incident. He turned the page almost dropped the book. Written in his handwriting was the following sentence over, and over: *Plant Theresa in the fields, then see what the harvest yields.*

There was the wet sound of tearing. Graham had heard the same sound when the hunters would skin out their game. Both Graham and Randall looked to the spot, and for just a moment, it seemed as if the entire wall fluttered like it was paper in the wind. The tearing sounded again and Graham took a step back. Then, it stopped, and the wall no longer shuddered. The candlelight brightened and only then did Graham realize just how dark it had been.

"What the hell's going on down here," Emmett asked as he entered the room.

Graham took the opportunity to rip the notebook page out and stuff it in his pocket before Emmett crossed through the linen sheet. The old man had the gun in hand again.

"Graham's been infected. He's going crazy," Randall said.

Graham's jaw dropped and he turned to the boy.

"That's insane! I'm fine," he said.

Emmett leveled the shotgun and motioned for Graham to take a seat. Graham wanted to argue, but the look in Emmett's eyes stopped that notion. He took a seat.

Emmett stood over him with the gun poised and ready.

"Open 'em," the old man said.

Graham followed the order and held his eyes open to let Emmett inspect them. After a moment, Emmett sighed and lowered the weapon.

"He's fine. We don't have to plant him in the fields," Emmett said.

Plant Theresa in the fields, then see what the harvest yields.

"What did you say?" Graham asked.

"I said you're fine. Well, at least you're not infected. Go get some sleep. The watch can take a lot out of you."

Graham nodded. Sleep sounded like a fine idea, as well as a drink of water. He glanced down at the puddle and frowned. Ripples rolled across the small puddle, and for a moment, the dark depths seemed to go down forever. Emmett gave him a slight shake on the shoulder and motioned for him to go.

"I'll make sure Randall is set up for his watch, then I'll be up," Emmett said.

"Okay."

Graham walked up the stairs. With each step, he could breathe easier, and an invisible weight seemed to slip off his shoulders. He walked outside and the night air felt good in his lungs. The sun would be up soon, and hopefully, with it, the light would bring some warmth.

* * * *

Graham ate some food outside with the horses. They smelled of hard work and purpose and reminded him of the village. Of the fields. *...see what the harvest yields.* Of Theresa.

He finished his dinner and returned to the lobby. Emmett or Randall must have set up the cots, but it didn't matter who did, only that he had a decent place to sleep. Graham crawled onto the cot. The stress and pull of travel melted away as he settled in for the night. Then, he fell asleep.

The sound of a shotgun blast ripped Graham from his slumber. He sat up and groaned as his road-weary muscles protested.

The sun was out, and given the way, the light poured through the window, was almost setting again. Graham tried to determine just how long he had slept when another shotgun blast echoed from the basement. He sprang up and ran down the stairs. Graham slowed as he neared the debris pile and the entrance to the room.

* * * *

Emmett hummed a tune which carried out into the stairwell. Graham put his body against the wall and peeked into the room. The sheet was up and obscured his vision, but he could still see the hunched over shadow of Emmett as he reloaded the shotgun. Randall was on the floor, with only his hand visible from outside the white cloth. Graham contemplated sneaking back up the stairs. He could get on his horse and be back to the village in a day if he rode hard.

"He was infected," Emmett said.

Graham froze.

"I had to put him down. It was the right thing to do. You know that, right?"

Graham took a deep breath and stepped across the threshold. The metallic taste of blood permeated the room and he almost gagged.

"I had to. We can plant him in the fields when we get home," Emmett said.

Graham walked slowly toward the white sheet. He reached out and grabbed onto the fabric and flinched when his hand contacted something warm and wet on the linen.

"How about you put the gun down, Emmett," Graham said.

The old man started humming again as Graham pulled the sheet to the side. The room was empty and the humming stopped mid-tune. Randall was gone, Emmett was gone. The old man's shotgun was on the ground.

Blood covered the floor, and there was a distinct path showing where someone dragged a body across the floor toward the brick wall. There was the sound of water dripping into a puddle, but the water on the floor was still as a pane of glass. That wasn't what held Graham's attention. The spot on the wall had grown. The black splotch covered the entire brick wall in a substance that reminded him of tar. It pulsed as if breathing and small, inky tendrils crawled toward the blood on the concrete.

* * * *

Graham turned to run and found Emmett and Randall standing behind him. They stared past him with eyes the color of burnt coals. He took a step back into the room but stopped when something brushed across his leg. It was cold and wet and promised him horrible things.

Graham reached back and found the chair. He turned and sat down to resume his watch.

✗

Schism in the Sky
Donald McCarthy

Humanity expands, but it does not evolve. It attempts to convince itself otherwise, with its spaceships, its colonies, its new worlds, but its wars, its hatred, its diseases all linger no matter how far humanity tries to extend itself. That's why I've chosen to live in solitude, on a barren planet without another soul to taint it.

For two years it'd just been my church and me. I received special permission to create a house of worship here and run it myself. The clergy had no interest in my mission, but liked the idea of having as many churches throughout the universe as possible, even if they served no one. The decline of the religious had caused a desperation in the clergymen and they were eager to come across as still relevant in any way possible.

My monk-like existence over those two years held nothing of note. I existed on a day-to-day basis by cleaning the church, growing food in the hydroponics shed behind the church, and taking small walks when the temperature cooled. When my solitude eventually came to an end, I grew excited, not for the human interaction but for what it signified.

The moment came when I stepped outside the church one morning and saw a man in a black suit. "I know why you're here," he told me. "I know all about your beliefs and what you're aiming to accomplish. So I'm prepared to offer you something unique if you'd be willing to indulge me and my peers." He laid out his offer and I accepted. Who he was, never became apparent; he represented Earth's military, but his order in the hierarchy remained obscure.

Two months after I made the deal with the visitor, my church's reign as the only structure came to an end. Five miles from my home, the military had set up a small bunker from which it could watch the testing of a new device, one the man in the black suit described as a new type of weapon. In exchange for welcoming the military to my planet, I got permission to join the spectators. "Where better to search for God than in a place where the world becomes warped?" he asked me. He probably didn't believe what he said, but I knew the truth: God would be there, in one form or another.

On the morning of the test, I swept the floors of my church; despite the lack of parishioners, I kept the church clean and even held mass for the empty hall on Sundays, feeling the need to remind myself of the order I'd pledged myself to. I was just finishing my duties when the front door to the church opened and a woman stepped inside, older, with gray hair, and standing at least six feet tall. She dressed well, black pants, white blouse, and a purple scarf. "Father Graham," she said. "I'm Doctor Elizabeth Xiang. If you still want to watch the experiment, then come with me."

The experiment. I loved that she called it that. Not the bombing, not the explosion, not even the test. The experiment. Made it sound both more and less ominous.

I leaned the broom against the altar and walked down the aisle towards her. I tried to read her, to find out why she'd come to pick me up instead of some lackey. I wanted to ask her outright, but to ask would be to give her power and I didn't want that; I'd enjoyed the comfort of independence the past few years. "I'm excited already," I said.

We stepped outside and I caught her flinch, probably from both the sun and the heat. I'd grown used to it, mostly, but there were days when the heat even got to me. I'd picked one of the cooler spots on the planet; the only place cooler would be in one of the mountainous areas and they harbored creatures that would assure me only a brief stay. I could hear them howling some nights. I never saw them, but their existence could not be questioned. Those sounds in the night weren't just the wind but cries from vicious creatures. I'd long wondered what they looked like, but I did not have the stomach to go for a walk in the dark, hoping to catch a glimpse. In the light of day, though, when everything seems less scary, they could be neither heard nor seen.

A wind, too light to cool us, but strong enough to blow up sand came through and Xiang coughed. "I'm this way," she said, inclining her head to the left. I followed her to her transport, a boxy vehicle with an open top, like an oversized matchbox. Ugly, I thought.

"The observation point is about five miles away," she said. "General Chiasicmo is already there."

I nodded and climbed into her transport. I didn't recognize the model; I'd only been away from humanity for a few years but technology moves at a lightning fast pace. I sat down in the passenger seat and she sat in the driver's. She activated a force field that created an invisible dome over the open top of the transport, cutting off the wind. With a tap of her fingers on the console, the transport lifted.

"So what are you doing here?" Xiang asked me, her voice harsh as if she'd already decided she hated me. The collar has a tendency to get that reaction from some.

"There's no speck of humanity here," I said. "I thought that'd allow me to get in touch with God."

"Because of the quiet?"

"Not at all," I said.

"Then why?"

I turned to look at her. Her voice had not lost the disdain yet her curiosity sounded genuine. Had she done research on me? Did she already know the answer to her question? The man in the suit knew me well enough, after all. "Are you a student of history?" I asked her.

She snorted. "I like how you picked the most pretentious way to ask that. But I know my history, yes."

"Then you know there's been more killing than can be counted. Enough to make you numb."

"Humanity has let down God," she said to me. She guided the transport in the direction of the mountains; they were hundreds of miles away, but so large that they scraped the sky. One did not need a North Star to figure out direction here.

"That's a common thought, but it's not the real answer," I said. "The clergy has, for years, tried to grapple with the central tension of faith: why would an all-powerful God allow such horrors to exist? That's where the idea of free will, of life being a test, came from. But why? Why test us and set up this rigged game? Why not just allow us to live well?"

"I'm guessing you think you have an answer," said Xiang.

"God made us in His image, it's said. Yet I don't know how any honest person can look at our history and say that God loves, or even likes, humanity." I could make out an outpost in the distance, a black cube among the brown sand. "God hates us, Doctor. Maybe God hates us because He hates Himself. Maybe He hated us the moment we were created. I don't know. On this planet, there's no reflection of Him or His failures so that's why I chose to set up shop here. If I get to one day feel the presence of God it'll be in a place like this, a place where His worst creations haven't stained the landscape."

I waited for her response. I remember the bishop back home laughing at me, almost in tears thanks to how hilarious he'd found what I'd said.

To my surprise, Xiang didn't argue my point. "That's very interesting, Graham."

I noticed the lack of my title but did not comment on it. Her level of respect for me would only affect me if I allowed it to. "I'm glad you think so."

"Have you felt anything while you've been here? From this angry God, I mean."

"No," I admitted. "Not yet."

"Your interesting take on religion does make me wonder why you allowed us here."

"Because you're designing a weapon that'll kill people," I said. "If you believe in my version of God then logically He'll be even more interested in this place now."

Xiang glanced away from her console to look at me.

"What?" I said.

"Nothing," she said. "I just wouldn't call this a usual weapon. Perhaps it's not even a weapon." Her fingers danced across the console and the transport slowed, before settling down in the sand. She deactivated the force field and stepped out, graceful despite her age. I'm at least twenty years younger and I had considerably more trouble hopping down. She didn't offer me a hand, for which I'm grateful; I don't think I'd survive the humiliation.

The outpost looked to be no higher than three stories, but I suspected it went deep into the ground. Two armed men stood beside a door that led into the outpost. The door was as black as the rest of the base, only its thin outline alerting anyone to its existence. Neither of the soldiers looked at me or Xiang. Impressive discipline; they'd make great monks.

Xiang halted half a foot away from the door. She waved her hand in front of it and the door slid up. "C'mon in," she said.

I took one last look out at the desert, the sun, and the distant mountains, wondering if I'd made the right choice by bringing specks of humanity to this place. I imagined I'd find out shortly.

* * * *

General Claire Chiasicmo turned out to be a razor thin woman with a lined face and bright green eyes. She waited for me, or more likely for Xiang, in the observation room, which, as far as I could tell, looked like any other room in the outpost in terms of an outside view: there was none. In the center of the room, however, a holographic projection shone out of the floor, showing a view from the sky or, perhaps, even from space. The shot was so wide, I could not even see the outpost, only the mountains, the desert, and-

"What's that green blot?" I asked, not bothering to introduce myself.

"Foliage," said Chiasicmo.

I bristled. "No one said anything about that."

Chiasicmo turned to the upper right corner of the room and for the first time, I noticed someone else stood in the room with us: the man in the black suit.

"We didn't think it'd be a problem," he said. His voice came clear, crisp, practiced. "It's just a little plant life. Hydroponics beneath the ground support them."

I debated arguing but figured it pointless now. "Why is it here?"

"For the test," said Chiasicmo.

I watched as Xiang walked to the computer consoles at the other end of the room. She gently pressed against the screens. "I'd love to know what the test is," I said.

Chiasicmo looked to the suited man once more. Did she answer to him? Or did she just expect him to humor me while she did real work? "I thought he was told," she said.

The suited man shrugged and said nothing, apparently fine with letting someone else indulge me.

"I'm supposed to know everything," I said. "It was part of the deal. I wouldn't have made it otherwise."

"Doctor Xiang, would you care to explain?" said Chiasicmo.

Xiang turned away from her computers, paused, and said, "No."

Chiasicmo smirked. "You'd think stars on your shoulders would get you somewhere."

I touched my collar. "Tell me about it."

She laughed and pointed to the projection. "The green fields are there because the bomb is there. But to call it a bomb is, well, perhaps technically accurate, but it doesn't do it justice."

"He'll be letdown," said Xiang, not stopping her work.

Chiasicmo ignored her comment and said, "I'm calling it a culture bomb. Doctor Xiang was an integral part of the creation of it, along with some coworkers. The idea is that war has gotten larger on a destructive level, but the weaponry hasn't become more effective at actually resolving conflicts. The death tolls are higher, but the wars are as plentiful as ever. So that's why we developed the culture bomb. Put simply, it destroys a group of people's culture, their existence. You cannot go to war if your beliefs never existed. You see, the bomb doesn't kill; it rewrites reality. Its explosion isn't with fire, but with time, reinventing the surroundings. A warlike people suddenly become primitive again, no longer a threat. They're still there, but not as they were and they're no longer anything to fear. There's a risk, of course. The enemy could become more powerful in reinvention, but we're trying to work that out. In the end, I think people will believe this bomb, however radical it might seem, will be worth it when more mass slaughter is barreling towards them. Would you rather keep bombing your enemy, knowing they'll return fire or would you take a chance and rewrite their existence?"

I couldn't tell if she joked. "Are you serious?"

"Completely. It's an ethical bomb if you think about it. It's not killing people so much as it's devolving them."

This sounded better than anything I could've hoped for. A device capable of eliminating aspects of humanity? It was a pitch right down the center for me. "So why the plant life?"

"We want to see what it does. Will it eliminate the plants or will the plant life change, become something new? We know what we want it to do, of course, but whether we're there yet is unknown." Chiasicmo patted me on the shoulder. "You're getting the chance to see a new frontier in history, Father."

My title came easily to her. Was she a believer?

"We should be ready to go when you are," said Xiang, a hint of anxiety in her voice.

The man in the black suit leaned against the wall, looking like a voyeur. A smile crossed his face and I wondered if he'd be happy no matter the outcome if he just wanted to see destruction.

"Let's begin then," said Chiasicmo. "Is there a countdown of some sort?"

"No," said Xiang. "I just authorize it and it'll activate."

"Go ahead."

Xiang tapped one of her screens. Anticlimactic, if you ask me.

Everyone watched the projection, waiting to see what happened. No luck, though, as the projection went out.

"What happened?" asked Chiasicmo.

Xiang already loomed over her screens again, tapping them with a level of energy that betrayed either anger or panic. "I'm not sure yet."

"How far away is the bomb from us?" I asked.

Neither Chiasicmo nor Xiang answered. The man in the suit held up two fingers. Two miles? Two kilometers? Some other unit of measure? I never got the chance to ask.

"Okay, we have weird readings from the first scanning range," said Xiang. "There's some sort of distortion. The readings are all over the place, like they're coming from different time periods."

"What does that mean?" asked Chiasicmo. She walked to Xiang's side.

"I'm not sure," said Xiang. "There's no plant life there anymore, though. All the readings agree on that. Temperatures are all over the place. There's a massive amount of carbon dioxide."

"Well, do you know what that means?"

"I have no a clue."

I knew what it meant. Not scientifically, of course, but on a philosophical level, I knew what Xiang's readings meant. God's hatred for humanity given form. He would only allow a device like this, one that could rewrite His reality, into the world if He thought it'd bring about such destruction. An honor to be there to see it, to know what Oppenheimer felt when he saw the first atomic bomb explode and realized the true nature of the world.

"I'm getting double readings now," said Xiang. "It's like there are two temperatures in the same place, like part of the air is being folded apart.

Or torn. Jesus. The entire scanning system doesn't know what to do. The oxygen readings are off the charts now and the carbon dioxide is gone. Yet somehow foliage is back? The other scanners are confused, too, and it's spreading. The distortions are spreading."

"I don't know what the hell you're saying!" Chiasicmo snapped.

Xiang stepped away from her consoles, hands interlocking. Her face went through every possible human expression at once. "It means we didn't know what we were doing. It means we're going to die."

It also meant, more than anything else, that I was right, always had been. But I said nothing.

The man in the black suit bolted from the room, went down the corridor, and, presumably, charged out of the outpost. I don't think the others noticed, though; they were too preoccupied with the fact that death now reached out for them. I pitied them as they considered what it meant to die. Neither moved nor spoke, both of them probably wondering what the future had in store for them if death marked the end or a new beginning.

I've often wondered that, too, I must admit. But not then. I knew I wouldn't die. I knew God would let me live. Of course, He would. We were alike in that moment. You see, I knew what Xiang's readings meant. Maybe the bomb worked; maybe it didn't. But the world distorted because He was making His presence known. He'd come to watch the bomb. We both had.

* * * *

I survived. This is not a statement of hubris, merely a statement of fact. I did nothing to cause my survival; it simply occurred.

When the distortion hit the outpost, although I don't even know if distortion is the right word, I blacked out. When I came back to consciousness, I saw the orange sky above me, but with a purple crack in it, almost a straight line, as if part of the sky had cracked while I rested.

I rose to my feet, dusted off my clothes, and looked around, seeing only desert and the distant mountains. No sign of the people I'd spent the last hour with. What happened to them, to the outpost? I still don't know for certain, although I'd arrive at some suspicions.

I began the trek back to the church, wondering if some sign of God's presence at this event would lay there. If He left a sign then surely it'd be at the church. An hour into my walk, probably a mile from the church, a rustling came and I looked to my right. At first, I couldn't quite process what I saw. Had the sand become animated? But no; instead, a creature moved across the desert, its skin the color of the sand. It walked on seven legs, each of them thin as a spider's, covered in hair. Its skin appeared to be hard, like rock, and two yellow eyes stared at me. Was this a creature from the mountain? Had it, too, come down to witness the event? Or was this a sign from God? Or, more uncomfortably, was this someone I'd just been with, rewritten into this spider creature before me? Not knowing just how successful Xiang's experiment had been meant I couldn't arrive at a solid hypothesis. I found myself wishing she were still here to explain things to me.

The spider scurried off, towards the mountains, its seven legs bending deeply at the joints. I watched it go, thinking about what could possibly be going on in its mind.

A voice behind me said, "Did life flash before your eyes?"

I about-faced and found the man in the black suit stood before me, his demeanor changed from before. His eyes were narrowed and he smiled like he knew all the secrets of the universe. Maybe he did.

"You lived, too," I said.

He shook his head. "You didn't answer my question. Did life flash before your eyes?"

"It didn't," I told him. "Did yours?"

"You don't understand. It wasn't *my* life that flashed before my eyes. It was all life. All of existence. I saw the entirety of it within just a couple of seconds. I was outside when the incident happened, remember?"

"You ran out," I said. "I remember." I can't lie; I took a little pleasure in reminding him of that.

"I did," he said. "There's no shame in it. I thought my life was over. That's the best time to be a coward because you don't have to be around to hear people judging you."

"What did you see around you when it happened? Other than all of life, as you say."

"I can't remember all of it." He touched his temple. "My brain is frying. It's like someone put a match to it, and the outside is crisping. I saw too much, Father. I am positive of that."

It hit me then what he must've seen. "Did you see Him? Did you see God?"

"I'm not sure."

"Do you think the bomb worked?" I asked.

"Oh, it worked, Father. It worked. Better than we could've imagined, I think. You should see what's out there now." He pointed behind me, but I saw nothing. He'd probably gone insane. "But we brought something down upon us, too. Something greater. I saw something I shouldn't have. I saw what's elsewhere. What's above."

My breath halted. I felt like a child, eager to hear a truth long withheld by my parents.

"Heaven doesn't exist, Father. Hell does. Hell is the place we thought

Heaven would be."

"What did it look like?" I asked, at once skeptical and eager.

"You want the surprise spoiled?" He coughed and put his hands to his head. "I wonder if I'll end up there soon, in that place He's in, with all the others."

"The others?"

"The ones like Him. The ones who understand the truth. His angels."

The ones like me, I thought. "Do you want me to stay here with you?"

He shook his head and then grimaced. "No. I want to die in peace, with just my thoughts. Forgive me if I don't see the need for last rites."

After giving him a nod, I honored his request. He screamed once, a minute later. I didn't look back.

* * * *

To my disappointment, the church remained untouched, with not even the smallest of signs that God had deigned to visit. Still, I prevented myself from falling into complete despair over the next few days. I thought of what I'd sensed before I blacked, of the spider, and of the words said by the man in the black suit. It all had to mean something, I decided. I just had to figure it out.

There was another distraction, too. The violet crack in the sky remained and thin slivers of…something began to come down from it, a little more each day. The slivers looked like frozen rain, but brown in color. I imagine their descent began the moment the crack appeared, but the slivers were then too high up for me to notice them. Day by day, the slivers came closer to the ground, as if someone unfurled rope from the crack and gradually let it down. The crack was a few miles from the church and despite my curiosity, I remained hesitant to venture there, not ready to face what could be another disappointment.

Not sure of what to do, I resumed my normal existence. I kept the church clean and tended to the hydroponic garden. I looked up each morning, the sky now permanently orange other than the schism, wondering if it'd be the day I'd have my revelation. I'd allowed the military here, I'd brought God's attention to this place so why wouldn't He acknowledge my existence after I'd so often acknowledged His? Why did the man in the black suit have the honor of seeing into the beyond?

A month after the experiment, when I'd almost lost all hope, I noticed the slivers finally reached down to the horizon. It was time, I decided, time to risk disappointment. I set off at once, not even bothering to bring water. The closer I came to the slivers, to the ground beneath the crack, the more I noticed how the schism reminded me of a mouth, with the slivers saliva dripping out.

I walked for a long time, wondering just how long it'd take to get to the opening in the sky. It loomed so large one could be forgiven for assuming it'd be only second away. But no, the walk took time and time again, the hours piling up. I stopped only once when I saw the body of the man in the black suit, face down in the sand. The insects had chewed away his skin with only wispy strands of muscle still curled around his bones. I paused for a moment, wondering if I should give him a prayer before deciding that was merely the lure of tradition hitting me. I resumed my walk.

About an hour later, I first saw the daffodils.

I assumed I'd become more dehydrated than I'd thought. Why I'd hallucinate daffodils I didn't know, but a hallucination seemed the only explanation; no plant life could survive in the desert unless someone tended to it like I did back at the church. When the daffodils did not vanish after I shook my head, I began to debate how they could be real. My mind cycled back, trying to think of any clues. I am ashamed to admit how long it took me to recall the foliage Xiang and Chiasicmo set up in the desert. That had been simple plant life, though, all green, not like this, not an entire field of yellow eyes watching me, which meant only one thing: the bomb worked. It reinvented the green plants into sunflowers. The man in black had been right. This is what he must've seen.

But if the bomb did work as expected then what explained the crack? That answer came to me quickly, at least. It was Him. He came to watch and the sky opened for him. He'd been in the sky above the desert the whole time, waiting for me.

I started to run through the daffodils, many of them as tall as me, pushing them aside, some of the petals flying off. "I'm coming," I said under my breath. "I'm coming." When I reached the other side of the field, I stood under the crack. I coughed, exhausted, and almost fell to the ground. I staggered forward and looked at the sight before me.

The slivers turned out to be arms, long arms that came down from the crack, reaching for someone, maybe for me. At the end of the arms were human sized hands, the fingers wiggling, urging me forward. Hundreds of hands came from the sky, all of them wanting me to grab onto them.

"You're here," I said. "You're really here."

I could feel Him in the air, above me, watching me. He knew I understood. He'd been there, with me, when the bomb exploded, watching, and He'd made His presence known; I'd just been too stupid to grasp His design.

"I knew you'd appreciate me!" I shouted, laughing. "I'm ready. I'm ready for you. I'm not like them, like the others. I'm different. I'm sorry I didn't realize you were here. But I do now. I do."

Two of the hands moved in my direction, both of them stopping before my face. I raised both of mine and brought them to the hands from the sky; they accepted my gesture, our hands wrapping around; I couldn't recall the last time I'd had such meaningful contact. Maybe never.

The hands began to rise, taking me with them. So effortless, gentle, comforting. I felt no strain as I left the ground and rose towards the schism, towards Heaven. I looked down and felt no vertigo. The daffodils stared up at me. Just beyond them, I spotted four sand spiders. I almost had an urge to wave to them, to the whole planet, to say goodbye.

Above me, I saw faces. Human, I think, looking at me, their smiles showing bright white teeth and their eyes an intense blue. They were ready to welcome me, to the place where God lives with the few of his creations that understand Him. They spoke, but I could not understand what they said. Whispers, cooing, as if they comforted a baby.

I felt blessed. The faces above me, the flowers below me, the sky all open just for me. What a fate! I might've even said it aloud, because the faces nodded, fervently agreeing with me. I smiled in return and their smiles grew even wider.

I thought it all so beautiful, at the time.

✗

To Roam the Universe, Forgotten and Free

Janet Harriett

Colin has called me back to the house. What used to be our house. I guess it's all his now. I don't want it anymore. I haven't been back here since I cleaned out the last memories that bound me to this place. Piece by piece, I reassembled myself from shreds that lingered, haunting the corners, until I was free of this place and it was free of me.

* * * *

The bridge on the road into town hardly deserved the name "bridge." The creek beneath it barely trickled except after a rain. I crossed it ten times a week, on my way to and from work. A once-white cross was stuck on the end of the guardrail. When I was running early, I would slow down to try to read the shadow of a peeling name that blended into the layers of grime. As the trees flew past a little more slowly, I thought I could see the faint, broken shape of a woman in a sundress, floating above the water. Most days, I drove by too fast to notice the cross or the name, or if the woman was there.

* * * *

On the bottom shelf of a bookcase in the corner, scrapbooks of the two of us blend into the background, already stripped of the memories inside. Between the covers, we are happy as we'll never be again. Visits to the botanical gardens, hikes in the mountains, days at the coast. Our trip to Chicago, the cruise to Jamaica, us standing in front of the Capitol taken by some random passerby Colin stopped because my selfies always turned out blurry. The albums are still there, but I've picked out all the seams that held me to them. There should not be anything left here that Colin can use to pull me back. Yet here I am.

* * * *

The name on the cross was Juliette. The last time I crossed the bridge, the woman in the sundress was there to greet me when my car stopped tumbling, the tires stopped spinning, my blood stopped seeping into the deflated airbag, and the pain of lacerations and broken bones faded so completely I did not even feel numb. At least she was more there than she was anywhere else.

She reminded me of an unnaturally perky barista after a 5:30 a.m. alarm jolted me out of the dream of being alive.

* * * *

The doorbell rings. I had promised Colin I would replace the broken doorbell button that coming weekend. I had every intention of really doing it that time, too. His father fixed it, though, the day his mother helped with my closet, and I've chipped the memories out of both. It can't be the chimes that bring me back to the house.

* * * *

In the moments before anyone knew I was dead, I dissolved into the universe. I was everywhere at once and nowhere in particular, humming in every vibration of energy that time will ever hold, in a state where there wasn't even a "me" anymore distinct from the energy permeating everything everywhere. There wasn't a now or a then, a here or a there, a this or a that. What had been me was perfectly, completely lost among time and space. Oblivion was peaceful and free of pain, regret, longing or love.

* * * *

Sam is at the door. Sam is the secretary-treasurer of the paranormal research society Colin belonged to when we met, ostensibly because of an interest in the technology. Colin always liked gadgets. He'd stopped going to the meetings when we'd become serious enough for him to learn that I didn't believe in ghosts. I wish I could tell him I was wrong.

* * * *

When the police broke the news to Colin, his thoughts sucked me back together and slammed me into him. He collapsed in a heap, and I had no choice but to watch. I wrapped myself around him and through him and kissed his forehead with lips that I no longer had, desperate for him to know that I still loved him even as my thoughts wandered from him. In a voice that was no longer a voice, I whispered that I was fine, trying to console him in an inconsolable moment. He shivered with the cold I unintentionally infused. More than anything, I wanted him to be okay. But almost as much as that, I wanted to be back out in the universe I had tasted so briefly.

* * * *

Colin is looking for me again. That is why I am back at the house. Sam has a van full of night vision goggles, EMF detectors, infrared cameras, and things I never bothered to learn the names of before I had to hide from them. Colin really is excited by the technology. I'm glad he's making friends; I just wish they didn't want to meet me.

* * * *

At my funeral, everyone remarked that they could feel my presence. Of course, they could; I had no choice but to be wherever so many sad people were remembering me.

It was the type of cookie-cutter funeral put on for people who died before anyone had put any thought into the readings or music. The service was full of the generic comforting sentiments assembled by professionals when the living were too paralyzed by their grief to consider what might be meaningful. The flowers were straight from a florist's catalog, full of the cloying, fetid lilies I hated.

Juliette came through the receiving line, her sundress fluttering behind the forty-first person that I didn't know who, with wetter eyes than the other forty, told my parents it was unnatural, having to bury a child. My parents shook the woman's hand, numb and polite, without a hint of recognition, and Juliette floated past unseen.

"I hadn't wanted to be buried at all," I told Juliette. "They got this whole thing wrong. I wanted a party, like Janis Joplin."

"This isn't for you," Juliette said. "This isn't even about you. It's about them. Even when they come looking for you, it's about their pain, not yours. We're dead, after all."

* * * *

Sam gives Colin a dead sensor. Before they leave, Colin takes it to the workbench in the basement and rigs it to run off an extra set of a completely different type of battery. He is happy for a moment, getting something to work, even if it won't do anything even close to what the hunters think it is doing. The hunters are looking in the wrong places for the wrong things.

* * * *

As the funeral faded into the past, there were longer and longer moments when Colin's thoughts would drift away from me, and I could waft toward oblivion again. I melted into the energy of the universe, chasing the haze where there was no me or them, just hints of people I thought I recognized. I never quite made it back, though. Whenever I got close, Colin would hear a doorbell or smell someone wearing my perfume, and his recall would jerk me back together, right back to him. Every time he brought me back, he was crying. At work, he'd tamp the pain down and claim allergies for the tears that leaked out or excuse himself to the men's room to weep silently in a stall.

* * * *

As they drive, Colin tells Sam about a wife who bears little resemblance to me. She doesn't have faults. She never argues with him, never puts off getting an oil change, never spends too much money or sneaks a cigarette after promising she's quit. But I am here, so he must mean me. The force of this ghost of a perfect wife weighs me down and chains me to the world that holds nothing more for me than the burden of others' expectations.

* * * *

Colin installed a second cross at the bridge. As he drove the spike into the road shoulder and bolted the cross to it, each blow of the mallet and turn of the wrench chained me fast to this place and to the quintessence he was building. It felt wrong being there as if I were intruding on his private moment with someone else.

* * * *

Sam parks the van where the road's shoulder broadens out a few yards up from the bridge. It's a narrow road. The night shadows are taking over visibility. They're meeting the club here. Someone should tell him this isn't safe, should make him go home and forget about finding me here. Forget about finding me anywhere. The temptation of a ghost is too much for Sam, and the temptation of me is too much for Colin.

* * * *

Colin joined the paranormal research society again. Sam and a few of the other ghost hunters remembered him from before he chose me over them, and they gave awkward shoulder-claps and condolences at his return. If they were at all competent, they had to feel me there with him. They had to suspect why he was there.

* * * *

"He's going to keep me here, Juliette. Why would he do that to me? Why would he keep me at the worst place in my life?"

"You're dead," Juliette answered. "He's not even considering that he's doing anything to you. That's the paradox of grief: all of these thoughts of you, but the living never stop to consider that they're compelling us to haunt them. That we would leave them alone with their mortal futures and happy lives if only they'd let us."

"How simultaneously thoughtless and thoughtful."

"This is great news, though."

"How is being forced to haunt a bridge in the middle of nowhere good news?"

Juliette drifted toward the galvanized mailbox that replaced the one I had taken out on my way into the guardrail. "He's not trying to keep you at home. He's trying to keep your memory alive in a place he can forget exists."

"I don't want to stay here. I can't stay here."

"It's not forever. Someday, you will be forgotten."

"Who remembers you, Juliette?"

"Well, there was you."

"Me? How could I…?"

"You wondered. About the name on the cross, and how it happened. You imagined that I had been walking along the shoulder on a summer evening and someone swerved. And so there I was."

"I'm sorry."

"It wasn't just you." She coalesced at the base of the cross. "Somebody put this here. And then she left, too."

"What really happened?"

"I don't know. It doesn't matter."

* * * *

Colin proposed the club do a ghost hunt at the bridge. Someone had to think that giving him hope was a bad idea, had to think that preying on grief went past a line. They weren't bad people, even the ones who made their livings assuring B&B owners that the cold spots and rattles were hauntings instead of indications that they needed to upgrade the furnace or flush out the plumbing. Some places really did have ghosts, when the hunters and the haunted wouldn't give them up. I would not be one of them. I would not be a ghost a moment longer than they forced me to be.

* * * *

The creek runs full under the bridge tonight, but the road is dry. The guardrail is repaired and plants have filled in the path my car took off the road. The trees have grown calluses where my car took off the bark. I've taken all the traces of what happened here. The only sign left is the gleaming stainless steel cross.

* * * *

I had never liked his mother as much when I was alive as I did when she finally convinced him that he could get rid of my clothes in his closet, my books on his shelf, my toothbrush in his bathroom. His mother was wrong, of course. Keeping those would bring me back, after a fashion. As she spread his clothes and his books out to fill in the spaces where mine had been, she pried the parts of me out of those places and left them for me to collect. I gathered what I could. Colin took the pieces I could not pry away from him, and he filled in the empty space between with glowing, soft-focus fantasies of what he had wanted me to be.

* * * *

Colin kneels in the mud next to the second cross. He's crying, not caring what Sam and the others might think. The grieving widower is appropriate here. With every jerk of Colin's shoulders, I want to touch him, to hold him, but reaching out to him reminds him I'm here. Every bit of comfort I can give him keeps me away from my own happiness that much longer. But I have an eternity. The universe will still be there if Colin remembers me a little while longer. Maybe I can stand it.

* * * *

I took everything he wouldn't notice was missing. For months after the accident, I peeled and scraped and scrubbed everything, trying to remove the sheen of memory before it hardened into a veneer of nostalgia and I was trapped forever as the ghost of a stranger who is supposed to be me.

* * * *

I reach out. I almost touch his cheek, as if I could wipe away his tears. But I can't wipe his tears, and I can't bring myself to stay. There's too much out there if only I can be forgotten. The ghost hand drops, but he's felt it and looks straight into the empty space where his pain and memories have summoned me.

"It's okay, Colin," I say. I want to call him his private pet name, but I can't. Not with the others here, even if they can't hear me. I think I say something else, but I'm not listening.

From behind us, Sam yells "I think I got something!"

* * * *

I tried to take all the memories and mementos and minutiae all at once. Colin held fast to the big ones—our third date, our wedding album, the last time we made love—and by trying to wrench them from him, I lost my chance to ever pull those in. What he knew he was missing, he'd look for, so I grabbed the detritus at the periphery and picked my way to the shards that were fused to the pedestal on which Colin put my ghost.

* * * *

Sam plays the audio recording for Colin. It's staticky, but in the crackles hide things that could be words. Things that could say "It's okay, Colin. I'm okay. You don't need to cry for me."

I've baited my own trap. If Colin has hope, I'll be stuck here forever. I scream so loud that I hope even time itself can't contain the rage, and it will have no place to go but into the past and over the near-words on the recording. Everyone shudders. Sam picks up an EMF detector and starts scanning. I strain against the force of Colin's thoughts, but I can't escape and I can't bear being stuck here. My blind, impotent rage only feeds the signals to the devices and the hunters' conviction that I'm here to be found.

* * * *

I got tantalizingly close to losing myself in the energy of the universe's forgotten consciousness. The last splinters of myself that bound to the ghost Colin created were almost impossible to claw back. Colin cried whenever he could feel one slipping away as I tried to wrestle another part of me away from him. His tears would have killed me if I weren't already dead. But, having tasted nothingness, I had to be free, had to get back there.

* * * *

"Calm down, or you'll be stuck here forever," Juliette whispers doubtlessly picked up by one of the microphones. I want the hunters to hear her, to know that I don't want to stay. That's not what they'll think she means, though. They probably won't even know it's not me. They'll take it to Colin as another message from me, and they'll spend hours debating the fuzzy words.

Juliette melds into me, and I focus on the faint residue of oblivion that she brings with her.

"You're out there when you're not around me."

"I coalesce at your behest. I don't even like dresses."

"Then why do you wear one?"

"Because that's what you imagined."

"And if I didn't?"

"I wouldn't. I don't do anything that you don't imagine."

"You said there was someone else who remembers you."

"She remembers who she wants to remember, and I've left her with that."

Around us, needles drop, and Juliette slides back into the universe where the hunters' instruments cannot find her.

* * * *

* * * *

Longer and longer intervals pass between when Colin conjures the ghost he has melded to the memories of me. In between times, I reach the oblivion of being forgotten, where there is no measure of time, where all of time is happening at once and forever. Then Colin remembers, and I am smothered and choked and squeezed back into reminiscence, which is always brushed with sadness. I will never be able to dissolve back into the universe permanently while pieces of me are lodged in Colin's imagination. I want him to be happy. But I want out even more.

* * * *

I am stuck to my ghost, floating above where I died, watching the hunters and wishing I had a cigarette and lungs.

A sharp-edged wire on one of the sensors pricks Colin's finger, and he pulls me into a memory he has not thought since our last hike in the woods.

"Yes," I whisper to him. "Remember when you got stung by the bee walking to the falls?" If the sensors hear me, so much the better. "If you would just let me get these last stingers out, it would stop hurting you so much. It would stop hurting us both so much."

I pull together every piece that I had reassembled from the lingering shreds of our memories together, all of what gives substance to the ghost he's created of the wife who never was. I tear myself apart from her, piece by piece, moment by moment, and set reality and nostalgia asunder.

I will be forgotten, and I will forget him. I will forget all the laughs we shared, all the hopes we had. The last piece I leave to her is our first kiss, which he remembers as more romantic and moonlit than anything ever really was.

I leave him to her, to the stranger he has created with my face and my life. And I leave her to him, to bear the weight of our memories together. Unburdened, I can permanently lose myself in the energy of all time and space. I can finally be perfectly and completely free.

✗

Rejuvenate
Lily Luchesi

"In pieces... They're in pieces..."

"I'm sorry, Ms. Corpus, there were no survivors..."

"An accident. The assistant will, of course, be punished to the full extent..."

"...have to close down."

"No, no, never. I'll never give this up. I'll never give them up!"

"Ma'am, you're in shock. Sit down, please, have some hot tea."

"Where are they? I want to see them."

"That's not advisable, ma'am..."

"Let me see them!"

"...not whole. The explosion...they were in pieces."

* * * *

It was the last performance of the night, the man who shoots himself from a cannon, and circus manager Endora Corpus surveyed her workers. This was a high-risk act, and every time they performed, there was a fifty-fifty chance the performer's body could be blown to bits. Those weren't great odds, considering the circus had nearly shut down years ago thanks to an accident.

The cannon hadn't gone off on time during a rehearsal, and the combustible materials had caused a massive explosion. It was only because of Endora's quick thinking and considerable skills that there *was* still a circus, that the same performers were still with her.

She ushered the performers backstage once the show had ended and then went out front, where she had seen some children hanging about, most likely hoping for a chance to get a picture with a clown or a tightrope walker.

Endora put on her best smile and went to greet them. There were eight children who couldn't be older than twelve chaperoned by two teenagers who looked bored out of their minds. The kids, on the other hand, were gushing about the show.

"Hello," Endora said in that bright tone adults always adopted when speaking with kids. "Did you all enjoy the show?"

She was met with a chorus of enthusiastic yeses.

"Too bad you guys only come around once a year," one of the kids commented.

"Well, we're an independent production, and we have to make sure we go everywhere we can," Endora replied. "And anyway, that makes us that much more of a treat, doesn't it?"

Again, a round of agreeance and dual eye rolls from the teens.

"Tell you what, how would you all like to go backstage and meet everyone?" Endora asked.

The kids began talking excitedly, tugging at the teens and begging them to say yes.

The boy checked his watch. "Well, we're all supposed to be back at the home in twenty minutes."

Endora waved a hand. "This won't take long. Come on, you don't want them to wait a whole *year*, do you?"

The girl with them nudged the boy. "Seriously, we can take the time. You wanna hear these kids till the next thing comes along to grab their attention? You *worked* to bring them here, don't forget."

The boy shivered playfully. "No way. All right, lady, lead the way."

"Kids, don't forget to say thank you," the girl said.

There was a chorus of happy thanks and then Endora led them all backstage. The girl walked up next to her.

"You know, ma'am, if you have time, I'd love to interview you for my school paper. It's not often you see women running circuses," she said.

"Certainly," Endora replied.

They were in the back lot, which was covered by tents as well for privacy reasons. The trailers were all hooked up to each other to make for quick moving and less hassle. There was one longer than the others that looked like it might be able to it every performer in there comfortably.

"Are you related to any of them?" Endora asked the girl.

"Nah. He is." She gestured to her friend. "I'm just helping out with the babysitting. It's a birthday treat for his sister. We, um…we live in a group home, you see, and he's been doing extra work around the place to take all the kids his sister's age here today."

"How sweet," Endora simpered. "Come, children. They rejuvenate in that trailer." She pointed to the large one with one long, red-painted finger. "You can go on in ahead of me."

She held the door open and ushered them all in and quickly entered after them, locking the door behind her. The stench inside this trailer was always extreme, especially after a week with no rejuvenation for the performers. Sickly sweet, thick in the nostrils, Endora loved it and breathed deeply.

The children were standing, frozen in terror at the sight before them. Every performer was lined up on a long padded bench. Every performer was dead. With the masking lights of the circus stage off of them, their graying skin and limbs held together by stitches were on full display. Eyeballs were rolling, unfocused. Blue lips parted, grayish tongues lolling out from between them. Hands hanging limply between splayed legs like tree trunks.

One little girl broke the silence with an ear-shattering shriek, and that got the rest of them going. They turned to run, only to find themselves blocked by Endora, who was smirking at them all, their fear feeding her more than any other sustenance.

"As you can see," she said in her pleasant, lilting voice, "you are all specially chosen to assist in the rejuvenation of my employees. You will be a part of the Corpus Circus…that is until your blood runs its course as the last batch has done tonight."

"Hell no, you psycho. Let us out!" the boy yelled, dashing forward.

Endora held out a hand and he stilled, becoming completely immobile. As did everyone else. The only things they could move aside from their inner organs were their eyes. Endora loved to see the fear in them. She lifted the smallest of them first, dragging the child's prone form to the furthest end of the trailer and setting her next to the corpse of their trapeze artist. She repeated this until every living person was next to a performer. One by one, still watching the mesmerizing terror in all of their eyes as they tracked her movements. From the storage area, she wheeled in a small cart filled with needles and tubes.

The needles were about six inches long, ten-gauge, and they attached to either side of the red-stained plastic tubes. The needles were stained and rusted from the blood of countless participants over the years since the accident had blown apart Endora's entire crew. Skin particles still lined the edges of them, and the other sides were stained nearly black from being inside the veins of the corpses.

"Now," Endora said brightly, looking at each child. "For the final act of the night, we require the audience's participation. Thank you all so much for volunteering!"

Endora had worked so hard to build her little company, and the thought of losing it all because of negligence on the technician's part was unthinkable. So she had gone back to her old profession, the one she had had since Biblical times, and reanimated her precious employees, stitching them together by hand; a long painstaking process which was a labor of love. She cast an ancient spell and they were alive once again…with one catch.

They needed fresh blood to be animated, which was where the "volunteers" came in.

They performed weekly, with no discernable pattern so they couldn't be traced to the mass murders, and they always put on a show in what you might say was the middle of nowhere. No one could find a pattern to the mass murders because there was none. No trace of tickets purchased could be found because they were cash only.

Endora knew how to cover her tracks after centuries of living amongst the delicious mortals.

After each child was hooked up, she hooked the teenage boy up to their strongman, because he required the most blood due to his size.

Finally, that left the teen girl, who managed a whimper as Endora came up to her and caressed her pretty face.

"You're quite beautiful; it'd be a shame to waste you…. You know, we could use a pretty little girl like you to greet our audiences." Endora stood up straight with a smile, the decision made. She snapped her fingers and watched as the girl's neck twisted at a one-eighty degree angle, snapping in multiple places. She let the corpse slump to the floor; she'd worry about finding an audience participant to rejuvenate her another day.

The little girl's blood had been fully transfused into the trapeze artist. Endora disconnected the transfusion tube and the trapeze artist stood, looking dazed as she lumbered out of the trailer into her own to preserve her body in a special solution until the next show. Tonight, Endora saw with satisfaction, her stitches did not need to be fixed with the participant's hair.

Endora picked up the girl's bloodless corpse and licked her lips as she gazed down the line of children, many of whom were dead already, nearly bloodless hunks of warm meat. She smiled. She was going to eat well tonight.

* * * *

As the caravan was driving from the small town they'd performed in, Poplar Grove, and headed into Chicago the next day, Endora made a typical stop to get the local paper. As expected, there was a headline about missing suburban children.

"*Eight children from local group home go missing,*" she read. She bought the paper and took it back to her own van, settling in to read the article.

"Yesterday, seventeen-year-old Toby Grace, and his younger sister Ava Grace, who is only eight, went missing, along with six other children Ava's age and another teen, Isabelle Crimini.

"All of the children lived at a local Catholic group home in Rockford,

Illinois, and had received special dispensation from the home to attend a traveling circus last night for Ava's birthday. They were supposed to be home by ten in the evening but never returned. Police investigated and found the van Toby Grace had borrowed from the home parked in a deserted bit of farmland owned by the county.

"The headmaster of the group home, Father McRory, said the kids were going to the Corpus Circus, which would be taking place where the car had been found. No evidence of any sort of circus taking place was found except for the recent tire tracks of many cars on the premises.

"Is this a case of mass runaway? Is it a kidnapping? The police are keeping quiet, but this reporter did her homework. The Corpus Circus has had a cult following in the paranormal chat rooms. It claims to be older than Jesus, and reports of missing children come every so often after rumors of a performance all around the world. Drivel? Maybe. But kids are going missing for over a century if reports are to be believed, and if there's nothing Underworldly going on there, then there is definitely something criminal.

"Problem is, there is no evidence that this circus actually exists. So, is it a crime, or is it something much darker?"

Endora chuckled as she closed the paper. There was never a trail left by Corpus Circus, nothing for the police to investigate, but there was always one conspiracy theorist ready to fire up the old rumors of magic, mischief, and murder.

It was how the circus lived, how they got their advertisement. Kids who thought it was a fun gimmick or adults who had obviously watched too much *Supernatural* in the past decade. Either way, it ensured a packed house every time and rejuvenation for both her and her employees. She hated the police, but she loved the press.

She tucked the paper away and went to the refrigerator, taking out a plate with a few child-sized hands wrapped in plastic wrap. The new press—and reassurance that people will keep their name alive and shrouded in dark mystery—called for a celebratory meal.

✗

Vigil Night
Lorenzo Crescentini

Where the last strip of land meets the waves, there Joahn is sitting.

He looks around, at ease. He contemplates the vastness in front of him, listens to the endless murmur of the ocean that comes at him running, and then backs away.

Sometimes a fish passes swiftly beneath the surface, Joahn follows it until it's gone in the wave, thus leaving its memory itself.

Time does not flow for Joahn. The world is a perennial present, a long now in which dawn follows dusk, light, and darkness.

His gaze falls on the pieces of armor scattered on the ground nearby. Are they his? They must be because he is still wearing a boot and an iron plate that covers his shoulder. He can't remember where is the rest, nor does he care.

* * * *

He lifts his hand to caress the thick beard he feels on his cheeks but holds it halfway when his attention is captured by a seabird cruising high over his head, cawing. The sun is at its back, and for a moment, the bird is a sparkling point in the blue of the sky.

* * * *

Joahn does not know how he came here. He tries to think about it, but all he can recall is a memory of when he was a child. He remembers that on Faire Day his father took him in the great square of the town, which on that occasion was filled with sounds, of smells and colors. He recalls his father's face, in that occasion the network of lines woven in his expression relaxed, giving him a younger look, his eyes becoming brighter.

"The winter will come, Joahn," those eyes said to him. "The winter will come and it will bring hunger and fatigue. But not today. Today is a festival day, and we can be happy."

He remembers the peak of the Faire Day, when the crowd opened and the great wooden cart arrived, carrying the Musicians. They came from outside, the Musicians, they were foreigners. They stood on the planks and played instruments never seen before, braiding notes and weaving melodies with an exotic taste.

They played and the people cheered, happy. And danced.

Joahn has barely the time to ask himself why this memory, in particular, came back to him, and it is gone.

* * * *

He looks at the sea and does not remember what he was thinking about anymore. Something to do with his childhood, but it is all too hazy. Also, he's not certain at all he ever had a childhood. Maybe he had always been there, sitting on that coast, staring at fishes and seagulls passing him by.

What does it matter, after all?

He's almost certain he had a name, something beginning with J, or maybe G.

The spray from a wave touches a corner of the armor and washes that thought away, too.

On the Eve of the Day of the Dead

Kraon climbed along the ridge and reached the top.

The shape of the commander stood against the backdrop of the campfires, like an ebony statue.

"Sir," Kraon said, nodding his head, "I reported the orders to the soldiers. I told them to be ready."

The man nodded in turn. He kept staring at the darkness beyond the camp's line of light.

Kraon joined him in watching. In front of them extended a vast bleak plain. Very far, at the edge of vision, a hillside rose into the night.

They had deployed the defense line in an optimal position, that made impossible for them to be caught in a trap. In the open field, warfare training would have caused an overwhelming superiority. They had two hundred trained men on their side, and yet the commander was worried.

"Joahn," Kraon said.

In front of underlings he would not dare to call him by name, and without his rank, even if he was an officer himself. But there, there they were alone, and he and his commander had been long time friends. They had fought together.

"They have no hope," he said. "They will never attack in the open field and, should they be such fools, we'll crush them."

Joahn glanced at him, then looked up at the sky. Kraon followed his stare and found himself gazing at the moon, reduced to a thin slice.

"It's a bad night," the commander said.

Kraon understood.

"The eve of the Day of the Dead," he said.

"Exactly. His power is strong now."

They stood on the top of a low hill. Below, all around them, the sound of armors knocking against each other: the soldiers were setting up camp in their battle gear.

JOahn went back to staring at the horizon.

It seemed to Kraon the commander was trying to pierce with his stare the hill in the distance, to go further in the dark to the rotten swamps of Raya.

Again it was the subaltern that broke the silence: "U'Nul is crazy, but not this much."

"We have no idea of what he might do," Johan replied, sternly. "The governor fancies he can keep the Raya forces at bay, but truth is nobody knows what hides in that place. Apart from death."

Kraon did not speak. The other went on: "They sent us here just because there exists the possibility the necromancer will try something. I asked for more men, but they didn't give'em to me."

He fell silent. Again he stared overhead.

The moon looked like a skewed, sharp smile.

* * * *

"Once I knew a foreigner that could read your future in your hands," said Raam. He stuck a picket in the dry earth. "And I'm not talking about cheap fairground stuff, those generic forecasts that can't but become true sooner or later. Like 'you'll go through a rough time,' or 'a happy surprise awaits you'."

Rikom said nothing and waited for his companion to go on.

"I mean she really saw what was going to happen," Raam went on. "I was visiting the capital, with an old friend. We go through this alley and a woman asks if we want to know the future." He started raising a tent. Then he stopped, and looked in the distance, engrossed.

"She was a beautiful woman, by the way," he added. "She wasn't from Iliar, you cold tell by her features and her garments. She looked like an easterner."

Rikom sat on the ground, pulled his sword out and started sharpening the blade. He looked up at the little scythe of the moon above them: according to some, that night of the year was unlucky. As far as he was concerned, he had spent enough wartime nights waiting to know each night can become cursed, with no need to call up superstitions.

Raam went on with his story: "So my friend smiles and says yes. She takes his hand and studies the lines of the palm, in silence. Then she lifts her gaze—and what eyes she had, dark and sparkling like obsidian—and tells him 'Your mother is about to die. I'm sorry.'"

Rikom stopped sharpening his weapon and turned to stare at him.

"And then what?" he asked.

Raam finished mounting the tent and observed it with satisfaction.

"My friend does not take it well. Pulls his hand back and is gone. I don't know exactly how to act, in part the thing strikes me as I know the lady in question, in part I feel like laughing because my friend took it that way. I toss a coin at the foreign woman and I run up to him. We stay in Iliar for a few days, then we go home to discover his mother died in her sleep the night before."

Rikom arched an eyebrow.

"I'm not saying she was a young girl," Raam said, "but she had never given any worrying sign. All in all, she was doing well and nobody could understand whatever happened." He looked at the sky and added: "It was a night like this."

"You superstitious?" Rikom asked.

Raam picked up his spear from the ground, stuck it in the ground and leaned on it.

"I don't know. Truth to be told, I never found myself in a situation in which I had to think about it."

"Except with the foreign woman."

"Except with the foreign woman."

"And what did you think that time?"

"That I was happy it was not my mother."

For a while nobody said anything. Rikom started sharpening his sword again.

* * * *

Joahn turned and said: "Do you remember Peodes?"

Kraos nodded. He couldn't forget and he knew what his commander was about to say.

"In Peodes, too, it was only to be a small garrison," Joahn said. "And it was a bloodbath instead. How many men did we lose on that day?"

Kraos did not answer, but the ghosts came to him. He saw in front of him a procession of shadows, saw those that had been his companions and that had met their death on that day, in the fiercest ambush he had ever found himself in. He remembered the eyes of the soldiers, that turned east as the horde poured forth through the swamp reeds. There was an awareness in those eyes, as their hands ran to the grips of their swords, and still, they knew the enemies were too many.

"We ran," said Joahn, and as he spoke images ran vividly in his underling's mind. "And we were able to save a fifth of the troops. Do you remember the man with the scythe?"

It was like somebody had hit Kraos with a stone. Not only he did remember the man with the scythe, but now that he was back in his mind, he wondered how could he ever forget him.

They were running, broken and desperate, and among the enemies in pursuit, he had appeared. He shouted, like a mad wolf. He was bare-chested and held in his hand a curved blade. He was not particularly muscular or imposing, but Kraos remembered the terror he had felt seeing the man jump and scream as he chased them, faster than they were, unencumbered by armor. He leaped from rock to fallen tree trunk, and as soon as he was close to a soldier, he cut him down with a cleave. It was like being pursued by a demon, the few braves that turned to face him were shredded. Then Joahn had turned and thrown his spear at the man. It had passed through his arm just above the elbow, the hand letting go of the weapon. The shouting man had stopped chasing them, and Kraos had seen him sit down and stare at them as they ran.

"This won't be another Peodes," the officer said. "I told the men to be ready to face an attack in any moment. Also, we are not on foreign ground. This is no man's land, they have no reason to attack us."

"We are close to Raya. Anything can happen."

"Do you really believe it?"

The commander shrugged.

"If a plant dies and is not pulled from the ground, the ground around it too becomes poisonous."

* * * *

"What do you know of Raya?"

Rikom had finished sharpening his blade and now was staring at it in the reflection from the brazier. He waited for the answer from his companion that, sitting, gazed at the horizon.

Raam did not answer. Rikom shrugged and went on: "I heard that the inhabitants are half human and half demon. Monsters that feed on human flesh. Creatures of nightmare."

"If there're no men," Raam replied, "where do they find the flesh to eat?"

Rikom snapped his fingers. He had not thought of that.

"I heard they are all dead," Raam said. "And that the only one still alive in those swamps is the necromancer, that is gone completely mad. They say the souls of all that die in Rya join the host that U'Nul summons and commands through his black magic."

Rikom put down his sword.

"They say," the other went on, "that the people in Raya died centuries ago, and that the old man survives by draining little by little what is left of their life essence. I don't know if some madman ever went there to check. If it happened, they never came back to tell the story."

"So you believe it?" Rikom pressed him.

Raam stood.

"I don't know. I don't know what's beyond that hill, but it's a dangerous place. Be it men, dragons or giants, Raya is an evil place. And should somebody attack us tonight, they will show no mercy. And neither we will."

His companion nodded. They waited in a solemn silence until Rikom started laughing, releasing the tension.

"To hell with it," he said, patting the other's armor. "Stop scaring me. I bet the next watch nobody will show up."

Raam smiled in turn. "Let's up the ante, would you? For instance, I have heard your wife's a pretty…"

Then he was silent. He was silent and looked at the hill.

* * * *

"They are coming," Joahn said.

He unsheathed his sword, and Kraos did the same.

"Let the bugles sound. We fight."

* * * *

The things that lurched down the hillside were gray.

Some walked, some had no legs and crawled, other still were dragged along.

If those things had ever been men, now they were rotting corpses that staggered about.

They were thousands.

When the first lines came in the middle of the plain, Raam heard the death rattle: it was a clammy and bloodcurdling sound, made by clucking mouths and festering joints.

And then there was the music. At first, Raam thought he was imagining it, but as the horde approached a melody became clearer: it was something he had never heard, played on instruments he could not recognize, a caressing dirge, disquieting, and gripping.

Raam heard panic spread through the camp behind him.

The people of Raya came forward, relentless. The plain between the hill and the camp crawled with them, the music was getting louder and Raam was sure those that played it were coming up the hillside and soon would appear on the crest.

The things he was facing were revolting and chilled his blood, and yet the thought of the players filled him with terror pure and simple. He had no idea what could pluck similar notes, and he did not want to find out because those were no common notes: the sound was beyond description, he heard strings but also horns, braided in a disgusting and sublime way. And even more obscene than that, he saw that the dead crowding the plain were moving in time with the music, in a sort of dance.

I don't want to see them, he surprised himself thinking. By the gods, I don't want to see the players.

As if intercepting his thoughts, the horde started opening up in the middle. It did it in a fluid way, like two flaps of skin separating at a blade's passage and, when the wound reached the top, a large and undefined shape appeared on the hilltop.

The thing started descending, advancing along the cleared path. As it came closer, the music grew in volume and the corpses started shaking with more energy, some even moving their fleshless bones in a clumsy dancing step.

Then the thing came closer and Raam saw it was a huge cart, the largest he had ever seen. On it were the Musicians, polished skeletons holding instruments made of bone and mud. They looked around with empty eye sockets, their mouth agape and their teeth exposed, as in laughter. And in the meantime they played, their finger bones touched the instruments and Raam understood why the notes sounded so horrible and familiar: it was not horns he had been hearing, but heartbreaking sighs mixed with arpeggios, they were the voices of tormented souls that tuned in with the melody.

Raam looked at the grotesque display and felt a chasm opening up inside, and from the bottom of it everything he had buried in his life was staring at him: there was the scream of the wind in the dark of night, and his mother petting him and told him not to be afraid, because there's nothing to fear, my child, there's nothing in the dark but the wind blowing in the trees. His mother that had died in her sleep and a foreign woman had predicted it and told him for a coin, and he had buried it down, as deep down as he could, and had tried to forget.

The abyss stared at him and inside it was the winter, hunger for him and his unborn children, there were killings and rapes and torture and all the evil that men do to each other as if to measure the meager time given to men in this world. Because if what he was seeing was true, if that total and desecrating parody of life was unfolding in front of his eyes, then what was the purpose of anything? What use to exist, to toil, to love if death was to hand them to a bacchanal of eternal torment?

He started crying and turned to Rikom, finding out his companion had reached the same conclusion, and cut his own throat. Now he was staring back at him, dying, laying in a red puddle, his eyes seeming to say "what can one do?"

Raam saw his companion's eyes roll back and show the white. He thought about the glittering eyes of the foreign woman, thought about his mother telling him fairy tales when the wind screamed too much. He picked up his sword and pushed it in his own heart.

* * * *

Chaos. Screams. Music.

Joahn and Kraos ran on the field, shouting orders and trying to organize the defense. They saw groups of soldiers run to the campfires and jump in, they smelled the stink of seared human flesh and molten metal. Some men were crouching on the ground and trembled like children while others, despite the terror, obeyed and were taking position.

The dead of Raya did not advance, they held their position and shook. At times a soldier's nerves failed him: the dead looked at him as he pulled out his sword and ran to them, then they grabbed him and they rent him with hands and teeth, never ceasing their dance.

Joahn looked at Kraos, finding the officer's face pale and covered in sweat.

"Hold on, my friend," he said, holding him by the shoulders. "I need you."

And then the music rose, even more, the cart moved by the side revealing what had been hidden behind it, a long line of skeletons marching in lockstep. Each skeleton was wearing a helm like the one they were wearing, with the same red plume.

New moans rose. Joahn turned to see a young soldier knife three of his companions before he stabbed himself in the throat, spraying blood on everything around him.

He was back to staring at hell.

At the center of the column, a number of skeletons advanced in a circle. In their midst, something shook and danced more than everybody else.

"Don't look!" Kratos shouted. "Don't!"

Joahn ignored him and kept staring at the shape he glimpsed through the skeletons. He could not see it properly, in that cage of bones, but it was completely black. It was human in shape, but its limbs were disproportionately long, and it moved them in such a fluid way they appeared to be liquid.

The column advanced and Kraos shouted again.

As the skeletons came to the front of the host, they split into two lines and moved away in opposite directions, left and right, like in the best of military parades.

Finally, the circle containing the creature came in front of them, all the dead turned to stare at it.

Through the ribs of the guards, Joahn caught a glimpse of an alien figure with burnt skin. It was holding a scythe.

The circle started breaking.

"Don't look!" Kraos shouted once more, hysterical.

Joahn turned. The officer had ripped his eyes off and now held them in his fists, the nerves dangling through the fingers, while globs of blood oozed from the eye sockets. Before he could stop him, Kraos let the eyes fall and stuck his fingers in his brain.

Joahn looked back at the skeletons making way for the black shape.

The dead started clapping their hands.

Joahn saw Him and went mad.

* * * *

He opens his eyes and finds himself in a deserted camp. Embers from spent campfires exhale the last puffs of smoke.

There's blood on the ground, there are weapons and armor scattered everywhere. Bodies, there're none.

Joahn stands up and starts walking, without a direction. Climbs on top of a small hill, he finds a banner stuck there. It is somewhat familiar, for some reason. He shrugs and goes on, forgetting the banner and the camp.

He walks for a long time.

At one point he realizes he doesn't know where he comes from.

He keeps walking until he meets the sea.

He sits on a stone and gazes in front of him.

Strange Jests

Jessica Amanda Salmonson

Alligator for Tom Waits

Walkin' down the street in an alligator suit
Tellin' ever'body, "Feed this alligator fruit!"
Got alligator shoes and an alligator's head
Been livin' in a swamp in a 'gator hunter's shed.

Bet a couple dollars on the inside track
Gonna buy a car from a slick maniac
Patent leather jacket and a shiny Cadillac
Headin' for a party at the Catfish Shack
Gwine to Sugar Hill ain't never comin' back
Gwine to Sugar Hill ain't never comin' back.

Coconut House

They drifted o'er a whale shark
They floated past a seal
A blue-bubble man o' war
An upturned keel.

They came to a tropic isle
They crawled onto the shore
They made a house of coconuts
And stayed forevermore.

Jemima Mae

Jemima Mae was a catfish
twenty-three hours a day
On the 24th hour she was Jemima Mae
and she took my breath away.

In a swimmin' hole lived Jemima Mae
beside it was a fishin' shack
Every 24th hour she came out to play
but then she had to go right back.

The Tardigrade

Water bear, O Water Bear
You've got warts but got no hair
You can survive most anywhere
When we're extinct you'll still be there
Lovely piggish Water Bear.

Dead Clowns for Christmas
L.J. Dopp

1

On a dark street, in a lonely town, a son leads his father to the window of a small shop.

"There he is, Dad," the ten-year-old said, pointing at the sign. It read, "Corpzo the Clown—NEW! $39.95."

Bryan Preston looked at the bent frame and decomposing face of the thing his son wanted for Christmas. "That's supposed to be a dead clown, son. Frankly, it's disturbing. And, what's with the pointed teeth? …What would your mother say?

* * * *

"Absolutely not! You bring that thing into this house and there'll be no Christmas for you till March, do you hear me, young man?"

"He just showed you the ad, Ally—no need to go Kathy Bates on the boy."

"You always take Hunter's side."

"I didn't buy it—I said to ask you."

"Brendan and Carter are getting Corpzos for Christmas—and even Sharille Henderson," Hunter blurted. *Uh, oh!* He'd panicked and showed his game card; Sharille Henderson was class president, and his mother was always shoving her grades in his face.

"I'm not raising Sharille Henderson, am I?"

"…You are when I get my report card."

"He's got you there—er… I mean, don't talk back to your mother, son."

* * * *

On Christmas morning, the Prestons were opening their meager Christmas gifts. Hunter's little sister, Brittany, shook the wrinkles out of her new sweater and thanked her mom and dad. She'd also received a new writing tablet from her father and some girly things her mom had picked-out, which she'd arranged in an area next to the small Christmas tree Ally had bought with her sewing money.

Little boys aren't thrilled with sweaters and socks, so Hunter had left them folded in their open boxes and was playing with his new Duncan fiberglass yo-yo, making it sleep and go 'round the world.

"Not in the house, Hunter!"

"*CRASH!*" went the yo-yo into a glass ornament, shattering it and shaking the tree, knocking a lot of dry pine needles loose.

"Hunter, clean up that broken glass and go play outside! I told you we shouldn't have bought that tree so early, Bryan. It's stupid when we wait till Christmas morning to open out presents. Now it's falling apart—we'll be lucky if it lasts till New Year's!"

"You got pine needles and glass shards on my new sweater—*waaaah-hhhhh!!!!*"

Brittany was only seven and very precocious; mom was already mad at her brother, so she could get some mileage out of a good Christmas morning fit—just ruin it for everyone and Hunter would get the blame.

* * * *

Outside, the sun was low in the eastern sky, and orange flames danced on the icicles lacing the eaves above the front porch. Hunter could see his breath and had his car coat zipped-up all the way to his throat. His fingers stiffened in the cold, but the yo-yo was unmanageable with gloves.

"Life's a bitch, ain't it, kid?"

Hunter looked around but saw no-one. "…Over here, under the porch," the voice said. The boy walked around to the side of the wooden porch and peered into the open space beneath the steps. Two red dots peered back.

"It's friggin' freezing out there, and I can't reach the doorknob 'cause I'm only a foot tall." Hunter struck a match he was not supposed to play with.

"Aaahhhh!—you can talk!!"

"Yep," the dead clown doll said. "All of us Corpsos are programmed with a dozen different politically incorrect phrases. But, some of us can… *improvise*."

"How did you get here?—Out of the store, I mean?" Hunter felt dizzy and thought he must be dreaming, but having the imagination of a child, rode it out like body-surfing a wave. "How can you speak extemporaneously if you're only programmed for twelve phrases?"

"Jesus, kid—never look a gift clown in the mouth!" Corpzo grinned through blackened, jagged teeth. "…Dead or otherwise. You gonna take me inside to meet the battle axe, or what?"

Still riding the wave, Hunter smiled back. "It's actually my little sister that's the problem." He picked-up the doll and went back in the house.

"Well, we can sure fix her ass."

"I told you to play outside," Ally Preston said.

"Thanks a lot, Mom and Dad! Hiding him under the porch really had me fooled. This is the best Christmas ever!" Hunter held up Corpzo so his parents could get a good look. Then, the doll opened its rotting lips.

"Always obey your parents," it said, in a different, robotic voice. That got his mother's attention.

"Bryan—did you buy this creepy but polite doll for Hunter?"

"NO! Not after what you told him. Besides…thirty-nine ninety-five—*sheesh*! You'd need a co-signer at that price—*Chucky* was only twenty bucks in the movie."

"It's blasphemous-looking! Like something from…*heck*."

"Honour thy father and mother," the doll said, using the correct English spelling of, "honour."

"Well…all right, he can stay… For now."

"Who wants to make some Christmas popcorn?" said Bryan.

2

In the weeks that followed, kids all over the small town acquired Corpzo dolls, and it wasn't so lonely anymore. And, they weren't the only ones; the Corpzo craze outlasted the Christmas season and became a national fad, not unlike the Hula Hoop rage of the '50s.

Teachers often allowed Corpzos into classrooms because they were usually smarter than their students, and served as private tutors. For some reason, no-one questioned why the dead clown dolls could talk, and after a time, even Hunter realized that they were controlling people mentally. Hunter's sister, Brittany, was a good example of that.

"Is the toast all right, Hunter? Not too crisp?" she asked, as she presented him with lunch in his room: a club sandwich on a silver tray, with a Dr. Pepper in his special frosted glass. "I don't mind doing it over…"

Hunter pulled out the toothpick with the olive and opened one of the four wedge-shaped sections of the club. "I prefer iceberg lettuce—this is Romaine." Corpzo sat beside the boy in his own chair. The dead clown doll had grown, and was now two feet tall; as it stared at Brittany, its eyes grew a brighter shade of red.

"I'll do it over! I'm sorry, Hunter—please don't let him punish me again—please!!" The doll grinned, as a dull whine grew in volume and its eyes began to pulsate.

Immediately, Brittany's eyes began to grow over with flesh, as if they were never there, but nothing hindered her screaming. She felt her eye sockets, now smooth skin—and stopped at her eyebrows, sobbing.

"Fix the sandwich or I'll let him…"

"NOOOOO!!" she screamed. *"My eyes!"* She turned to leave and tripped over Hunter's skateboard, but crawled to the door, anyway, begging, "I'll get iceberg lettuce and a new sandwich—please make him give me my eyes back!" Corpzo bet him she wouldn't make it down the stairs, and when they heard the screams and the thumps of her body bouncing its length, Hunter had to give the doll his yo-yo.

Tables were turning everywhere as the young owners of Corpzo dolls—mostly boys—took the lead roles in their families and ended the concepts of homework and punishment, forever.

And, the dolls continued to grow in size.

* * * *

One day, Hunter and his friend, Brendan, were tossing a Frisbee in the March wind. Their Corpzos sat nearby on the cement walk, playing craps. "Boxcars—you lose," said Hunter's Corpzo. The dead clown dolls were now three feet tall, and fairly dangerous when angered. Little Sharille Henderson was turned into a pillar of sea salt by her Corpzo—they didn't seem to like girls very much.

Soon, a Corpzo became a reporter on the local news channel, and in time, another took over the anchor desk at one of the networks. Once they grew to five feet in height they could join the police force and even run for office. Laws were changed to accommodate the Corpzos, and "abuse a clown, go to jail" became the national buzz-phrase.

In China and Russia, communist Corpzo dolls took over and had all the nukes dismantled. By July, there was a new world order run by the Corpzos, and most humans worked in Corpzo mines and factories—except for their human-child familiars: they were treated like little kings.

Hunter had become the mayor of his small town, and was running for governor of Iowa. His mother, Ally, had been stuffed and mounted on a small base at the edge of the yard, facing the street with a big ring in her hand. Corpzo had turned her into a lawn jocky, and Bryan was happier than ever, tinkering in the garage with his ham radio rig. Corpso had let him live because he was so agreeable, and approved of Hunter's advancement in Iowa politics and involvement in the new regime.

3

One day it came: the giant circus in the sky, half the size of Cleveland. With a mile-high big-top and huge neon-lit rides that could be seen from the ground, the floating carnival slowly spanned the globe, passing over cities and farmlands, frightening adults, but capturing the imagination of the children.

Several of the enormous rides had roller-coaster tracks, and others had Flash Gordon-style rocket ships fixed on spokes that rose up-and-down as the rides spun in place. The second day, cotton candy fell from the circus in pink-and-blue clumps, like manna from Heaven, into the hands of children all over the world, who could see the attractions and longed to ride them.

On the morning of the third day, the rockets and roller cars began to detach, and fly away from the circus. Off into the sky, they streaked, with dead clown dolls piloting them; down they dipped, landing on Earth to scoop up willing children. The clown pilots could only fit a few children in each rocket, but there were a million rockets—and, empty seats at dinner tables all over the world.

Parents who protested were bribed, and if that failed, turned to sea salt, or curb jockeys, or worse! Sharille Henderson's father had been made an early example of what can happen to those who cross the clowns: his body had been drawn and quartered by clown cars in the small town's square. His rotting head now housed a streetlamp.

Clown cars became standard issue in U.S. police departments. A tiny Nash Metro painted like a black-and-white Maria would arrive at the scene of an alleged crime—usually, a protest against Dead Clown Dogma—and a thousand clowns would pour out, all five feet tall and dressed like zombie stormtroopers, but sporting orange Bozo rings and round, red noses that honked when squeezed.

* * * *

Hunter's Corpzo was Prime Minister of the Dead Clown Authority, and seemed to rule over all the other Dead Clown dignitaries, who would occasionally visit the Preston home. The boy had been appointed President of New Clown America, and even though he was mainly a figurehead, he still had some power. Bryan had remained Hunter's guardian, although adults really had no purpose but to continue working, and feeding the children who were still on Earth; so many had gone to the great circus in the sky, playgrounds and parks were empty and toy stores were going out of business.

One day, after making his sister Brittany, now turned into a dachshund, eat a stack of cork-covered drink coasters, he pushed Corpzo a little too far. "Why can't you do it, Corpzo? I'm the damn President, and I demand you make wings grow out of her back! I want Brittany to be a flying dachshund with horns, so I can shoot her down with this!" And, at that, Hunter pulled out his father's 9 mm Glock 19.

"Put that away, kid. You don't want to go shooting that thing in the house."

"You sound like my mother used to. You're no fun anymore!"

"I made you what you are today, kid, and frankly, you're not cutting it."

The boy seemed stunned by this reproach. "What do you mean?"

"I mean you're a greedy little bitch, that's what. No matter what I give you, you want more!"

"I'm human, and "greed," as you call it, is the American way," Hunter said, racking a round in the chamber. "I don't like you anymore, Corpzo. I think it's time I got a new doll—maybe a G.I. Joe, this time."

"Kid, you're not human—you're a character in a story, that's all... words on a page. When the reader finishes, you die. I, on the other hand, am a cliché villain, and will always have a place in literature and entertainment."

"Liar!!" cried Hunter, his hand trembling. "I don't believe you!"

"Come on—wake up and smell the Starbucks, kid. Haven't you noticed your parents are a cheap spoof of a '60s sitcom family? Who the hell 'takes in sewing' in 2017? Or, tinkers in the garage with his ham radio set? The clues were all over the place."

"Screw you, Corpzo!" With that, Hunter fired two slugs into Corpzo's face: "BLAM, BLAM," blowing out the back of his rotten, dead-doll head, spraying circuit-board and fiber-optic wires—as well as plush toy stuffing—all over the floor. A Cracker Jack prize and old set of keys were among the gears and tiny blinking lights that had comprised the brains of Corpzo.

"Well, what do you know?" said Bryan, picking up the keys. "Doesn't it figure? They're always in the last place you look."

"What have I done?" said Hunter. "This wasn't supposed to happen!"

"Reminds me of that episode of *The Brady Bunch*, where Marcia..."

"Shut up! Shut the hell up, dad!! I'm sick to death of your pop culture references! And, you had no business leaving this handgun around where a kid could find it!"

"BLAM, BLAM!!" went the Glock, again—and, down went dear old dad.

* * * *

But, a funny thing had happened when Hunter shot Corpzo; nobody had ever shot a dead clown doll before. Quick as a wink, the dolls began to decompose—all over the world! They just crumbled into dust, and except for one Corpzo air traffic controller, and another who plunged a bus off a mountain road in Yucatan, there was little damage caused by their "discorporation." The great circus in the sky slid quietly into the sea; but, near a beach, so most of the children who had been taken by the rockets returned safely. ...Not that they were happy about it.

Parents began taking over their households again, and the 12-year-old governor of Arkansas was even sent to bed without dinner. Hunter was hailed as a hero by the adults, but hated by the children of the world, and he was miserable. "If only I had another chance," he said to himself, "I wouldn't screw things up this time... Stupid, G.I. Joe action figure! What have *you* ever done for me?" With that, he heaved the soldier doll into his toy chest, slammed the lid, and went to do his *homework.*

4

"Come on, Hunter, wake up—it's Christmas morning!" His father pulled back the covers, grinning. "Your mother is making waffles."

"Wow, dad! What a weird dream—it was so real!"

Minutes later, Brittany was shaking out her new sweater. She thanked her parents, and laid-out her gifts under her side of the tree. Bryan was filling his new pipe, and ever upbeat, offered his appreciation: "Thanks Honey—it's just what I always wanted."

Hunter wasn't impressed with his sweater and socks, and left them neatly stacked in their open gift boxes, preferring to play instead with his new, black Duncan "Imperial." His dream had faded to a dim glow. He couldn't remember any of it, but was melancholy, now. Ally was collecting the wrapping paper and ribbon for next year when the yo-yo smashed a Christmas tree ornament just above her head.

"Darn it to heck, Hunter—take that thing outside!"

"Sorry, mom..."

* * * *

The sun was low in the east, and its orange reflection graced the tops of snow banks, made icy Slip-n-Slides by the morning dew. Hunter could see his breath, and had his nylon parka zipped up all the way. He removed his gloves and took out the yo-yo, looked around but saw no one, heard nothing.

Hunter felt a dark emptiness, a wistful longing for the dream he couldn't recall—his only thought a grim, growing fear that his story was coming to an end. Then, for some reason, he walked around the front porch and peered into the darkness beneath its steps. When two red dots peered back, he smiled, and knew that somehow, this was going to be all a good Christmas after all.

✗

The Tale and the Teller
Darrell Schweitzer

Who is the teller and to whom is the story told? Listen: there are voices, and the wind, and the sighing of the sea. Listen.

If you make your way a hundred miles up the Merimnian coast, you come to the Cape of Mournful Remembrance, and, beyond that, pass into a curious country, where high tablelands reach to the edge of the sea, then drop off sharply, revealing black, granite cliffs.

Now white ruins protrude out of the earth like old, broken teeth, but once a great city stood there, called Belshadisphon, a name which means "City of a Thousand Moons." So it was: in the days of the Empire of the Thousand Moons, it was capital of half the world. Yet there remain only ghosts, and wisps of mist; and, of nights, when the tide rushes into the caves that honeycomb the whole landscape, you can hear millions of souls crying out, all those who died in the wars that brought the place glory. Not for sorrow, not for vengeance. Just crying, wordlessly, faintly, like tide and wind.

It was called the City of a Thousand Moons because, in the great times, the very gods appeared on brilliant nights, rising out of the sea in their luminous robes, wearing masks like full moons, drifting up the cliffs and onto the tableland, to walk among the pillared palaces of the great city, some of them even, or so it is claimed in stories like this one, to give counsel to the emperor on his throne.

You can still see the moon-masks. They have turned to stone and lie across the beach and the tableland like so many scattered coins.

Suffice it to say that when I came to that place it was because my soul was weary and my tales had gone flat as stale wine. I came, I thought, to heal, to recover my lost fancy, or perhaps even to encounter some prophetic apparition which might reveal profound secrets about myself.

I came expecting a miracle then. Thinking I deserved one.

Be careful what you seek, lest you find it.

* * * *

"Oh, shut up if you cannot tell it as it needs to be told," said the other. "Tell of *that* night, when the moon and the sky and the mist were all as you see them now. Say how the emperor and his court had gathered for the immemorial rites, at the time specified by his astrologers. The empire was gone by then. No gods came anymore wearing stone masks. The courtiers wore paper masks to impersonate the gods, and the emperor wore one of thin and beaten gold, sitting in state in all his ancient dignity to receive their counsel; and around them the city yet stood in its magnificence, if more inhabited by shadows and echoes than aught else, but not yet broken by time or the rough hands of barbarians. Someone said that the emperor and the rest were like actors still on the stage after the play has ended and the audience has gone home. Maybe so, but the gowns of the lords and the ladies were still perfectly arrayed, brocaded with jewels, and the crowns they all wore were like stars drawn down from the heavens; and their vast and intricate dance was like the movements of tiny elements in some enormous clock, all of them turning slowly around the throne of the Emperor of the Thousand Moons, who was even then only half of the world of men, and half of the world of spirit.

"He himself spoke no word, nor did he make any motion—until he raised his hand suddenly, and all the others stopped; and a hush fell over those present, while the wind blew softly and carried moon-glowing mist rippling in through the great arched windows, over the smooth floor.

"Then there appeared before the emperor the Lady Eschalla, whose name means something in the ancient language of the empire. I forget what. It does not matter. This was his own daughter, the most beautiful woman who had ever lived on Earth up to that time or perhaps ever after. Perhaps I exaggerate, but not by much. Say only that the empire, having almost passed out of the memory and awareness of mankind, still possessed one inestimable treasure, which was she, whom her father loved; and she came arrayed as befit her worth, too dazzling to fully look upon. Certainly those who beheld her as she danced through the mist that night never saw any other, even in their dreams, *or ever could*.

"But I am ahead of myself. I have intruded into the narrative. Forgive me.

"That was when the thing happened, as the lady danced in the manner prescribed by ritual and prophesied in the stars centuries before. *Then* it was that Koviades the sage, the foremost of the emperor's advisors, violated the ancient ritual when he leaned to his master's ear and whispered, 'Lord, I am afraid even the gods will be envious of this.'

"And, shockingly, the emperor, who should have known better, laughed a little and said, 'Let them, for I am not envious of the gods.'

"What a fool he was! That is how you get yourself tangled forever like a fly in a golden web.

"No god from above descended. No god drifted up from the sea on moonbeams wearing a stone mask. But a god came, issuing out of the earth like a dark mist; and he was none other than King Death himself, no filthy specter, but clad as befit the occasion in all his magnificence, in a robe that gleamed faintly like the night sky on a moonless night. He held in his hand a staff of bone, glowing a pale white. His crown was of dim, red fire, and his face long, pale, and expressionless.

"It was he who came swirling through the mist across the smooth floor, who bewitched the emperor's harper so that he still played the stately dance tune while all the others stood aghast. It was he who took the princess by the hand and led her in great spirals around the floor, once, twice, thrice, in widening gyre until he had danced her out of the hall and over the cliff and away before the Emperor of the Thousand Moons could even let out a cry of protest.

"Oh, his cries were terrible thereafter, but it was too late. He sent his soldiers down to the base of the cliffs, then to search the whole country-side, even into the caves of the Cape of Mournful Remembrance. But they did not find her, and many who ventured into those caves never came out again.

"Koviades hanged himself out of guilt, thinking to appease the gods, but it did no good. The gods of the sea and sky didn't care. As for King Death, he had what he wanted. The Empire of the Thousand Moons passed out of history that night, into legend and story. Death had come there and death remained, in the form of a plague, which took the courtiers all at once, their faces distorted and blackened, blood streaming from every pore even as they were driven by madness to continue the dance and stumble clumsily about the great hall, and out into the streets, and over the cliffs, until many fell into the sea to their destruction. All the while the harper played, bewitched into a frenzy. The common people, too, danced, having heard the music, having seen King Death and the Princess Eschalla in their dreams.

"In the end there remained only the emperor on his throne, and the harper, whose name was Vardanes, who stood in silence once the frenzy of bewitchment had passed. By whim, or malign design, the plague had not touched them.

"I think you have already figured out that this man was no ordinary musician, but another of the greatest and final glories of the empire which was no more. First there was Eschalla with her beauty, then this Vardanes, whose hand on his harp-strings could charm dragons down from the sky or monsters out of the sea, who could make stones weep, and yes, could inspire even King Death to dance. I think the gods grant such things out of cruelty, so that men may suffer more from the longing after them when they are finally lost.

"So the emperor suffered, as he sat there and wept, and then, maddened in his sorrow, offering fantastic rewards, he bade the harper go down into the underworld and fetch his daughter back."

* * * *

Now the teller paused, and I broke in.

"I know this story. I have performed it a hundred times, though in my version the harper and the girl have different names."

"Don't be so smug. You don't know how it ends."

"He brings her back, but something goes wrong."

The moon had set. The other huddled in shadow amid the ruins. The mist was clammy and cold.

"There was indeed a terrible price."

I confess I was getting impatient, despite the atmosphere, the ruins, the mystery of that night. Take it as a sign of how dead my soul had become. I said haughtily. "I'll finish this. Let me tell the rest."

"Don't be an idiot. There's one idiot in the story already."

"Yes, yes, yes. The harper goes into the underworld. He plays before Death and strikes a bargain, right?"

"But he wasn't the first."

"Not the first?"

"No, the idiot was a fisher boy named Adronax. He was a nobody, not a musician nor a courtier nor a knight, not suited to be a hero at all, but, idiot that he was, he somehow got it into his head that he should be. He saw everyone he had ever known going mad and dying. Perhaps he really was very brave, or just an idiot. Anyway, it was he who wrapped himself in a black cloak to conceal himself and put wax into his ears so he would not be bewitched; and it was he who rowed a boat to the cave mouths. By moving swiftly, he had outraced the plague. He stole inside. He could not hear the sorrowing or angry or pleading voices as anything more than whistling wind and the rush of the tide. He groped his way into the darkness and found some jewels and shreds of cloth from the Princess Eschalla's gown where they had been torn against the rocks as King Death bore her down, down, out of the world entirely. It was he before whom, at last, the tunnel widened out into a cavern vaster than the eye could take in, a world beneath the world, lit by its own bloody red sun, the light of which had been dimly reflected in King Death's crown. There demons flittered through the air like flocks of sparrows. There the millions of dead lay, half buried in the earth or in the stones. There he crossed five black rivers, each passage costing him some vital part of himself, some energy, some memory, some fragment of his soul.

"When he came to the black stone palace at the center of that land, he was little more than a phantom himself, a husk, but still he bravely announced himself, and was conducted by skull-faced guards before the throne of King Death himself—who, having put aside his finery, now reigned as a filthy specter. The princess was there, seated beside him, her face like wax, her eyes empty of all expression. Adronax realized, then, the cruel joke of it all, for having made this heroic journey and come to the point where he should try to make a bargain, *he had nothing to offer.* So maybe he was just an idiot after all."

* * * *

I wanted to argue. I didn't know that part of the story. I didn't like it very much. It seemed to me that the fisher boy was actually well-intentioned. He was only trying to save his country and the princess. He certainly hadn't done it for the reward. How could he have even known about the reward unless some crier went shouting it throughout the land? I don't think there was time for that. I don't think he dreamed it either, for somehow the wax in his ears shut out the terrible dreams too. It was a mystery. Another cruel joke of the gods. Suddenly the weariness of my soul overwhelmed me. Any arrogance melted away, and I knew I was but one more idiot among the rest, with nothing to offer.

Then I paused, reflecting that even self-pity is a kind of pride. I tried to let it go, like a captive wind released from a sack.

Now, in the darkness, I could see very little. One of those stone disks lay half-buried in the earth. Here and there were a few bits of marble, which might have been a dancing floor.

My companion seemed very thin, like a bundle of sticks wrapped in a black rag.

I asked very quietly, "But the harper went too, didn't he?"

"Oh yes, Vardanes went. He played his harp and sang as he made his way through the caves. His song was nearly as magical as his harping. No soul can ever rest that has heard him sing. But for the first time ever, the voices in the caves were silent, as even the dead were amazed.

"In the end, King Death wept. When Vardanes confronted him, he was clad in his finery again, as he had been on the night when he bore Princess Eschalla away, and his pale face wept red tears.

"They made a bargain. King Death spared the harper and allowed him to depart, and commanded him to take that which lay before his throne, that which was wrapped in a black cloak.

"So Vardanes took the burden over his shoulder. It was very light, like a bundle of sticks."

* * * *

"But he paid a terrible price. It was part of the bargain. There fol-lowed, too, unspeakable folly and even more unspeakable cruelty."

"Who is telling this story, you or me?"

"I don't know. I think it is telling itself. I think it goes on, like a hurled spear, piercing one breast after another, leaving a trail of sobbing ghosts behind. I only know that what Vardanes had to give away in the bargain was his music, *that of his hand and that of his voice, so that when he made his way back through the caves to the Cape of Sorrowful Remembrance the dead were screaming at him. He had no wax to stop up his ears. Soon he bled from his ears. He bled from every pore. Still the winds tore at him and hurled him against the rocks. But he could not die, because King Death had spared him.*

"He found the fisher boy's boat. The outgoing tide bore him away. It was only then, weeping, that he discovered his unspeakable folly, which was that, in the frenzy and terror of the moment, or maybe even out of pride as he struck a bargain with King Death, he had failed to look within the black cloak. He saw that he had rescued, not the princess, but the use-less idiot, Adronax. When he saw that he had failed and he knew that he had given up his voice and the music of his hand forever, he tore his harp asunder and tried to strangle himself with the strings.

"And this was the unspeakable cruelty: that, longing forever for the sound of that lost music, he could not die. *King Death, laughing, had chewed him up and spat him out like a rotten grape. It was King Death's little joke. Vardanes could not die, even after many centuries, even after time wore away the stones of the City of a Thousand Moons. The emperor passed away, into shadow. His body collapsed inward onto itself, a thing of boneless dust, dissipated by the wind which scoured his throne clean."*

* * * *

"That's it over there. That lump of marble. It was a throne once. No one sitting there now."

"Whatever happened to Adronax?"

"He couldn't die either. King Death had given him back. He could only grow older and older, contemplating his idiocies."

"And Vardanes, the harper?"

"He withered. He shrank. He became a tiny, croaking thing. Adronax kept him in a bottle."

"He threw it into the sea eventually."

"Yes, but it washed up again. I have it right here."

"It's empty."

"It's just possible that the dried-up husk of Vardanes soaked up enough seawater that he came to resemble a man again. But that is an illusion. He is only fooling himself. Perhaps he wanders in other lands and has lived other lives, but he is only a second-rate imitation of what he once was. He has forgotten much. He wouldn't recognize himself if he met himself. But I think that he still hears the music. He even remembers the Princes Eschalla dancing in all her beauty. Those things he cannot forget. It is unspeakable cruelty, as I said."

"Who is telling this story?"

"Adronax, the idiot. It is his doom to tell it over and over again until it ends."

"Which one of us is Adronax?"

* * * *

Like a hurled spear it goes on and on, piercing breast after breast, leaving a trail of mournful ghosts behind. I am he and he is I and yes, we remember the music. We have gone down to the sea again, where the moon-faced masks of the gods lie scattered on the beach in the moonlight like coins. We walk on them like the paving stones to the water's edge, find a boat, and thus make our way once more to the caves. We have no voice with which to sing, and no harp or any skill with it, and yet, maybe just because the tide is low and the wind is still, there is only silence as we pass through.

* * * *

Perhaps by now even King Death has died and the throne of the underworld is vacant. But we do not think it so. We expect to find him there, waiting, in his splendid robe and fiery crown, with the Princess Eschalla by his side as his queen. Then recalling our lost eloquence, all our memories, we shall tell him the story until the both of them weep red tears, and then we will strike a bargain, in exchange for the ending.

✗